“WHY CAN’T YOU [illegible]’

“You said you did not want to be bored by my tale,” Tessie replied.

“Well, that was before you saved my life and I hadn’t the faintest inkling what a devilish fine shot you are!”

“A fine shot is no recommendation for marriage, my lord. And I told you, saving your life was payment of the tab.”

“Extravagant payment.”

“Indeed, but then I was horribly hungry and sadly in need of a chamber. I do not deceive myself that I should have succeeded in either had you not intervened.”

“True, but it took little effort on my part.”

“Yes, it is a shocking thing what rank and a haughty demeanor can achieve.”

Nicholas grinned, but those subtle marks of pain were back. Tessie noted it instantly, for his brows furrowed and there was telltale moisture upon his brow.

“Try sleeping,” she said. “If there was some laudanum somewhere . . .”

“There is. Joseph carries it. For . . . emergencies.”

“For acting the spy, you mean.”

“For acting as government’s agent, Madame Sharp-Tongue.”

Tessie grinned, for he was obviously nettled. “I shall get some, then. And a cotton shirt. You will feel better clean.”

She slid down from the bed, glad of something to do other than fall under the spell of those mesmerizing eyes and the sheer lines of his body, hardly decent under the bedclothes. . . .

A RAG-MANNERED ROGUE

Hayley Ann Solomon

ZEBRA BOOKS
Kensington Publishing Corp.
http://www.kensingtonbooks.com

ZEBRA BOOKS are published by

Kensington Publishing Corp.
850 Third Avenue
New York, NY 10022

First Printing: September 2002
10 9 8 7 6 5 4 3 2 1

Printed in the United States of America

One

"Mr. Dobbins, you will kindly remove your arm before I either scream out or do you serious injury."

Miss Hampstead's voice was calm but dangerously firm. Her dark eyes flashed brightly. Little ringlets persisted in escaping from her somber bonnet, trimmed, as it was, in colors of half mourning. Its redeeming feature—a merry, twirling feather, now looked somewhat worse for wear. Tessie thought of it as the last straw on her present haystack of troubles.

She tugged at the bonnet's lilac ribbons and wriggled on the hard perch seat. Her furious words appeared to have *no* apparent effect, for the negligent arm still crept about her waist, persisting in its unwelcome attentions.

Tessie breathed hard from a virtuous desire to practice patience. If she had it her way, she would simply heave the driver *straight* onto the Great North Road and take off with his cattle. But *that,* she knew, would be unladylike. She sighed and tried again.

"*Dear* Mr. Dobbins, in case you are deluding yourself, I should mention that I would not permit you to touch me if you were the last man on earth. So *do* be a dear and let me go before I feel obliged to create a fuss!"

But Mr. Dobbins, who was *very* fine in an ill-fitting olive riding coat with an extremely high collar, did not seem to care about threats. He took his eyes off the horses and the narrow stretch of road simply to enjoy Miss Tessie's satisfying curves. Then he compounded his sin by setting his arms squarely about her waist again, scraping a good deal of carriage paint on the only signpost in miles, and causing his elderly high steppers to sweat.

Tessie hurtled forward but managed not to land in an undignified heap. Nevertheless, her gown was made hopelessly dusty, the hems acquiring two grubby brown stripes across the front. She dusted them down crossly, noting that her tormentor *still* did not have his team under control. He clearly had not the faintest notion how to handle a team. She murmured a few sterling words of advice—for she was an excellent horsewoman—but was, naturally, ignored.

She prepared, rather fatalistically, to be ditched. After two hours of traversing the countryside with the hapless Oliver Dobbins, she did not repose the *least* confidence in his skill with the reins. Consequently, she resigned herself to the inevitable collision, clutching hard at her perch and squeezing her eyes tightly shut. When a phaeton curled quickly around a nearby bend, she heard it, and accepted her fate calmly.

Or at least, as calmly as her volatile nature permitted. At the last moment, she could not refrain from opening her long lashes, grabbing the ribbons, muttering a few choice epithets—and, I am sorry to say it, actually yelling.

"You will ditch the gig, you unutterable beast!" Tessie's eyes gleamed in fury, a fact that Mr. Dobbins, hardly ruffled by the clouds of dust that the near accident had caused, ignored. He merely coughed, tugged ineptly on the reins, and smirked when his horses pulled up a mere matter of inches from the oncoming phaeton.

This, due more to the skill of the *other* driver, who had swerved neatly, narrowly avoiding the ditch on the opposing side.

"You complete fool! You . . ." Words escaped Tessie. Well, ladylike ones did.

"Hush, Miss Hampstead. It is of no use to squawk. I am perfectly accustomed to insults."

This Tessie *immediately* had the proof of, for the gentleman in the phaeton pulled to a halt. Within a very few seconds he'd jumped from his chaise and begun a lively series of abuses, beginning with Mr. Dobbins's hamhandedness and ending with a derogatory remark, interpolated with several choice epithets that Tessie silently appreciated and, sadly, rather admired.

Upon sighting Tessie with a profusion of lovely curls still escaping her dull lilac straw, he colored up and began "pardoning his language in front of a lady."

Whereupon Miss Hampstead nodded demurely, relieved that he could have heard nothing of her *own* colorful expletives seconds earlier. She was actually saucy enough to bat her lashes, an act that had the effect of making the gentleman in the phaeton falter a little, his annoyance trailing off in a flurry of jumbled exclamations that even the most avid listener could have made no sense of whatsoever.

Tessie did not seem to mind, for though the *words* were not immediately apparent, the intentions were. For a fraction of an instant, she nearly applied to the gentleman for assistance, for he looked young and kind and charming, even if a little too eager to tool his horses around the bend at breakneck speed.

But then a second, more sedate carriage drew up behind, and Tessie realized he was one of a party—probably his mama and his betrothed—and *her* presence would likely be irksome. As a very high feather emerged from the window, followed by a fashionable poke bonnet and a pair of inquisitive eyes, the impression was confirmed. Further, the difficulty in describing her own reprehensible circumstances to the satisfaction of all seemed perfectly impossible.

So she held her tongue and extended her hand regally, hoping that no introductions needed to be made. She had her wish, for Mr. Dobbins was in no mood for civil banter.

None of this interlude seemed to phase Miss Hampstead's would-be seducer, for he merely fiddled with his reins and got his ill-matched beasts trotting again, although hardly in tandem—a fact Theresa's tired derrière was now becoming accustomed to on the hard seat.

"What was I saying?"

Miss Hampstead adjusted her hat.

"You were saying," she answered sweetly, "that you were perfectly accustomed to insults."

"Ah, yes. So I was." He nodded in satisfaction, long sleeves flapping against his reedlike frame. "What I am *not* accustomed to is a pretty little armful. *That,* I am happy to say, I am bound to rectify this afternoon."

"I will shoot you first, you silly creature. I should *never* have asked you to take me up."

"Oh, but then you would never have reached London, would you?"

Since this was unanswerable, Tessie contented herself with glowering at the wretch and tilting her chin significantly toward the horizon. Out of the corner of her eye, she could see that this stratagem was pointless, for Mr. Dobbins was affording her yet another infuriating smirk. He continued as if unaware of her annoyance.

"In point of fact, my dear, I should never have agreed to the excursion, for a more tiresome, quarrelsome vixen as you have proven to be I cannot imagine. So, you see, neither of us are best satisfied, but we are bound to endure."

Tessie ignored the unpleasant beating of her heart. She was not afraid, for she was far from puddinghearted, but she would have been a great fool not to take Mr. Dobbins's threats at least a little seriously. Still, she did not think it at *all* necessary for Mr. Dobbins to know that he had overset her, so she retorted with spirit.

"If that means bumping all down the road pulled by a couple of job horses and enduring lascivious glances for the next few hours, do pray excuse me. I declare I can hardly stomach the notion."

"You do not have to stomach it, merely comply with it. You have excellent shoulders, Miss Tessie. I have always thought so, though for some perfectly skatter-brained reason, your grandfather was *never* so kind as to afford me a closer look. I would have offered marriage, you know!"

"Marriage? Why in the *world* do you think Grandfather would have countenanced that?"

"Because our lands march together and it would have saved him the cost of a London Season."

The answer was almost *too* prompt for Tessie. Her eyes glimmered with sudden mirth.

"Never say you actually had the nerve to put that to him?"

"I did, though the old goat behaved so disgracefully, I withdrew the offer instantly."

"For which, I own, I am heartily grateful."

"You may not think so at the end of this day, Miss Hampstead, for I find it is no longer convenient to marry you. Your dowry is apparently disappointing, if village rumors are to be believed?"

There was just the faint interrogative in his tone that made Miss Hampstead color slightly, for it was to answer precisely this question that she'd been so determined to find her way to London.

The offices of Mr. Devonshire, the Viscount of Hampstead's solicitor, was of far more significance to her at this point than viewing the Elgin Marbles or even the Tower of London.

It was *there,* she knew, that she would be able to ascertain, at last, in precisely what circumstances she stood. But none of this was any of Mr. Dobbins's business, though he eyed her keenly.

Too keenly, she thought. But if he thought her portion sufficient, he might be distracted away from his current deplorable intentions. Accordingly, Tessie swallowed the preposterously unladylike comment that hovered teasingly on her lips and assumed an air of haughty disdain.

"Disappointing? I would hardly call sixty thousand pounds a year disappointing, Mr. Dobbins!"

The eyes sharpened for a moment, then the tips of a rather elongated mouth slackened in disbelief.

"Never smoke without fire, Miss Hampstead. And though your bonnet is rather fine, your gown is . . . shabby."

"Oh!" Tessie was incensed, the more because she knew the remark to be true. Truth to tell, after putting away her blacks, she had no gown suitable for half mourning besides this pink and a pearly mauve in the bandbox. She satisfied herself that more could be procured in London, but to be told as bold as brass that she was "shabby" was the absolute outside of enough. And now those creeping hands again . . . she pursed her lips and wriggled.

Mr. Dobbins seemed satisfied by her silence. Smug, really. At last, thinking he had made a rather significant point, he concentrated on the reins. Tessie watched the autumn leaves fall from the trees and contemplated the enormity of her scrape.

She had tumbled into it quite accidentally really, for how was *she* to know that she could be so horribly mistaken in Mr. Dobbins's character? Or that London could be so very far? She was positive that every bone in her body would be aching before they reached the next posting house. But that, of course, was not the worst of her problems.

Her problems were prodigious and tangled. She would be hard pressed, for example, to explain *exactly* how it came to be that she, a gently bred female, the granddaughter of a viscount no less, should be trotting off to London in horse and trap unfit for the knacker's yard. Worse, why she should be unaccompanied by *any* female of respectable age, lineage, or relationship to her, and worse yet, why she should even now be fending off the most unwelcome advances of a certain Mr. Oliver Dobbins, late of the village of Greenford?

Certainly, if the viscount had been alive, none of these strange circumstances would have occurred. She would doubtless be preparing for her first London Season, arguing over ball gowns—she had most unsuitable taste—and dashing through the park on the high stepper she was *sure* she could have wheedled out of his lordship.

If Grandfather Hampstead had *not* died in a carriage accident, she would have driven sedately to London in his chaise, on soft squabs and accompanied by outriders. *Certainly* not in so ramshackle a manner as this!

Miss Hampstead tried her very best not to look guilty. But her features, piquant beneath the straw hat, were far too expressive for her liking. She knew, of course, perfectly well that she should have waited for the full period of her mourning to be over before attempting this unsuitable excursion. Further, she knew that she should have sent word to Brighton, for dear old Finchie, despite being newly married at the grand age of seven and forty, would doubtless have hastened back to chaperone her.

But Tessie, try as she would, could *not* think that poor Mr. Moreton, once coaxed out of his bachelorhood, would welcome such an outcome to his marriage trip. Even so, Miss Fincham—no, it was Mrs. Moreton now—was just the redoubtable sort of person she needed.

She would have been quite able to depress the pretensions of such a person as Oliver Dobbins. Not that Tessie was not perfectly able to do so herself, but her methods were less socially acceptable than Miss Fincham's.

Had she not been told time and time again that ladies do *not* shoot gentlemen? They do not even, as she had once shockingly put it, "plant them a facer" no matter *how* much they were deserving of such treatment. Females of *quality,* as Miss Finch frequently liked to instruct, raised their eyebrows coldly, pointedly remarked upon the weather, or at their most cutting, bobbed the slightest of curtsies and turned their backs.

Well, that was all very well, of course, but if you were stuck in a rackety gig with a bonnet to hide your pretty but haughty eyebrows, and it was impossible to make *any* kind of curtsy, never mind turn one's back, there were rather few options left available.

Tessie had tried the weather but had not progressed very far, for there is only so much one can say about a crisp autumn day that is cold but not biting. Besides, she would rather choke than converse with a man whose stated intention was to divest her of her maidenhood at the nearest posting house.

She sneaked a peek at the scurrilous rogue she had trusted her venture to. Yes, he still had that odious smirk upon his sallow countenance—the type of smirk she longed to put an end to by ditching the team and grabbing the reins herself. But the road had too many bends and twists—far too risky. Besides, though the horses were as lame as donkeys, Tessie could not wish to see them hurt, and they might be if she decided on such a course.

So she abandoned *all* attempts to be ladylike and contemplated biting Mr. Dobbins's whip hand. This was currently curling about her waist in a manner that was as sly as it was distasteful. If she leaned forward, she could just manage it. It did not signify in the *least* that the feather on her bonnet would be sadly rumpled. However, on reflection, the taste of his horrible tan riding glove in her mouth was something she could not relish, so she settled, first, on giving him a sporting warning.

"Unhand me, if you please!"

For answer, a faint, supercilious snort. "Kindly remove your fingers. They are poking me."

"Stroking, you mean."

"Poking. And I meant it about my pistol."

"Nonsense. A woman never means such things. And even when one does, one can rely on a poor aim equaled only by an equivalently poor temper to ensure no lasting harm is done."

It took all Tessie's self-control not to prove him hazardously, disastrously, and irreparably wrong. But if there was one thing her grandfather had taught her, it was to take her skill seriously. She was in the habit of joking that nothing could be more fatal than to kill someone. But the truth weighed heavily with her, for Tessie, sad to say, was a hothead.

A hothead with a strangely remarkable eye, a superbly trained balance, and an enviable swiftness that always caused a chuckle to rise in the throat of the old Viscount of Hampstead. It was a combination of which poor Oliver Dobbins was wholly unaware, for Miss Fincham had always disapproved heartily of such goings-on and would never permit a word of such matters to pass beyond the gates of Hampstead Oaks.

Now the urge to reach into the reticule that bounced demurely upon her dusty pink skirts was almost overwhelming. Tessie bit her lip and concentrated on the pretty trim hat her half-mourning clothes now permitted. She would *not,* she told herself, shoot unless she truly needed to. The temptation, quite frankly, was strong. But she demurely played with the elegant ribbons of her reticule and satisfied herself with a mere remark.

"You are admirably sanguine, Mr. Dobbins. I congratulate you on your smugness. I'm sure I hope it is not ill founded."

"And *I* congratulate you on a sharp tongue. A woman's only weapon, but you appear to keep it well honed."

"Ah, you give me such ample opportunity!"

Again the sweet smile and a tug at the reticule ribbons. These gay, curling wisps no longer appeared quite as jaunty, but Miss Hampstead was concentrating so fiercely on *not* shooting Mr. Dobbins that she did not appear to notice overmuch.

The gentleman, disappointed by her inattention, frowned and fell into a thoughtful silence, broken only by the passing of the common stage, the chime of some distant church bells, and the rumble of their carriage wheels.

Presently, the dust road turned to cobble. Mr. Dobbins, who had lost interest, for the moment, in continuing a conversation in which he appeared to be the loser, seemed intent on killing his stumbling beasts. Miss Hampstead sighed, nobly refraining from offering advice, though her instincts told her that the left chestnut was pulling and probably needed to be reshod. Also, though they had been traveling for several hours, the horses had not been watered, which to her was as cruel as it was foolish.

The ride continued, consequently, in silence, though Miss Hampstead was necessitated from time to time to remove creeping fingers from her person. She thought London had never seemed so far.

Two

Just past the Postlethwaite toll, on a little fork in the road that leads, in one instance, to a small ivy-clad cottage, and in another, just a few miles beyond, to the regular mail coach route, a furtive glance was cast at the countryside. To untrained eyes, the scrawny man with the thin, majestic features and the pinched chin appeared quite benign, for he was sporting a tweed greatcoat with two respectable capes and did not brandish any particular weapon.

This, of course, in stark contrast to the gentleman—and one uses the term loosely—beside him, who was burlier, dirtier, and pleased to be holding both a blunderbuss and a nasty type of pickax that somehow appeared menacing.

One would be wrong, of course, for the bonier man was by far the more dangerous, he being the handpicked emissary of a certain Mr. Philip Grange, whispered of in most circles, wanted by Bow Street, and feared about London with a great trembling of nerves.

Satisfied that there were no stray ears to hear the clandestine nature of his discourse, the bony beckoned the burly, waving aside the pickax with irritation. Purely, one supposed, from force of habit, he leaned close to his companion and muttered some grim words darkly. " 'Is royal 'ighness rides tonight. After the meeting, Fagan, I want yer to follow 'is cavalcade down to Kings and Knightbury. See wot yer can spy out."

Then, balking, it must be supposed, at the rank breath that beset him, he stepped back and waited for his companion to nod reverentially, as was his due. He was disappointed, for the burly one was more acquainted with gutter fights than with reverence, and merely wiped his nose against his blunderbuss arm.

"Like as not, I'll spy some wenching."

"Clothead! Of course yer will! 'Alf our information comes by 'is maids and mistresses! No, I mean see if 'e meets wiv anyone. Rumor 'as it there is a spy among us."

"Among us?"

"Aye, among us God-fearin' Luddites. We can't take chances. The whole matter is a hanging offense, Lor' 'elp us."

"Killin' the king? Cause for national praise, belike."

"Hold your tongue, and 'e's not king yet."

"No, nor like to be, thanks to a dozen able coves."

"A dozen able coves and one spy."

"Wot? Lor! I see wot yer mean!"

"Yes, well, it takes yer a bit longer, Fagan, but if the penny 'as dropped, at last, I'll not be complainin'. And neever will Master Philip."

At this, the burly one shivered, his eye narrowing.

"Oo do yer suspect?"

"Not certain—got a list of possibles, but need proof."

"Oo are the possibles?"

"Danvers from Sideham, Marley from Trent, and Murray 'Iggins from . . . blimey, can't think where 'e's from. Midlands somewhere. The others seem all right and tight, but yer never can be shore."

The man who answered to the name Fagan sniffed. "I'll nosy around."

"Be sure that yer do. We don't want no more mistakes.

The master is not pleased, which is somethin' that you, Fagan, should be worryin' about." Then the bony one cracked his knuckles beneath tan riding gloves of indeterminate leather. Fagan, most uncharacteristically, shuddered. Then, collecting himself, he glared balefully at the bony one, whom he personally thought a bit soft, and nodded. His beaver bobbed several times for emphasis.

"We'll find 'im, guv."

"Good. The matter should be simple, really. They 'ave all been furnished wiv little passwords. The spy will have had 'is from Whitehall. Unfortunately for 'im, that will be a sight different from yours or mine. Master Philip thinks it quite a jolly sort of thing. Almost smiled, 'e did. We used Lijah Josham, who we know is a ferret, God rot him, to rootle the password back to Whitehall. 'E'll get comeuppance tonight, 'e will."

"And when 'e does . . ."

"Aye, guv?"

But the bony one did not need to say more. He merely made a swift movement with his finger across his rather fine neckerchief. Fagan understood perfectly.

"Wait!"

The low-perched gig rumbled off with a great click of wheels and a smattering of mud that caught at Miss Tessie's bonnet and half her paisley shawl. Muttering in a most unladylike manner, she wiped off the smears with her pale gloves. The results were unfortunate.

The lady looked crosser and squinted into the mists. There was no sign of the antiquated gig—it could not be elevated by any stretch of the imagination to the rank of a chaise—with its rusting spokes and creaking springs, but she could hear its distant rumbling.

For a mad instant, Miss Hampstead actually regretted her fast reflexes that'd caused poor Mr. Dobbins to howl in pain and once again lose control of his steeds. Undoubtedly, if she had more tolerance and a better check of her temper, she would still be wending her way to London.

She sniffed. She felt rather forlorn out in the cold, and although Mr. Dobbins was naturally an odious snake, he was at least company. It was mean of him to set her down without all her luggage, however much she may have stomped on his boots and ground her delicate feet into his shins.

"Hah!" She scolded herself firmly for weakness. Mr. Dobbins was *not* company, he was a lecherous old scarecrow with bony fingers and the worst pair of lame chestnuts she ever had the misfortune to encounter. If the conveyance traveled another three miles this day, she would be amazed.

Prosaic, Miss Hampstead decided it was now quite pointless—not to mention beneath her dignity—to pursue the matter further. Howling or chasing after the gig would merely be excessively birdwitted. She therefore refrained from calling out again, dusted herself off, and twirled around daintily in her stout half boots of sensible jade leather. A few shy drops of rain caused her to stop in her tracks and consult the sky pensively.

It looked likely to rain. She could possibly still purchase a seat on the mail, but by this time she would almost certainly have missed the stagecoach to London. Even taking the faster mail, it would be nightfall by the time she reached Grosvenor Street, and there was no saying what suitable accommodations could be arranged. One thing was certain—she would *not* stay with Lady Haverlea, who treated her mama so shabbily, no matter *what* the connection!

No, it was surely better to spend the night in front of a warm fire and continue on in the morning. By all accounts, the hostelry that rose before her in a cheerful mass of gray stone and rosewood shutters was excellent.

But how vexatious to have on only a half-mourning traveling gown and muddied shawl! Not to *mention* no chaperone or proper baggage . . . Miss Tessie bit her lip. In London it would not have mattered. The city was sufficiently big to permit anonymity. She would pass for a merchant's daughter or a governess, or even a superior upper servant. Here there were bound to be questions. Country folk were all the same. Quickly, Tessie assembled some sort of story, then turned toward the neat cobbled path leading up past the stables. Just her luck to have hailed Mr. Dobbins, when if she'd only had a little patience, she could have wheedled Jack, the carrier's boy, to take her up in his chaise.

She shook off her childish pout and replaced it with the wider, more sensuous smile of a beautiful woman halfway through her eighteenth year. It was wasted on the cobbler's boy who eyed her saucily as she passed, but it lifted her gloom a little. No point pining and repining. She was not a wet goose! Indeed, no! Miss Theresa Evans Hampstead was made of sterner stuff, as anyone with half a wit would attest to. And if she was *not* to be conveyed to London that day, she might just as well step out of the drizzle.

Rain was dripping from her bonnet, but she scornfully ignored the rather sobering notion that she doubtless looked a fright. Pure vanity—she had no time for such nonsense. She clutched at her valise and marched forward.

The posting house, now that she had passed the stables and taken a closer look at bright awnings and cheerful plant boxes, seemed warm and inviting. She could just make out a fire through the windows, and even though it was morning, tapers burned merrily to offset the heavy, gloomy drapes and the dullness of the day.

Of a sudden, Miss Theresa Evans Hampstead—otherwise known to all her intimates as Tessie—was hungry. The forty-two gold sovereigns weighed heavily in her reticule. She felt rich. And, though annoyed at Mr. Dobbins's lack of chivalry, she was nevertheless pleased to see the last of him. Poor company he was, forever prosing on about this or about that. And boastful! He had bored on in his dry way a full six miles about his hunting prowess and several more about riding unicorn.

Miss Hampstead sniffed, though the corners of her mouth tilted upward rather wickedly. She doubted whether poor Mr. Dobbins possessed three horses frisky enough to put it to the touch. But when he had tried to kiss her at the Postlethwaite toll, it had been the outside of enough. She really did not regret stomping meaningfully on his hessians, even if it *had* resulted in a long and bitter tirade about "fanciful chits who needed taking down a peg or two." Not to mention, of course, being deposited but two miles later at this unknown outpost miles from anywhere fashionable and probably far removed from Upper Grosvenor Street, her preferred destination.

Mr. Dobbins's ardor, she presumed, had waned to all but nothing.

Tessie shrugged. She'd wanted an adventure, and now she had it. She dusted down her traveling coat, and with a slight tweak of her bonnet, she stepped inside.

"Might I organize a room for the night?" Her voice was like soft velvet, belying her youth and obvious shortcomings of dress. Her gown, she knew, was positively provincial, and though her pearls were of the finest quality, they were presently hidden from view by a high-cut collar that itched most uncomfortably. Still, despite these disadvantages, her color was high, her eyes sparkled with their usual animation, and her skin was almost translucent in its unusual pearl-white purity. Her hair was tucked in coils beneath a cottage bonnet of tawny trimmed straw, but even so, thick, dark ringlets escaped their pins and peeked out most invitingly. She smiled encouragingly at the innkeeper, unaware that even in the shadows her lips were a sultry pink, bordering on a subtle shade somewhere between roses and violets.

Despite certain obvious deficiencies, she bore herself well.

The innkeeper, calling orders to the ostlers, did not seem to mind her muddied shawl or the stained gloves. He was just smiling upon her in a benign and avuncular manner, when a shriveled-up woman twice his height and half his girth appeared from the kitchens. She marched over to the oak counter and glared balefully.

"We are full up, mistress. Like as not you'll find something at the Cock and Candle."

"But that is not respectable!" Miss Hampstead stood her ground firmly. She was young, but she was not a bubblehead. The Cock and Candle was no place for a young lady, however much she sought diversion.

"Quite right, missy. Respectable is as wot respectable does!"

The innkeeper's wife—for so she appeared to be—muttered these incomprehensible words while her husband shifted uncomfortably on his stout feet. The utterance was quite unintelligible to Miss Tessie but not the tone. She colored but tilted her chin rather dangerously, her eyes sparkling with sudden anger.

The innkeeper, hardly reassured by this gesture, wiped his hands upon the capacious apron that enfolded him, and coughed unhappily. The newcomer might not look or *behave* like quality, but she *spoke* like it. Further, she was turning up her nose and arching a very fine pair of dark brows in a manner suggesting that she was neither pleased nor patient.

Now she spoke firmly, with just a trace of hauteur. "I have forty-two gold sovereigns in my possession. Have the goodness to show me to a suitable chamber."

The innkeeper picked up a jug of ale and looked meaningfully at his stick of a wife. Several of the occupants of the taproom looked through the open door and eyed Miss Hampstead appraisingly. She did not appear to notice, for she was concentrating fiercely on looking regal.

The innkeeper's wife laughed.

"Lawks a mercy, just look at those airs and graces! A duchess she might be! A duchess wot has never hair or hide of a stick of baggage. Nor maids nor outriders neever."

There was a general murmur of amusement about the room. Tessie felt her face heating, but she refused to be drawn.

"I shall not require a private parlor, but washing water will be excellent and a hot brick in the sheets. . . ."

"Did yer 'ear that, Percy? She *requires* . . ."

Miss Hampstead was not used to her orders being dismissed. Certainly, she was not used to being treated like a tavern wench rather than a lady. She was too resourceful to be desperate, but her situation was uncomfortable. Certainly, it was over her dead body that she would take herself off to the Cock and Candle, no matter how late the hour. She masterfully—and regretfully—resisted the urge to box Mistress Audley's ears.

So intense was her concentration on maintaining her temper that she did not notice a gentleman, dressed all in cream, with a tiny froth of ice-white lace around his neck, approach the party. *She* may not have noticed, but the company did, for Mistress Audley's lips stopped mid-sentence and her husband's ample stomach bowed slowly to the floor.

Towering above her, she heard a gentleman's firm but languid tones. He appeared to be finishing Mistress Audley's sentence, for Tessie's tingling ears heard ". . . soapy water and warm sheets. I believe that is not too arduous a request."

Miss Theresa's spine tingled. Worse, she felt her knees misbehaving horribly, and her flush had deepened, for no particularly discernible reason, to crimson. She longed to whisk around and gaze at her unexpected champion, but she did not dare.

Suspended, for a split second, in agonies of indecision, Miss Hampstead, needle sharp, made a quick assessment. Oh, a gentleman, undoubtedly that, but how tiresome. He would leap to the same conclusion as the innkeepers.

Tessie knew full well that her behavior was extraordinary for a gently bred lady. Even an *unconventionally* reared gently bred lady must have qualms. The qualms struck her now more fully than even on Mr. Dobbins's gig.

The tips of her gloved fingers quaked—how much more so must the rest of her be trembling! She deserved, she supposed, to be considered fast. Normally plain spoken, Miss Theresa Evans Hampstead did not care to think of the other, more ruthless terms he might have applied to her. Undoubtedly, she was being brazen, but she had precious little choice.

When she was in London, when she had seen her solicitors, she could transform into a decorous lady—at least she hoped she could—but not now. Now she needed her wits about her, and most of all she needed not to be recognized. The gentleman with the baritone voice and the sardonic eyes—yes, she had peeked—was just the sort of nuisance she could live without. If a whisper of this journey reached any ear of consequence . . . but he was speaking.

She could not hear what he was saying, but suddenly

there was much bowing and scraping. Then she was being promised a sumptuous feast, beginning with what she hoped was rabbit stew. She was particularly partial to this treat, having caught and cooked many a hare in her tender years.

Now, remembering her manners, she thanked the gentleman, who was regarding her, she thought, rather coldly. If his shoulders were not so haughty, and his bearing not so rigid, she might have thought him handsome. Those arched brows were especially defining. . . . No. She amended her first impression. He had a scar above his right temple that marred his symmetrical features. Intriguing, she speculated, rather than sinister . . . Damnation! He *was* handsome. Just a shade too supercilious for her tastes.

The gentleman was now regarding her with faint amusement, as if he perfectly understood her every thought. She felt, rather wildly, that she preferred his coldness.

"I am gratified sir."

"Most young ladies *are,* I believe." There were several sniggers in the nearby taproom. Tessie drew herself up to her fullest height. He deliberately misunderstood her! And with such a bold glance as to bring a sudden warmth to her cheeks. But she was no greenhorn, and she would *not* allow him to indulge the belief that she could fall victim to his gentlemanly charms. Indeed, now she looked, he had *several* imperfections, for though his hair was jet black, there was the odd strand of silver easily detectable, and his brows had dark arches that were wide, rather high, above those wickedly blue eyes. "Too blue," she thought, "for a gentleman."

"You misunderstand me."

"Do I?"

"Indeed, for it is not *you* that gratifies me, sir, but your obvious status."

"How humbling."

Was his mouth twitching? She suspected so. Nevertheless, she continued in a civil tone. She would consider the matter a penance.

"It is mortifying that your word should bear more weight than mine, but since it does, I take leave to thank you."

The indignation in her tone was evident, causing a rather more definite smile to appear on the face of the gentleman. Unfortunately, it was both superior and indulgent, which made Tessie forget her civil intentions and suffer the desire to kick his shins.

"Quite so, Miss . . . ?"

She pulled herself together. "Evans. Charity Evans."

"Ah, how . . . *appropriate.*" His disbelief was palpable.

Did he realize she was using a false name, or was it simply her choice that was amusing him? Charity. Yes, she saw the joke in that. A little against her will, her eyes twinkled.

"I do not mean to be seen as a charity basket, sir, though I concede if you hadn't spoken for me, I may well have found myself at the parish door. This *despite* the fact that I have—"

"Forty-two sovereigns in your pocket." He finished the sentence for her with something between a frown and a gleam of amusement.

"Not my pocket, sir, my reticule."

"Ah, yes. Pray enlighten me on this point. *And* the rest of the taproom. The door stands ajar, you know."

The reproof was unmistakable. Worse still, it was well founded, for Theresa *did* know. She could see several hats and the curl of tobacco smoke out of the corner of her flashing chestnut eyes. She was behaving like a sapskull, and she knew it, for it did not do to boast of riches in a watering hole such as this. Normally, she would not have *dreamed* of doing so, but she had been most put out by the innkeeper's attitude.

"If I were you, Miss Evans, I would be more circumspect in my confidences."

Theresa flushed. It did not help in the least that the gentleman was right.

"I am used to dealing with petty thieves, sir."

He raked her up and down with his eyes, so that Theresa felt distinctly uncomfortable. But she managed, by dint of tilting her chin up defiantly, to match his gaze stare for stare without wavering once.

The gentleman did not seem to appreciate this fine display, for he merely drawled in a bored tone that he might have guessed. Then, by way of incensing her further, he continued.

"What a very uncommon female you are, to be sure. And now, I really must leave you to enjoy your repast. I hear the clatter of china."

There was nothing for it but to curtsy and to murmur something inaudible under her breath. The gentleman apparently took her thank-yous as his due, for he merely nodded curtly and took up his cane. But there was an odd, indefinable expression in his eyes that made Theresa wonder whether he had heard the muttered expression that had issued from her modest lips and passed for a "thank-you." All in all, she hoped not.

Three

The innkeeper himself led the way to a private parlor and there, to her disappointment, she found nothing so plain as a rabbit stew, the posting house being very superior by nature and employing a French cook. The only remove she recognized as being eminently English was a cod's head, and this she disregarded immediately as entirely ineligible. No matter how hungry she might be, she *could* not consider the eyes in the light of a delicacy.

So, after some thought, she accepted a dish of steaming oysters à la crème, a generous helping of vegetables, and several slivers of green goose, which she recognized from the other meats, despite its villainously French name. When the servant departed, she found herself quite alone, and ate ravenously, for it was several hours since she had thought of anything so mundane as food. She was just swallowing the last mouthful when the door opened and the stranger of earlier stepped in.

"Ah, you have eaten, I see."

"Where I come from, sir, it is a courtesy to knock." Was she mistaken? Did his eyes grow bluer? It certainly seemed so as he stared down at her from his mocking heights.

"Where I come from, madam, it is traditional for a young lady to be chaperoned."

Since this was quite unanswerable, Miss Theresa scowled and considered overturning the cod.

The odious man must have been a mind reader, for he lifted the platter off the table and placed it well out of her reach. Then, almost unconsciously, he removed one of his gloves and plucked out an eye. "Ah, a cod's eye! It must be years since I have indulged in such a treat." He popped the delicacy into his mouth and chewed, much to Theresa's disgust.

"Is there a reason you are intruding upon my meal?"

"None at all, ma'am, save that there appears to be only one private parlor and I had judged you to be finished."

"You were mistaken, then."

"Indeed. I am also rather hungry."

A flash of amusement crossed Theresa's features. "You want me to invite you to dine with me!"

"On the contrary. That would be . . . frivolous besides being highly improper." His voice sounded forbidding.

Theresa neither paled nor quaked in fright, something she half suspected the gentleman intended.

"You sound exactly like my dear Miss Fincham. *Do* give over being such a shocking bore and pass me an orange jelly."

She smiled and batted her eyelashes. She had no idea why she was behaving so outrageously, but neither did she care. She thirsted for adventure, and here it was, in the guise of a *very* personable gentleman who would be just perfect if he were not so unpardonably high in the instep.

"Have a care, young lady. *I* may be immune to your charms, but I warrant half the occupants of the common stage shall not be so discerning." He filled a glass with an amber-colored liquid and tasted it musingly. "If you want your virtue to remain intact, I suggest you keep those delectable lashes quite out of sight. Preferably in your chamber. It is a great pity you do not wear spectacles, in fact. And though I can find no fault with your dress—it is modest enough—your features are altogether too piquant for safety, and your lips—well, we shall say no more of *those*."

"And why not, pray? Your sudden reticence astonishes, when you have, up till now, deemed fit to pronounce on all *else* about me!" Theresa's color had risen at his derisive little speech. She had dropped her spoon and was now standing, challenging, on the other side of the intimate Queen Anne table.

The gentleman's voice was deceptively velvety. "You are deceived, my dear. I have hardly *begun* pronouncing, as you call it. And my reticence was intended to spare your blushes—an uncustomarily civil gesture on my part. No . . . no . . . do not interrupt. I believe I have changed my mind after all. I *shall* say more about your lips. . . ."

"You jest!"

"I never jest about such things. Yes, as I suspected. Innocent, but kissable. A little too wide, perhaps, for prevailing fashion but soft and pink and I daresay pliant. . . ."

"Oh! You are nothing, I see, but a rag-mannered rogue!"

His attitude became crisper as he set down his glass. "Save me the spasms. I am merely warning you in the *roundest* of terms not to flaunt your obvious charms too openly."

"I think I know how to conduct myself, sir!"

"I think not, if the display you have just edified me with is anything to go by. Yes, yes, those pert, pouting lips, too. I repeat: Have a care, though naturally your affairs are no concern of mine whatsoever."

"I am glad that you realize that!" Tessie found it hard to keep the pique from her voice.

"I do, else I would doubtless take pains to find out *which* country seat you have escaped from and *which* young greenhorn you are set on eloping with. Such a bore. I suppose I would also have to procure you a governess—preferably a strict one—and return you to the bosom of your anxious family. Then I would have to spend *days* assuring them your reputation—not to mention your virtue—is still intact. Horrors! I suppose, if I was to do the whole thing properly, I would also have to call out the gentleman stupid enough to have offered for you in the first place!"

"No one has offered!"

"My condolences."

"You are vulgar and insufferable!"

"So I have been told. If you are not eloping, you must be escaping your governess and very likely a severe and well-deserved tongue-lashing. Spare me, if you please, the particulars." The gentleman's tone was curt enough to gall even a saint, and Tessie was many things—all quite adorable—but certainly no saint.

"I have never been scolded in my life, so keep your reflections to yourself!" Here Tessie's indignation vied with strict truthfulness, for in fact she was forever being scolded, but there was no need for this sarcastic, arrogant beast of a man to know anything of the kind.

How annoying, then, that he could lift his eyebrows so disbelievingly. Worse, that his lips were twitching ever so slightly, just enough to afford Miss Hampstead the lowering impression that he knew perfectly well she was telling outrageous lies.

"Never?"

"Never!"

"Well, I must say, you offer a tempting prospect."

"Oh!"

"Yes, the deficiency is rather evident, alack. Possibly with firmer schooling you might have proven charming. And decorous."

Tessie was stung. "In the normal way, I *am* charming. And decorous." She had no idea whatsoever why she was caviling with this gentleman. Surely it was better to give him a disgust of her than to cross swords with him over a strawberry trifle? For a young lady wishing to preserve her anonymity, she was being strangely perverse. She could not help feeling exultant, however, when he discarded his indifference long enough to finally inquire into her circumstances.

"Come," he said. "You pique my interest a little. If you are not eloping—and I must say, I am, by and large, relieved to hear it—and you are not escaping punishment—here, I am somewhat less relieved—"

Miss Hampstead scowled.

"What *are* you doing careering about the countryside in this . . . novel fashion?"

For an instant, Tessie nearly told him. He was not exactly a *likable* gentleman, but he was the first person who had even vaguely shown an interest in her since Grandfather Hampstead had died. What was more, he was clearly not a fortune hunter, for everything about him spoke of elegance and hauteur in a grand degree.

But then he tilted her chin upward and held her face carelessly in his own rather large, kid-gloved hands, and she bit her tongue firmly. He was treating her like a child and, indeed, he had even threatened to return her to the country! No, she would conduct this particular adventure quite on her own.

"I believe you acknowledged *that* to be no concern of yours." Her tone was even, masking the sudden erratic beating of her heart. For a fraction, his fingers lingered on her chin, then he shrugged and dropped them to his elegant side.

Tessie was left with a vague feeling of disappointment, though she could *not,* for the life of her, understand why. The gentleman bowed. Rather mocking, Miss Hampstead indignantly thought.

"How true and perfectly sensible of you. The last thing I need is a hoyden's confidences when I have concerns of my own to attend to. If you have not yet finished with your dessert, have the goodness to hand me a couple of slices of that ham. I will wrap them in the table linen and dine upstairs."

"No need, I have finished."

"Nonsense. You have merely toyed with your trifle, and I *know* you intend eating the orange jelly."

"Not anymore. You have quite ruined my appetite."

The gentleman was annoying enough to appear unrepentant. Indeed, his mouth quirked just a little, so Tessie knew he was more amused than guilty.

He arranged a table napkin rather artfully, turning down three of the folds. Then he compounded his sins by tasting the escargot straight from the silver tureen—Tessie could not abide such French concoctions—and remarking to the thin air that she was "sulky as *well* as pretty." He continued his discourse to the air. "A veritable mantrap." Then he addressed her once more. "And now, if you will pass me the ham, Miss . . . what was it? Norton? Manning?" He regarded her inquiringly, his eyebrow just slightly inclined. Miss Hampstead, perceiving this, and also the fact that he was, indeed, supremely attractive were it not for his traitorous scar and his odious superciliousness, could not think. Or, rather, she could not immediately retrieve the diabolically random name she had supplied herself with earlier.

"Um . . ."

"Um? Miss Um?"

Tessie looked confused and guilty in equal measure. The gentleman seemed quite unperturbed as he selected two apple turnovers and a perigord pie. These he tied carefully in a damask square before carving the ham himself.

"Ah, Miss Evans—recollect, my memory serves me better than yours—perhaps I shall just call you Charity. We are on *such* good terms, after all!"

Miss Hampstead scowled. "Drop the sarcasm, sir. It is beneath you. And you might as well know, you odious man, that my name is not Charity either. That was a *dreadful* trick to play on me!"

"Only dreadful if I were to use the information against you. By the bye, I have a title. Though I don't expect you to kowtow to my consequence, I find I prefer my given name—Lord Nicholas Cathgar—to 'odious man.' Forgive me if I seem pettish."

"You do, *Lord* Cathgar."

"My apologies."

"Accepted, with reservations."

Was there an appreciative gleam in Nicholas Cathgar's eye? It disappeared too quickly for Miss Tessie to be certain.

"I shall not flatter you by inquiring into those reservations. You have slipped up easily on the matter of your name. Take care, my girl. Subterfuge is best left to masters."

"Like yourself?"

Something flickered in his blue, oh, so deep, deep blue eyes. Shocking in a man, really.

His tone was clipped. "Undoubtedly. But we digress from the point."

"Which is?"

"Which is that you are as green as a goose. No, *don't,* I beg you, interrupt—agitation is really a remarkable bore."

He regarded her in such an amused, languid fashion that Tessie was in danger of throwing a teacup at his head. Apparently oblivious to her glowering countenance, he continued.

"I merely mention this, you know, out of"—his voice took on a wicked tone—"charity."

Miss Charity Evans, otherwise known as Tessie, did

not feel charitable. Not in the least. But Nicholas, once started, felt inclined to continue.

"There are many in this very posting house who might take a goose and wring its neck. Or, worse, they might, feather for feather, *pluck* it." His hand left his collation and drew yet another line down her chin. Tessie shivered, whether from this action or from the cold, clear threat behind his words, she could not say.

"Have a care, my pretty little Miss Nobody. I do not need you hanging on my shirttails right now, but I would be failing in my duty if I did not at least offer a word of caution."

"Consider it offered, then."

The man nodded. "And if I were you, I would lock my door and sleep with my reticule under my pillow."

"I always do."

"Excellent. I shall say farewell, then, while we are still in this state of harmonious accord."

Miss Hampstead smiled in spite of herself. Then, forgetting that she was wearing an appallingly outmoded gown, she stood up from her high-backed chair and permitted herself a stylish curtsy. Graciously, she also extended her hand.

It was taken, so that she once again blushed, especially as it was held rather too long for strict comfort or propriety. Also, his eyes seemed to be bewitching her own, for she could not seem to remove them from his face. How odd that she should feel this way, when they had been at daggers drawn practically from their first meeting. Not that he hadn't been all kindness, of course, rescuing her from the inferences of the innkeeper's wife. No! It was not *kindness* that compelled him. Not *kindness* that made him look at her so, so that her legs trembled like the molded fruit jellies still adorning the table.

Her eyes were now released from their lock as his own traveled down, quite gently really, to her lips. These he regarded speculatively, causing curious tremors in little Miss Tessie, tremors that lasted for a hundred years at least. Or so it seemed, for Miss Hampstead's wits seemed to have gone temporarily astray. Those roguish blue eyes still hovered devilishly upon her mouth, teasing as his haughty demeanor did not.

Tessie knew, for her lips were monstrously dry and her tongue, perforce, had to moisten them softly for some relief. It was not a jelly that she felt like now, but a custard. Soft, sweet, and intolerably undisciplined. She would have disgraced herself, she was sure, by tilting her chin up and inviting those lingering kisses. Had his hands not released her own, and tilted her chin himself, she was positive she would have helped him. But how salutary that she should be so tempted by a rake! And how handsome he was, despite having such a thorny and lamentable disposition.

Yes, it is a sad fact that, virtuous as she was, Nicholas offered a most tempting prospect, and unlike the heroines of most fairy tales, Tessie was *not* valiantly immune to his abundant charms. Her earlier annoyance with him had, perversely, vanished into thin air.

For once she lived up to her assumed name. She was in *perfect* charity with him. That is, until she opened the limpid eyes that had fluttered shut like bashful butterflies. Yes, it was most mortifying to catch an expression of sublime amusement upon his perfect features. Also, the laughter lines across his sensuous mouth and the crinkling corners at the edge of those mesmerizing eyes.

"Good night, infant."

"I am *not* an infant, but a woman grown."

"Don't tempt me, little woman grown."

"You are pleased to mock, sir."

He bowed, but the bow held regret rather than mockery. Miss Tessie was too innocent to discern the difference. All she noticed was the straight lines of his jaw, and the delicious fall of his cravat. To her, they seemed practically perfect. *Everything* about Lord Cathgar was practically perfect. She sniffed.

Four

"Do you require a handkerchief?"

"No."

"Good. It is just that you sniffed."

"You know perfectly well I sniffed because you are provoking."

"Provoking because I did not kiss you?"

"No!"

She was met with a quizzical glance that was annoyingly fascinating. She scowled.

"Telling farradiddles, again, Miss Charity?"

"I vow and declare you are the most odious, supercilious, overbearing, rag-mannered—"

"Yes, it is sad, is it not? Such a great catalogue of sins. . . ."

"You interrupt!"

"Indeed, for my time is not unlimited and you appear quite resourceful in your choice of synonyms."

Blue eyes—glittering blue—held her dark ones, rather too mockingly for strict comfort. Tessie struggled to find a suitable answer but felt awkward in the face of such worldly perfection.

Lord Cathgar had no business to be so . . . incomparable. Contrarily, she found the fact of his perfection provoking. *Especially* since he regarded her as a babe from the schoolroom, which somehow was more provoking still.

She knew she was behaving like a ninnyhammer, but with her legs quaking and her heart beating far faster than was normal in a young lady of her tender years, there seemed little she could do to change matters. If his lordship chose to think of her in leading strings, she should welcome such a misguided aberration. Her sensible side was really still most sensible.

The irritating smile appeared to widen, as if he read every one of her stray and nonsensical thoughts. It was particularly galling in the light of his own obvious polish, address, and perfection. He was a paragon, marred only by the existence of a single scar that shadowed his right temple.

A dangerous scar, that. One that offered temptations to a lady seized with a sudden desire to run her fingers along it. But Tessie was not that lady, oh, no, she wasn't! She was the demure young thing who swallowed hard, placed her hands well out of harm's way, and choked on her own civility.

"Farewell. Thank you, my lord, for dinner. If we should meet again in another setting, I should be pleased. I think."

"A gratifying change from the usual gushing sentiments. I must congratulate you on novelty. You *think,* indeed!" But the eyes were laughing again, and damnably infectious, so Miss Hampstead forgot her chagrin and took leave to laugh too.

"If you *should* ever run across me . . . ?"

"Yes?"

"You won't . . ."

"I won't?"

"You know! I daresay it is not quite respectable to be traveling unattended to London—"

"Dining with hardened rakes . . ."

"You were never invited, if I recall."

"I was, but we shall not squabble, my little mistress

of the understatement! Suffice it to say, you are *right*. *None* of your activities appear quite respectable."

"I, however, *am."*

"Quite respectable?"

"Indeed." Though Tessie blushed, for if thoughts could damn her, she was no better than a common strumpet. It was unpardonable that Nicholas should cause such wayward thoughts in her pretty little head! *Surely* it was not *she* who should be blamed in the face of such provocation?

For it was apparent that he required no padding in his doeskin breeches, stretched taut across the muscles of his thighs. Nor did he require any assistance with shoulder padding, or even with corsets across his stomach such as his royal highness had most sadly become reliant upon. No, he must surely take full blame for the disturbing nature of her thoughts and the pink that tinged her cheeks just looking at him.

Yes, he looked at her now in that dry way of his that was maddening.

Once again his voice was odiously indifferent, though his eyes, such a startling shade of blue, were hooded.

"Then you must accept my compliments. And chagrin."

"That I am respectable?"

Nicholas inclined his head.

"Oh! You are insufferable!"

"Undoubtedly."

"And . . . and . . . !"

"Hush, hush, my dear. Much as I would dearly love to exchange witticisms of this nature, my time, sadly, is limited."

"Then by all means leave, sir!" Tessie, contrarily, felt disappointment. She would rather die than have him know, though, so her tone was careless. Lord Cathgar eyed her keenly, then half smiled.

"I shall have to, regretfully. Though I hope to resume this fascinating conversation on my defects in the not too distant future. It is really rather salutary, I find."

"My lord . . ."

But Lord Cathgar's appetite seemed to have returned. He was meticulously spreading some butter on a thick wedge of crusty, still-warm bread.

"Spare me, if you please, the dull explanations! I find them all sadly tedious."

"But this tale . . . if it comes to the ears of the *ton . . ."*

Tessie watched Nicholas bite into his bread. He chewed for what seemed an age before swallowing. She could have screamed when he took a second, somewhat heartier bite. Then his eyes lit with resignation, and something more. Tessie could not tell.

"No, Miss Charity, if it will appease your sudden qualms, I am *not* a tattletale. Your secret, such that it is, is safe with me."

Tessie breathed. This might sound ridiculous, or too absurd to mention, but in truth she had been holding her breath, quite unconsciously, for nearly a full minute.

Certainly during the whole of the crust-eating episode. Her whole enterprise, she knew, would be for naught if this passing stranger chose to ruin her reputation. He could so easily do it. A whisper here, a passing remark there . . . Tessie chose not to let her imagination run any more riot than these two calamities. Now she exhaled slowly, and Nicholas grimly noted the small O into which her lips subsided.

I say "grimly," for Miss Tessie was cutting up his peace, a circumstance he did not find congenial, or in any way explicable, for he was generally *quite* immune to feminine wiles. Now he glared at Miss Hampstead, and took a few moments to comprehend quite what she was talking about.

"I thought it would be. Safe, I mean. The secret. You

know. I am a very good judge of character, though Finchie says . . ." She was prattling. She knew it. She knew it from the odiously smug air of the man who pinched snuff before her very eyes, who cast aside a butter dish, and who swept away a dust particle from an already immaculate sleeve. She felt the heat rise to her cheeks, whether from annoyance or embarrassment, she was too naive to tell. At all events, she very thoroughly lost the thread of her discourse. It seemed perfectly natural, then, to glare at him ominously.

He merely looked quizzical, an expression Tessie found disturbing. Then, in answer to a crooked finger that somehow drew her far too close to his annoying features, she eyed him with a wary smile upon her wide lips. He touched them for a fleeting instant. Again Tessie could hardly breathe, her eyes fluttering up to meet his own.

Lord Nicholas Cathgar's expression was unreadable, yet *still* she forgot to exhale. There was a certain tension about his jaw that made it perfectly impossible to look away. The moment seemed to lengthen, until amusement crept into those sultry blue eyes of his. Wicked for a gentleman.

"Exhale, little one."

Again the finger just touching her lips. Tessie realized she was behaving quite extraordinarily foolishly. The man was laughing at her, and still she could do no more than shiver at his touch, no, his half-touch. . . . Nicholas laughed. Then, very gently, very lightly—excruciatingly lightly—he kissed her at last. When he had, he put her from him firmly.

"Did I say green? I was wrong. Not green. *Lime. Shockingly* lime. Lock your door, little goose. I have never seen anyone more extraordinarily ripe for the plucking."

So saying, the gentleman traced his finger around her

mouth once more, and tapped his beaver in a mocking salute. Then, while Theresa was still shaking like a blancmange at his careless touch, he had the temerity—he actually had the temerity—to take his leave.

This before she could dream up a biting enough reply, which would have included such snippets as her being a deadly shot and quite up to snuff. Miss Hampstead bridled in indignation. Quite why, she was not certain, for her feelings were all aflutter, but she definitely knew nothing—nothing—could pardon his negligent pocketing of his package of delicacies. He was definitely an unfeeling monster to leave her thus, amid the array of jellies and first removes.

For there was no doubt that left to her sweetmeats, she was suddenly not so very hungry after all.

A gibbous moon half lighted the courtyard below Tessie's chamber. She was tired but not yet ready for sleep, the excitements of the day still upon her and the strangeness of the chamber a sharp reminder that she had thrown caution to the winds and there would be no turning back.

No returning to the country manor that had been her home, or not, at least, until she had established her credit in town and dismissed the lazy lackabouts who were managing the estate and allowing it to grow to seed. They had told her some twisted story, interspersed with many high titterings and tut-tuttings, that she was not so very rich after all. Not, in fact, an heiress, but merely the pensioner of some town sprig or other, who had no inclination to either visit her or set the land to rights. And this, after Grandfather had worked so hard with his irrigation schemes, and had hired Nash himself to design the gardens and the topiaries and the enormous hothouses with running water. It was not to be credited. Grandfather had told her clearly the disposition of his will, knowing that she had a mind as sharp as his own.

He had not permitted her to witness the signing, when Mr. Devonshire, his solicitor, had been summoned. This, she knew, was solely because she was the primary beneficiary. It would not have been fitting. But he had told her where she might find the keys to his dueling pistols, jewels, debts of honor, and snuffboxes. He had also given her carte blanche to his stables.

Now, after a tragic carriage accident, he was dead, her half mourning was over, and she had the strength of character, at last, to discover for herself exactly what her circumstances were. She knew of a certainty that Lawson was lying. Grandfather was a rich man—he had *not* left her and her dependents destitute, as the land agent appeared to imply.

But it troubled her that Mr. Devonshire had not responded to the queries she'd penned. It worried her, too, that there seemed to have been no quarterly stipend paid, and while the farmhands all seemed to be fed, many were staying on out of loyalty to her rather than because of any wage they were earning. Lawson's books, when she asked to review them, looked perfectly acceptable, but they were based on the premise that the estate had no income. This she knew to be patently untrue. So, it was a matter to investigate. . . .

The water was cold by the time she made her ablutions, but she was used to paddling in freezing streams, so made no objection. She merely toweled herself quickly and stepped into the crisp night garments she had thrown into her valise. These nestled arrestingly among a book of "recipes, charms, and soothing tisanes"; one morning dress of unfashionable cut, one high poke bonnet, one pair of silk stockings, and her tooth powder. Mr. Dobbins had made off with her curling papers, her pins, a morning dress of pale lavender, sundry smaller items like ribbons and handkerchiefs, a selection of half boots, some Grecian sandals, and a splendid evening dress of rose pink.

She sighed for this, for it really was enormously fashionable, and that small side of herself that was still thoroughly feminine delighted in it. Still, nothing was irreplaceable. The balance of her needs, she reckoned, could be procured in London.

She tried not to think what would happen if she did not encounter Mr. Devonshire quickly or expeditiously. Her heart gave that familiar, unpleasant little jolt that she always contrived to ignore.

Worrying, as Grandfather always said, was senseless. If things went well, it was a waste of energy, and if they did not, they wasted the pleasant moments one had before knowing things were not good. Besides, Tessie had no choice.

Mr. Devonshire was not traveling to her, ergo, she had to travel to him. If she'd had the felicity of a male escort or a chaperone, she would undoubtedly have seized the chance.

Indeed, she had not acted for a full quarter, hoping that some more suitable arrangement might arise. But, apart from Mr. Dobbins, who was more lecher than protector, there had been no one traveling to London. Her maid, Elizabeth, had contracted childhood measles and besides being feverish and spotted indicated strongly her propensity to be sick even on a private post chaise, which she had twice traveled in, once to Bath, and once accompanying Miss Tessie to Astley's.

Miss Hampstead, recalling this incident, deemed it the lesser of two evils to travel alone. Now she sighed as she pulled out her clips and tugged thoroughly at her ringlets, brushing them straight, only to have them bounce back when released from the spikes of her brush.

Outside, she could hear the horses being led to stables, their hooves loud against the cobbles. There were soft voices and several rather loud ones, obviously replete from the posting house's brandy, dessert Madeiras, and fine after-dinner ports.

A couple of bucks laid bets outside her window, but Tessie was too tired to take note of the odds. Gentlemen were so foolish that way! Grandfather, too, played deep games, wagering this, or wagering that, without the smallest hesitation. How many times had he lost a fabulous emerald pin, or a perfect cabochon sapphire, yet not two nights later dropped a string of pearls in her lap, or a tiara upon her head. How she had giggled at that! She supposed it must be locked away somewhere, if he had not lost it again.

She could hear some bells chime the hour, and a wagon roll in with large milk pails and churns of butter. Cool at night, she supposed, and straight off to the icehouse, for the cellars were reserved, in a house as superior as this, for wine. From the kitchens she almost could smell the cheeses, though she was not perfectly certain.

She peeked out of one window. Though they were adorned with elaborate shutters, they were fixed open, affording her a marvelous view of the square below. Water was streaming onto the cobbles. Maids, off duty, were waiting for their beaus and brothers, lit, for a moment, by the lamplighter. He was standing like a sentry at the posting house's door. It all seemed so strange and . . . busy. Tessie could just make out the new gas lamps. Like little yellow fireflies, they flickered in the distance. She turned from the window, yawned, and tested the door. Locked securely, of course. She tossed her head. She did not need a stranger's wisdom to warn her to do *that!*

Some of the men below sounded extremely bosky. She would pay no attention whatsoever to their ribald songs. And, of course, she would withdraw Grandfather's pistol from her reticule. She had decided after some thought to take only one of the very well-balanced set. Two would have been far too weighty, besides offering a temptation to any adversary. Now, her dark hair flowing past her shoulders—no, maybe just a little longer than that—she tucked the sleek, well-designed pistol under her pillow and pulled back the sheets.

True to Nicholas's orders, they were well aired and a hot brick warmed gently between the coverlets. On a small night table stood a neat, untrimmed taper in a simple holder, a bottle of cod liver oil—why, she could not fathom—and a tall cup of milk. No, she discovered on tasting, it was not purely milk at all, but, rather, a hot posset. It tasted vaguely of rum and nutmeg. Not the sort of thing she was usually partial to, but then, there was nothing usual in this night at all.

Extraordinary how every creak of the floorboards made her jump, as if she were just a silly widgeon rather than the skilled markswoman she knew herself to be.

That was the trouble really, Grandfather had brought her up to be a boy rather than a girl. But it was pointless going over old ground. She was who she was and soon enough she would know where she stood in the world. And if it was without a feather to fly with, so be it. She would make a plan. But she *felt* like an heiress, and Grandfather had told her so categorically . . . on these familiar thoughts Miss Theresa Hampstead fell into a sleep that would have surprised her. She didn't think it was possible with the peculiar mixture of country clatter and town bustle. Besides, the stars were shining too brightly by half.

One floor and a hallway down, Nicholas was discarding his high shirt points and gold cuffs. He was clean-shaven and ordinarily would have sunk into a tub of hot water and attended to the matter of his day's dark stubble himself. It was not offensive, merely a shadowy patch outlining his stark cheekbones and determined chin. To-night, however, he waved the razor away and ignored the waiting bubbles.

"The Luddites are meeting at ten after midnight in the crofter's barn."

"Oh! So that means, me lor', I am to spread that muck all over yer face and clothe yer in hose not fit for a prig-gin' varmint!"

"In essence, Joseph, yes."

"Well, me lor', pardon me language an' all that, but if ye want a piece o' me mind . . ."

". . . which I don't . . ."

The valet continued on without a blink of an eyelash. "Ye will jus' stay indoors 'ere and mind yer own business. Mighty 'armful some of those Luddites can be."

"Which is why, despite your deplorable cant, I con-tinue to employ you. If I am in the slightest need of any assistance, I rely on your discretion and your fists."

"Ah, well, it is not for nuffin' I've trained wiv a mas-ter."

"Quite so. Now, if you will be so kind as to pass me the, eh . . . muck?"

"Now that is wot I *don't* 'old wiv, me lor! It is not respectable like, and me a valet an all. . . ."

"Easily remedied, Joseph. I can demote you to the scullery. . . ."

"Ha-ha, always quick wiv a jest, me lor, but think of me feelings! Me sensibilities and such! Me, who 'ave dressed yer father before yer in powder and patches . . ."

"Reprehensible . . ."

"Quite, though it was all the rage, I might tell yer. . . ."

"Joseph, do I have to dress myself?"

"Not if yer be sensible like and try the new hunting coat Scott sent on this mornin'."

"Joseph! I am losing my patience! I am not interested

in tailors, but in treason! It is no laughing matter what the Luddites are doing. If we are not careful, we will be in the midst of revolution. Here, Joseph! Not in France, or on the damned Spanish peninsula, but here! In England! Lord save his majesty, the country deserves better from us. And the prince regent . . ."

"Blimey, sir, the prince is losin' popularity as we speak. There are some as wot say—"

Joseph stopped.

"Do you see? Already malcontents are gossiping. The Midlands are in uproar, and I am not just talking about frame breaking. Revolution is muttered more broadly than merely on the lips of a few disgruntled textile workers. With King George deranged . . ."

"Mad."

"See? People are not mincing their words. Precious few—saving Queen Charlotte, perhaps—expect him to recover. Already he has had relapses. For the Luddites—and factions like them—this is a God-given chance."

"They are afraid—"

"Afraid of progress, Joseph."

"Afraid of freakin' *starvation,* me lor'."

"Maybe. I sympathize with their fears, though most, I am tolerably well informed, are groundless. But there is a dangerous fragment, Joseph, which is willfully destructive. I fear these people with flames and axes. They care nothing at all for progress or for the new mechanization."

"Lor' luv them, why should they?"

Nicholas sighed. "Because their salvation lies within it. I shan't bore you with the details, only ask that you watch my back. Among the well intentioned there is a greater threat: The Luddite cause is being used by practiced interlopers. The type of bloodthirsty anarchists that foster chaos, looting, and wanton death. Mark you too: I would wager my last sovereign that it is not mechanization that is their full agenda, but *France.* Vive Napoleon!"

"The coves in the barn tonight?"

"We suspect so. We also fear for the life of his royal highness. He is an obvious target and does not help by maintaining a singularly rigorous social calendar. The scope for assassination is large."

"Wot's the plan, then?"

"I don't know, which is why I am going to such lengths to find out."

"Wot lengths, me lor', if yer don't mind my inquirin'?"

Nicholas allowed himself a brief, rather engaging grin. "As if you cared if I did! The plan, *when* you have deigned to exchange my clocked stockings for those vile garters, will be to intercept a certain Mr. Murray Higgins of Blackforth. Tie him up, gag him, and await orders."

"What shall *you* be doin', me lor'?"

"I shall be attending the meeting."

"As Mr. Murray 'Iggins?"

"Swift, Joseph. I must congratulate you on your comprehension."

"And I must congratulate you on bein' touched in yer upper works."

Nicholas smiled a little wryly. "It is a pity we have stopped beating our servants. We used to do so, you know, for impertinence."

"I'd rather 'ave a whippin' than carry you 'ome dead on a carrier's cart!"

"Elegantly phrased, Joseph. And in a strange way, I am gladdened by your sentiments. Now fetch me that calico shirt, if you please. And filthy up those boots, will you? I must look like I've been riding for hours."

And so, with a sigh, a few choice mumblings that Nicholas steadfastly ignored, and a vigorous shake of a curly, dark head, the valet set to work. It did not take long, of course, to grub up a pair of immaculate boots, but certain other of the preparations took a good deal more time. Joseph did not grudge it in the least.

Theresa woke with a sharp sense of alertness. Instantly, her hand was at her pillow, but though the shadows were long, it did not take a moment to realize that her door was still firmly locked and that there was no intruder in her small chamber but a little button spider crawling slowly down the wall. She relaxed a trifle but could not shake off the notion that something was not as it should be.

Tense, she straightened her rumpled undergarments, then discarded the rose-trimmed coverlet. It was cold, so she stepped over to the grate and prodded at it with one of the heavy pokers left for this purpose. The flinders ignited to flame almost instantly, lighting the little room with a soft red glow that should have been comforting but was not. Still shivering, Miss Hampstead paced up and down the chamber, her thoughts wondering distractedly—and for no good reason—to Lord Cathgar. He was undoubtedly below stairs or across the hallway, or, at all events, *somewhere* in this godforsaken posting house. The thought was strangely comforting, like warm milk and honey at bedtime. No, like sweet sherry, or something more wicked perhaps . . . brandy, or dark Madeira. . . . She wondered why she was behaving so foolishly. Her heart was still beating faster than it ought, and though she was not given to foolishness, she could not help thinking of the leering eyes of the men in the taproom and of her rash announcement regarding the forty-two sovereigns safe in her possession.

He was right! She *was* a fool and a greenhorn! He, the unnamed he—for she was not so lost to decorum as to think of him as Nicholas, even in her head—had been far too prominent in her wayward thoughts all evening.

So infuriating, too, when he did not care a button for her. That much he had made obvious. And how annoying, when this was precisely as the sensible side of Miss Tessie wished. But the sensible side was sleeping now, and all Miss Tessie's demons were storming at his rather piquing indifference. She moved restlessly to the window. It was quiet now, the lamplighters long abed, and the maids, too, belike.

The moon shone on a dappled horse tethered quietly beneath a shuttered window. She squinted through the leaves of an apple tree growing tall beside her window. The fresh scent revived her. Enough to hear muttered tones and see the silhouette of a figure loping toward the Great South Road. Tattered he was, and carrying a small lantern for illumination, though the moon was enough. There was something about his bearing, though, that set her heart racing even faster than its present abnormal rate. When the lamp temporarily lighted on a certain scar across the temple, the room echoed with her gasp. When she looked again, however, a common beaver had been firmly squashed over the offending flesh.

Then, to her outraged senses, there was a distinct scuffling at the heavy oak door to her chamber. She heard rather than saw the old handle being depressed. The wood quaked as if being forced. Then, her ears alert, she heard the faintest sounds of drunken laughter. Soon, soon she heard also the heavy jangle of keys upon a ring. . . .

It was less than a second before Tessie understood what was happening. Someone—some abominable, ill-meaning lout—had gained possession of the keys to her chamber.

But no! It was more than just someone. There were whisperings and sniggering and the scuff of boots on the landing.

Tessie sighed. It was those damnable forty-two gold sovereigns! Not to mention, of course, the spite of the innkeeper's wife. Doubtless she'd handed over the keys with a rare smirk to her thin, reddened lips. Well, a pox on her!

Tessie had no intention of being relieved of her fortune. She considered screaming, but the walls were thick and she did not think she was at *all* modestly enough dressed for rescue. Her only option was to put a bullet through the boots of the first man who entered. That, or make a swift escape.

Escape, though feeble, was probably best. By the sound of the laughter, she would be dealing, not with one, but with *three* drunken rogues. She would gladly shoot holes in *all* of their boots, but there was the small matter of reloading, not to mention the scandal . . . no! For now, she would be perfectly sensible. Even Grandfather, who was as game as a pebble, would not have hazarded the odds.

The chamber was small and sparsely furnished, so it was a mere matter of three swift steps and a small fumble for the pistol. Cool and heavy in her hand, she breathed a calm sigh of relief. Time. The little beauty would buy her time if she needed it. With regret she abandoned her open valise but reached for her reticule. She threaded the fastening ribbons through her wrists and felt around for her boots. They were reassuringly at hand.

The noises were growing louder outside her door. There was a scraping of metal and a hard thump across the oak. Then several loud hushing sounds and a couple of bars of Spanish. A soldier's song, and not one fitting for her delicate ears. Unfortunately, she understood every word, the viscount having educated her most unsuitably for a female.

She was less shocked than was strictly seemly, for she was more concerned with her escape than with her sensibilities.

Single-handedly—the right, as always, spared for the

pistol—she flung her stout morning boots straight through the window and out, into the night sky. One landed on a whispering branch of the apple tree, the other with a sickening thud on the cobbles below.

Tessie held her breath. She was positive the rogues would be alerted, but they were not. The Spanish warbling grew louder, shielding all thuds from suspicion. As she exhaled a little, the key was finally inserted into position. A split second later, Tessie's pistol was ready. Trained at the keyhole, she knew that at the veriest click, she would fire.

Nothing. Then a grumble, and the jangle again. It must, she realized, be a very large set of keys. Despite her fear, her eyes began to twinkle. She hoped each key looked identical and that the thieves were as drunk as they sounded. At *that* rate, she could remain in her chamber all night. The handle turned again. Miss Tessie changed her mind. Though habitually brave, she decided the tree offered a kindlier prospect.

One among them might be sober. Or brute enough to force the door. Wasting no time whatsoever—for Grandfather had never held with feminine delays and hesitations—she unloaded her weapon and cast her legs over the sill. It was second nature to grip the first branch of the apple tree. This with a steady left hand, so she could swivel to face the window. Slowly, she extended her right hand, pistol and all, to grab an upper branch.

Another key, she could hear, was being inserted. The men seemed to be quarreling, for voices were raised and there were footsteps . . . but these grew fainter as she steadied herself for a moment. Then, in the twinkle of an eyelash, she had clamored down the tree, regardless of all bruises or scratches to her person.

Her boot, providentially, was waiting for her. But not the first, which she had neglected to collect from the uppermost branch.

"Botheration!"

She could hear voices upstairs as she shook at the lower branches, hoping that the shaking would be enough to dislodge the offending—but necessary—footwear. It wasn't, so she was forced to lace up the first, thrusting the pistol into the capacious pocket of her gown. Then it was a matter of standing perfectly still with her back to the apple tree as a shadowy figure thrust a head out of her window. He was pushed aside by a burlier shadow, and there appeared to be some kind of scuffle from within.

Tessie did not wait to hear what the outcome of this was, for she was desperate for her boot. She could go nowhere without it, and was disinclined to even make the attempt. Consequently, while some kind of debate was occurring upstairs, she shinned up the back of the tree as fast as her ladylike undergarments would permit, and buried herself for a moment in the leaves. The boot was still too high to reach, but if she whittled herself a twig, she would be able to dislodge it without too much effort. Accordingly, she selected a suitable branch and worked at quietly breaking off a stick.

By now her senses and her night vision were rather more acute than they had been. She had already decided that in an hour or so it would be safe to return to her room, for no one would think to burglarize her twice, and she could brazen it out in the morning. The only people not expecting her at breakfast would be the rogues and possibly the innkeeper's wife. They might gape, they might even have their eyes on stalks, but they could hardly claim to know anything of the matter. She would calmly pay her shot and leave by the first available post.

In the meanwhile, there was still the problem of the boot. And the tree, though strong, was scratchy. Also, it was strange to be out of doors in one's nightrail, with several strangers ready, doubtless, to cut one's throat. For an instant, the redoubtable Miss Tessie sniffed. To her horror, a tiny tear lurked at the back of her shining bright eyes. She scrubbed it away scornfully and worked at retrieving her boot. The laces appeared tangled, but some forceful prodding yielded rewards: Before long, the leaves were whispering loudly as the boot made its way down several branches. Right, fortuitously, to where she sat.

Minutes later, she was ready to make her descent. But wait! She wavered a little, for a rogue, not two feet from the apple tree, was industriously coshing a gentleman over the head. His science was excellent, for it was a neat, clean blow that he delivered, such that his victim had no notion of the misfortune that had befallen him. Indeed, he dropped almost instantly to the ground with no more than a winded grunt.

The rascal was working quickly, pulling a large cravat from his pocket and gagging the man expertly. Then, as if it was his everyday custom—which indeed it probably was—he dragged the poor fellow away from the illumination of a gas lamp and regarded him thoughtfully.

Tessie squinted through the leaves. *Not* a good moment, she thought, to descend. Her pistol felt very comforting in her pocket. So much better than smelling salts, though a fit of hysterics would really have been perfectly suitable at that moment. But she restrained herself.

The victim, though not a gentleman, was undoubtedly a man of substance, for he wore a thick, dark coat and had alighted from a chaise. This was even now tooling off to the ostlers, its coachman quite oblivious to the troubles his master. Tessie could see very little of the stranger's face, for it was dark and there was a tangle of tree in her way. He did, however, sport a rather large fob watch, for Miss Hampstead could just see the glimmer of silver as its chain spilled from his pockets.

Curiously, the felon hardly seemed interested. Rather

than prigging the item—as any self-respecting pickpocket would surely do—he tucked it back neatly.

All this Tessie had noticed in less than an instant, in the half-moonlight and half-light. Strange how detail, which should be *less* obvious in the night hours, sometimes becomes *more* so. Either way, she perceived that she should now quite probably scream but did not care to draw attention to herself. So she watched as the rogue cast a glance around the courtyard, nodding in satisfaction at its emptiness. Then, with a wary eye on a neighboring barn, he proceeded to carry his victim—as if he were no more weight than a pound of flour—the small distance it took to reach the foot of the apple tree.

Tessie, still hidden in the branches above, dared not move. Her eyes flashed indignantly, however, as the man systematically tied his victim to the trunk of the tree. He was humming a brazen tune. He seemed to be waiting, though his eyes were trained on the barn rather than on his victim.

It seemed hours, though it was probably minutes, before Tessie nearly *did* cry out, more from surprise than from fright, for the man in the tattered clothes was back, and *this* time there was no doubt about the scar.

Tessie's heart stammered painfully in her chest. What could this mean? Was the arrogant gentleman who'd rescued her a spy? A highwayman? She had no answer, for his eyes traveled to the prisoner only briefly, and his words to the rogue were curt.

"It is on. Another fifteen minutes, I should think. Was there a password?"

"I forgot to ask."

"Forgot . . . Lord, Joseph! You coshed the man senseless and forgot to *ask?*"

"I thought 'e'd be better senseless than strugglin'. As for password, you said nuffin' of that, me lor'. Best forget the 'ole matter. It seems to me a damn silly plan, savin' your lor'ship."

"Don't lordship *me,* Joseph! And if there was another route, I'd gladly take it. Frankly, there isn't. I just met Fagan on the Great South Road. I don't like it. Something is wrong."

The rogue's manner changed at once. "A trap?"

"Could be. If Higgins awakes, for God's sake, ungag him. He might have something to say. In the meanwhile, the meeting gathers. Fifteen of the men are already assembled. I just hope these rags serve. Higgins seems more respectable than I'd imagined."

"Take 'is coat."

"No time."

"Then switch 'ats, me lor'ship. That beaver is . . . is . . ."

"Outrageous?"

"Aye."

The man with the scar grinned. "Very well, Joseph. I'd be loath to offend your sensibilities. Here. Now give me his hat. That do?" He jammed the thing unceremoniously on his head and untethered the piebald horse. It whinnied a little as he mounted. "I shall do a circuit and arrive from the north."

"You're a fool, me lor'."

The gentleman—for all his tatters, Tessie knew he was *that*—laughed.

"And *you* are insubordinate!"

"Better that than dead!"

"I'm not sure!" Then the bantering tone died. "Joseph . . ."

"Aye, me lor'?"

"Watch my back."

"For very certain, me lor'."

"If I don't return . . ."

"Aye?"

"Keep an eye on that wench upstairs. She is doubtless up to a pother of mischief, but I find that I like her."

"Aye, me lor'."

Here Tessie nearly emitted a quite audible gasp, for the rogue was clearly speaking of her! At least, she *hoped* he was . . . impudent, rag mannered . . . but she could not stop feeling a distinctly unmaidenly glow of happiness. His impudence should be outraging her. She should call the watch on him and his head-coshing confederate. He should be taken up in irons. . . .

No time for irons; he was gone, with a grimmer look on his handsome countenance than Tessie would have liked. In fact, the shivers of apprehension she now felt bore no resemblance to the delicious shivers of a moment previous.

The villain prodded his victim urgently. There was no response save for a mutter.

"Murray 'Iggnis, you have *got* to wake up!" This in a hiss. It was sufficiently audible, however, for Tessie to hear. Her descent of the tree became more reckless. The leaves shook and the villain—or so Tessie regarded him—gasped as the branches parted and Miss Hampstead landed with perfect poise just two feet beside him. Instantly, his strong arms coiled around her like a snake.

But Tessie, still gripping her pistol, begged him sweetly "not to make such a cake of himself."

The villain, shaken, released his grip a little, warily removing the pistol from her grasp.

"Careful. I think it might be primed. I heard a click as I dropped to the lower branch."

"Beg pardon, miss, this is no place for young ladies."

"Then it is fortunate that I have lost all claim to that title. My behavior has surely sunk me beneath all reproach. Now, wake that man up. . . . I don't believe I know your name?"

"Joseph, miss." This with a grin, for Joseph knew instinctively that this must be his lordship's wench. Uncommonly pretty she was, though not in his lordship's usual style.

"Very good, Joseph. Now do, I pray you, release me altogether, for though I am quite partial to reptiles, I have never yet relished the grip of a boa constrictor."

Joseph, who knew nothing of foreign shores or the creatures thereon, and who might otherwise have missed Miss Hampstead's irony, chuckled. Living with the earl had increased his knowledge of matters relating to the Peninsula and the colonies, and, of course, the far of Americas. . . .

He instinctively permitted Miss Hampstead her freedom, though he retained the weapon with raised brows and checked it himself. Miss Hampstead murmured her thanks, and knelt in the earth, feeling the victim's pulses with interest.

"It's a shakin' 'e needs. . . ."

"Nonsense. He is awake. No, don't kick at him, foolish man! It will make him feel queasy. If I had sal volatile I could revive him at once. Wait! There is cod liver oil in my chamber. Disgusting stuff. It will do, though he won't thank me for my trouble."

"Miss . . ."

"Oh, don't miss me! Shin up, will you?"

She gently removed the gun from Joseph's restless hands.

"The bottle is very close to my counterpane. I would do it myself, only there are some ruffians I should very much like to avoid running into, and they already have succeeded in breaking down the door. If they are still there, of course, don't go in."

This last a second thought as she smiled sweetly at the bemused Joseph. He, it might be said, was experiencing a gamut of emotions he later described to the second housekeeper as "quite haranguing," for besides being ordered about by a little chit of a thing who was as cool as you please with a mightily unsuitable weapon, he was also hard pressed to watch his lord's back, a matter of the most singular importance. So, what with one thing and another, he was shinning up blimey apple trees and muttering darkly, terrified that the cove would wake hisself up and stab the little mistress in the back, a thing he *could* not like, for me lor' had said . . . well, never mind what his lor' had said. . . .

In the meanwhile, poor Joseph was doing precisely as he was bid, bewitched by Miss Tessie's smile and her matter-of-fact handling of the pistol, which she now pointed quite merrily at the tree-bound Murray Higgins.

Five

It was a small matter to retrieve the cod liver oil, for besides an empty glass that had once contained the aromatic hot posset, there was nothing on the table save the blue-bottled decoction. The door had not been forced, though it had obviously been opened. Joseph could see the great key still in its lock, and the taper-lit hallway gaping beyond.

He snatched the bottle, clamored back to the windowsill, then heroically disregarded several sundry scratches to his face as he wormed his way down. The little miss, who he'd decided to trust despite severe misgivings, held out her hand peremptorily.

"Well done!" Miss Tessie's smile was warm but brief as she unstopped the cork. "Untie the gag."

Bemused, Joseph obeyed and hoped to heaven he would not incur the wrath of his master.

"Good." She grabbed the bottle, sniffed at its contents, then held poor Mr. Higgins's nose as she poured a considerable quantity calmly down his throat. The result of this barbarous onslaught was that Mr. Higgins choked himself conscious. While he spluttered, Joseph kept guard, cocking the pistol a dozen or so times every time he heard the most trifling of noises.

There was a maid who walked through the avenue leading to the courtyard, but she was laden with several long platters from the tavern and did not cast her eyes around her. Then a mongrel stray growled, but it appeared Joseph had a way with dogs, for he very soon loped off, having sniffed—and found satisfactory—the valet's elegant unmentionables.

Now, in the shadows of the moonlight, Tessie bent over Mr. Higgins and felt, not for his pulses, but for his fob. It was strangely elegant, wrought in silver and studded with tiny gems Tessie could not but think of as diamonds.

"It is close to fifteen minutes. I pray there is time."

Joseph nodded, thankful that the shadows hid his blushes. While he could ably snuff out the life of any hardened criminal, he felt at a loss, somehow, in the company of a gentlewoman attired in naught else but her nightrail, no matter how modest that attire might be. (Tessie's was disappointingly modest, for though she had longed for diaphanous silks, Miss Fincham's views on such matters had always been made prodigiously plain to her.)

"What the—"

"Ah, you are awake. At last! What is the password, Mr. Higgins?"

"Password?"

Tessie was firm, her chin tiptalting dangerously.

"The password, Mr. Higgins."

"What the devil . . . ? There *is* none."

"But there is. And if you don't care to tell me within the next three seconds, I shall put a bullet through your heart."

"You are deranged."

"Quite possibly. However, we stray from the point. The password . . . ?"

"Silks."

"Understand that if you play May games with me, I shall not be pleased. The password once again, if you please?"

"Silks, I tell you!"

"Very good. Joseph?"

"I am goin'. Belike I shall meet up with me lor' as he rides down. They are gathering already. I hear 'ooves upon the footpaths."

"Hurry, then."

"Aye."

Joseph, caught between keeping an eye on the wench and serving his master, chose the latter course. The wench, he reckoned with reluctant respect, could look after herself.

The barn was hardly comfortable, but it sufficed. Hay bales had been stacked neatly into businesslike rows, and it was cold, so each man wore a warm coat against the chill. The windows were covered in woven cloth—dark navy, so the lanterns could not be detected from outside. There were several of these lit, heavy and scattered all about, from front to back. The remaining gloom was alleviated somewhat by an open fire near the entrance. Wisps of smoke coiled toward the doorway, where a sentry, dressed grimly in the foggy gray of the Midlands, stood guard. Each Luddite entered and spoke his piece quietly.

Nicholas, looking nothing like himself, removed his hat and nodded curtly to the guard. The only chair in the place—a heavy oak confection that looked out of keeping with the barn—was occupied by a surly-looking character referred to throughout the night as Fagan.

Nicholas, being waved to one of the makeshift seats, selected an inconspicuous hay bale near the back and folded his arms.

" 'Is majesty, bein' mad, is no 'elp to us no more, savin' 'is grace. Would we could still 'ave the ear of 'is majesty. Farmer George, for so we 'ave called 'im and so 'e 'as become. But the reign of George the Third is over, me mates, for regency or no' it is not flamin' likely 'e is goin' to recover 'is senses."

"Long live George IV!"

"What bloody madman said that?"

There was a scuffle and an angry murmur, wherein Nicholas regarded the flames of the lantern steadily, and met no one's—least of all the miscreant's—eye."

"It is MacAlistair of Tottam, said that."

"Stand up, MacAlistair."

A thin gentleman with a bulbous nose and several red, spidery veins about his face rose from the hay bales. He chuckled, not at all put out by several sets of eyes glaring at him ominously.

"Lord love us, does none of you kens 'ave a sense of 'umor?"

There was a whisper and a small sigh, then an answering gleam from two of the northern gentlemen.

"Sit down. This is not the time to be joking, Kenneth MacAlistair. That soddn' bastard is squanderin' all the freakin' wealth of the kingdom! 'E needs to go, for else there will be looms and what have you all over the isles. The day will come when an honest man don't 'ave no bread to eat nor no ale to drink, think you on that! We need to get rid of the machines, gentlemen! The workers need work!"

"Aye! Aye!" There was general assent in the room.

"There is a plan afoot, even now, to rid the realm of the Prince of Wales. Nothin' but trouble, him! Now, if you look to France . . ."

"France is naught but a quagmire of Frenchies, and if you've taken a loikin' to that new Bourbon chappie . . ."

"Indeed I 'ave *not,* parding me language, but some among yer coves 'ave 'eard rumblins' . . ."

"Wot sort of rumblins'?"

"Napoleon is free, that's wot. Now, *'e* is a fella to support the Luddite cause. . . ."

The voice rattled on, and no one listened more intently than a certain gentleman seated to the back, the scar at his temple seeming more livid than usual. That Napoleon and the Luddite cause were rather hard to reconcile on an intellectual level seemed irrelevant. Someone was manipulating these men, and someone, whoever he was, was good at it. Honest workers were red hot for action, drawn into this mood of conspiracy like ignorant moths to a lingering flame.

When the meeting drew to a close, each man was allotted a task, and the burden of carrying the message through to his own county and borough. Pens and ink were not permitted, for besides being unsafe, they were not the tools of workingmen. Every detail had therefore to be committed to memory, every man suffering the grueling task of reciting the names, the dates, the places that had been spoken of so secretly, so furtively, for the safety of the Luddite cause hung on each separate instance.

Finally, the speaker hushed the low voices and held out his hands for attention.

"Gentlemen, I 'ave saved this moment for last, for I thought it might amuse you. You see, we have a traitor in our midst."

Nicholas's face remained perfectly impassive.

"Be'old before you Mr. Murray Iggins. 'Iggins, we have rumbled yer lay. Yer are a spy for the king. Leastawise, for 'is right royal 'ighness. An if yer think yer can quibble, let me inform yer that our password changed last Saturday at ten from silks ter silence. You did not know, for you were, at that stage, canterin' off to God knows where, bleatin' of our plans."

There was a tumultuous roar in the barn.

"Hush! Do yer want the watch down on us? Now, Mr. 'Iggins, what say you?"

"A mistake, gentlemen. And a 'orrible one at that."

"No mistake! A certain Mr. Murray 'Iggins was spotted by a palace guard—one of us—locked in earnest conversation with the Lord High Chancellor. That's nuffin' to snigger at!"

"Tommyrot!"

"It is *not* tommyrot that 'is royal 'ighness's cavalcade to Vauxhall was changed from Bruton Street to Upper Wimpole, nor that our sharpshooter is now moulderin' in Newgate, charged with treason and such!"

"I know nothing of that."

In this, Nicholas spoke the plain truth, for he had had no prior notion whatsoever that the Murray Higgins he was impersonating was actually in the service of his majesty's government. The matter would normally have struck him as absurd, but, being within inches of his own probable demise, he quite refrained from laughing.

"Lawks alive! It will take a sod more convincin' than *that!* And Mr. Grange, let me assure you, is *not* a slow-top!"

His lordship had heard of Mr. Grange. Indeed, it had been his particular mission to infiltrate the Luddites headed up by this person, for "Mr. Philip Grange," as he preferred to be known, was as infamous across the Channel as he was in England.

Known by certain circles as "the chameleon," he was said to hold high office. Not in England, of course, but in its erstwhile enemy, France. A Parisian born and bred, Mr. Grange was actually Monsieur le Duc du Marie—a new title, born of an equally new emperor—Napoleon. Sadly, Napoleon was even now languishing—or Nicholas hoped he was—in St. Helena, and the title seemed to be worth as much as the paper it had been written on. Nothing, in point of fact.

So, Monsieur le Duc, not content with inciting revolution in his native country, now sought to sow its seeds in England instead. Apparently, he had a burning hatred of the English, though he was related in blood to one of the noble houses of the land. This made him doubly villainous, for he could switch from English to French like his namesake, the chameleon.

Where there were whispers, so was there Monsieur le Duc, stoking at those whispers, igniting small fires of discontent. The Luddites, the free traders, the vassals oppressed by corn laws, all of these were cultivated by Mr. Philip Grange, who understood their desires and pandered to their vanities. Nicholas had been charged with observing his methods, with reporting on dangers. He now stood in grave danger himself.

"Kill 'im!"

"Lordy, no! That is a 'angin' offense!"

"So is burning looms, and we do it!"

"For England we do! This is murder!"

"An example, an example!"

A lantern overturned in the excitement. There was a scuffle, in which Nicholas saw his chance, his reflexes as swift as his intelligence. He threw a punishing left at the man called Tallows, beside him. Then, with no one immediately at hand to restrain him, he dived past the open fire and for the door. Too bad Fagan, less concerned with the lanterns than with pleasing his master, rushed upon him and pinked him with a cunning device concealed up his sleeve. Nicholas saw the flash of steel just before he ducked, averting more immediate harm to himself, though blood flowed freely from his shirt. He divined it was a flesh wound, however, for though the graze stung, he could still breathe freely.

"Blackguard!"

"Tie 'im up, gentlemen."

"What will you do with him? 'E looks naught but trouble."

"Trouble? 'E is naught but a coward."

"You'll not be killin' 'im!"

"Snaffle it, Millwardshire! 'Is blood will not be on

your lilywhites! 'E will live to tell us all 'e knows. After that . . . It is not up to the common likes of you an' me. Now go, all of yer! And one at a time, mind. We don' want to draw no attention to ourselves. Trouble it is when folks start reportin' on 'avey-cavey behaviors. Stubble the lanterns, will yer? The moon is 'igh enough for our needs."

So saying, Fagan turned to his prisoner with a rare smile illuminated by the flames. He had a large mouth, quite handsome really, were the effect not spoiled by one cracked tooth and two gaping holes where his molars should have been. Nicholas, seeing the smile, was not inclined to return the gesture.

It did not take the resourceful Miss Hampstead long to make her prisoner talk. Indeed, she felt rather amiable toward him as she eased his bonds a little.

"I am dreadfully sorry you are being treated like this. It is not my habit, you know, to threaten violence."

"Is it not? I would have thought you a veritable old hand at it!" The man's clipped tone was wry as he looked into the barrel of pretty Miss Tessie's rather businesslike gun.

"No, Grandfather would not have a bar of it, you see. My temper is too vile."

"I shall endeavor to remember that. May I sit up, Miss . . ."

"Evans. Miss Charity Evans." The lie slipped easily off her tongue. Tessie thought it was only fair to be consistent.

Unlike her teasing gentlemen, he seemed to notice nothing amiss in the extraordinary name but merely nodded as he shifted his weight a little.

"Ah, Miss Evans, then. May I sit up? This tree stump

is beginning to pall on me, and I have the most diverting notion that I might just cast up my accounts."

Rather than recoil in horror, Miss Tessie looked stricken. "Oh! If you do, it will be all my fault. It is the cod liver oil. Nasty stuff, alas, but that password was urgent."

At mention of the password, the man's eyes focused and he stopped fidgeting with the bark of the tree. Apparently, his dinner was safe, for he did not cast up his accounts as threatened.

"Miss Evans, answer me truly, if you please."

His voice held a pleasant lilt that seemed surprising in a man of his origin. Tessie made no comment, though she eyed the man speculatively. His low tones held both urgency and authority, which was really most diverting considering the circumstances.

"Why should I?"

He continued. "You will agree that while I am bound and you are in possession of that excellent pistol, there is no immediate threat to your person."

Tessie's mouth curved. "Yes. . . ." But her fingers closed quite naturally around the trigger.

He shrugged as best he could under the circumstances.

"I suppose I shall have to accustom myself to that thing, but I do implore you to point it at my arm rather than at my heart. You might sneeze."

There was a moment's silence as Miss Hampstead eyed the prisoner warily, for though it is true he was tied to the tree, he nevertheless had recovered remarkably quickly from his crushing blow.

Worse, in her opinion his voice sounded rather too animated for comfort, and she had the distinct impression he did not take her seriously enough. She put her finger to her lips.

"Hush! I would not relish, you know, being overheard."

The prisoner lowered his tone to a whisper.

"Not for anyone do I hush, but I value my life, and you seem a remarkably bloodthirsty female."

He then ignored Miss Tessie's baleful glare and continued.

"Now let me hasten to my point, for I fear there is no time to be lost. I am presently helpless, so you are under no *immediate* threat, though I can't answer for the same at any time in the future."

Raised brows from Tessie.

The man continued. "In fact, I can vouchsafe that I very possibly might strangle you, but not now. So do be a dear and satisfy my curiosity. Are you a Luddite?"

Miss Tessie, a small twinkle lighting her eye at this rather fierce soliloquy, bent her mind to the question.

"A *what?*"

"A Luddite."

"I don't *think* I am, though I am not familiar with the term. Is that a form of bluestocking? If so, it is quite possible, for I am rather well versed in the classics and the globes, Grandfather having—"

"Miss Evans, I am afraid I must bore you a little with my prattle. If you are *not* a Luddite—and decidedly, you are not, and no, the term does not bear any resemblance to the bluestocking society you have just alluded to—I fear you may—*we* may—all be in grave danger."

"You already are, I believe."

"I mean *real* trouble. Not the sort of prank where one is merely coshed over the head and bound to a tree."

"I am not partial to tricks, Mr.—"

"Lord, actually. Though the title is strictly a courtesy, I assure you. And this is no trick. . . ."

Tessie's eyebrows rose. "A second son?"

"Third, actually. To the Duke of Atwater. But that doesn't signify . . ."

"No, I see that it doesn't." In the shadows, Joseph returned and paced restlessly.

"He has the password?"

"Aye, but I mislike it. Something is wrong."

Tessie cocked her pistol again and looked directly at her victim. "Talk, my lord, but be quick about it. If you hoodwink me, you shall pay dearly for it, his grace or no."

"I am not Murray Higgins, as you have probably divined."

There was an audible gasp from Joseph, who had heard little of the earlier whisperings. "*Not* Murray—"

"Was he *meant* to be this Higgins?"

"Aye, in truth. A Luddite through and through."

"I am no Luddite. I am an emissary of Lord Castlereagh. Higgins is incarcerated. It was a small matter to switch places."

"No small matter. Do you have proof of this?"

"Is it likely? I did not expect to have to prove my true identity. The reverse, in fact. It is ironic, is it not, that I can give you proof absolute that I am Murray Higgins."

"Provided by Castlereagh?"

"Provided by friends to his majesty's government."

"We are at an impasse. Joseph, what do you think?"

" 'E talks too proper fer a Luddite. Oi believe 'im."

"So do I. *Laudem virtutis necessitati damus.*"

The prisoner stared at her as though she had gone quite mad. At length, he asked the obvious question.

"What do you propose?"

"Translate that, if you please. I doubt that Murray Higgins, whoever he is, would be trained in the classics."

Lord Christopher Lambert blinked. He felt damnably foolish trussed to a tree—and uncomfortable besides. His head ached and the success of his delicate mission was suspended, precariously in the balance. The chit was regarding him with an air of smug expectancy that made him catch his breath. In less dire circumstances he surely would have laughed aloud. To be required to dredge up his Oxford Latin in such conditions truly seemed to be the outside of enough.

Six

"Laudem virtutis necessitati damus. Laudem virtutis necessitati damus."

The Duke of Atwater's third and most troublesome son coughed. He tried not to think of the bump that must brewing upon his handsome—yes, he had always regarded it as handsome—head. Instead, he concentrated on remembering some smidgen of the classical education his parents had paid so dearly for.

"Laudem virtutis." He closed his eyes as if in pain. Then he opened them again rather whimsically.

"My, my, you *are* a bluestocking. Now, let me think. . . Quintilian, unless I am more rusty than I thought. Ah, yes. I take your point. *We give to necessity the praise of virtue.* Your excuse for treating me thus?"

"Indeed." Tessie smiled perfunctorily, for her thoughts were now racing ahead of mere niceties.

"Untie him, Joseph, for we may well have need of him tonight. My apologies, sir, and tell me, if you please, about 'silks.' That *was* the password for tonight, was it not?"

Tessie's brain was agile enough to single out the most crucial point in this debacle. If the password was sound, Nicholas's impersonation might not be discovered. He might be as safe as houses, *quite* unneedful of any feminine rescue. On the other hand . . .

"I was given it by Lord Castlereigh himself. The password, of course, refers to the looms. I believe the source was unimpeachable."

Miss Hampstead sighed a little in relief. Her fingers relaxed infinitesimally around their dangerous resting place. She probed just a little further, however, for she was a tenacious creature, as Finchie was always expostulating.

"But it *could* be a trap?"

"I begin to think so. Something feels not right. The road, sadly, is fraught with these possibilities. . . ."

But Tessie, tearing down the cobbles in her cotton nightshift, heard no more of Sir Christopher's explanations. It was left to Joseph to follow her command and unbind his prisoner, muttering dire curses about "females in flamin' petticoats" and "masters who were as obstinate as striplings in leading strings." Still, it did not take *all* of Sir Christopher's genius to see that the man was apparently attached to *both* these erring creatures, and that his curses, though colorful, were uncommonly fond.

"Set the barn on fire and 'im in it!"

"Nay, stanch the blood and wait for Mr. Philip."

"Let us go, I say! No one said ought to me of prisoners! They are more trouble than they are worth."

"Mmm . . . cut 'is throat, then. We don't want no talkers."

" 'E won't if 'e's charred in the fire."

"What if some bleedin' groom sets the alarm? It will look mighty smoky, 'im tied up an all."

Nicholas, listening to this discussion with an interest that was not entirely surprising, could not decide which of these fates he was more partial to. On balance, he decided neither, but unless Joseph was clairvoyant and therefore poised outside for a rescue, he could see no immediate manner in which escape could be accomplished.

His wound was not significant—he rather thought the rogues had overestimated it—but this slight advantage paled to naught when set against the odds. That Mr. Philip Grange was expected on the hour did not help.

As a matter of fact, this factor alone made immediate escape imperative. While the man called Tallows hastened, vengefully, to procure a coil of rope, Nicholas ignored his aching arm and the thirty eyes focused upon his person. His keen ears gave him cause to hope that his trusty valet was, indeed, outside, for he could swear he could hear stealthy steps on the flagstones. Still, it could just as easily be Mr. Grange arriving early, so he flexed his muscles as his arms were taken roughly and bound behind his back. It was a soldier's trick that he trusted would serve. By flexing, the rope, though taut, would loosen as he relaxed.

Tallows nodded significantly and the procession from the room began with low utterances, the gloom growing greater with each lantern dipping on the outside. Soon, it was just Fagan, still grinning, and Tallows, who vowed he would like to throw a satisfactory right.

"Don't be so callow, 'e's already bleedin' like a freakin' stuck pig. Save 'im for Grange." This from a thin, reedy man with a tweed coat and two faintly familiar capes. Nicholas struggled to think where he might have seen them before. When the man's knuckles cracked, the arguing subsided into silence. Not a nice man, Nicholas thought with irony.

Some moments passed. They could have been hours, they could have been seconds. Perceptions are strange when one is desperately trying to release one's bonds. The reedy man smirked.

"Indeed, please do."

The voice from the door was chill indeed. Nicholas, never one to despair, now did so.

A gentleman, marvelously dressed in impeccable buckskins, with a coat so nipped in at the waist one wondered at his ability to breathe, took several mincing steps into the room. To the untrained eye he appeared a dandy, for he sported a fan, and his shirt points were so well starched, they actually tickled his chin. There the resemblance ended, however, for the menace in his demeanor was perfectly unmistakable, even to the untrained eye.

"Good evening, my lord."

"Mr. Higgins," Nicholas Cathgar, peer of the realm, corrected Grange. His efforts, sadly, were not rewarded. He perceived this at once, for Grange's lips thinned into an ironic twist and his eyes narrowed into slits of disbelief.

"Ah, come, come, let us not persist with this foolish nonsense. Mr. Higgins—very sadly, I am sure—is rotting in Newgate. Let us not concern ourselves with such paltry matters, but cut at once to the quick."

There was a troubled interruption from some of the fellows, but Grange's eyes never left Nicholas's.

"Watcha mean, paltry matters?"

But Grange, apparently, did not hear the Luddite interjection. His gray eyes were still focused entirely on Sir Nick.

At last Cathgar spoke. "Which is?"

"Which is, my dear fellow, who your sources are."

Grange clicked his fingers and instantly, the last lingerers, the puzzled audience, straggled from the room. Even Tallows took up his lantern, casting a final vituperous glance at the impostor. His eye was already swelling into slits.

Mr. Grange turned cold, fishlike eyes upon him, so that he yelped a little, stuttering several small explanations that trailed off into his spittle. The man said nothing, but it was perhaps a matter of seconds before the barn was effectively empty. Mr. Grange—or Monsieur le Duc—looked about for the reedy figure in tweeds, but even he, it seemed, was gone.

"I haven't the faintest idea of what you are referring to."

"But naturally. You are not yet acquainted with my methods."

The man stepped forward and gazed directly into Nicholas's calm sea-blue eyes.

Nicholas ignored the prickling sensation up his spine. Instead, he concentrated on loosening his hands. He was weak, for the loss of blood was taking its toll, but not too weak to kick. If the man came any closer, he would. It was a matter, he supposed, of baiting him.

"I don't commonly consort with traitors."

But the ruse did not work, Mr. Grange finding this sally amusing rather than infuriating.

"Then you shall find it an instructive experience."

"Why are you doing this? Not for the Luddite cause, surely?"

"Good Lord, no. Stupid fools. But we tarry."

There was a scuffle outside. Something unlike the heavy booted feet of Tallow and his peers, fading into the night. Nicholas's ears quivered, alert to every nuance. Someone coughed, and he could have sworn it was a female. Then, a moment later, he was certain, for a vision appeared to his tired, bewildered, hallucinating view.

It was a vision that ordinarily would have appealed to his sense of the ridiculous. It might, had the circumstances been different, brought a light dancing to his eyes and a curve to play upon his rather masculine lips. Not tonight. His shock, frankly, was dire.

For Miss Tessie, far from being tucked up safely with her forty-two gold sovereigns, was standing at the barn door. Yes, a veritable nemesis with her hair flowing down in a tangle of curls almost to her waist, a modestly frilled nightgown tucked in swathes around inviting curves, and the look of the hellion upon her animated face. Nicholas did not know whether to be alarmed or pleased that she was brandishing a very businesslike pistol. On the whole, he thought, for the fleeting half-second that he had, that he was pleased. Her stance was admirable and her aim apparently immaculate, for by the time Mr. Grange was alerted to the danger, he was crumpled on the floor, alternately moaning and cursing.

To anyone paying close attention, Mr. Grange's dialect slipped just for a fraction. He was French but spoke English like a nobleman. When it suited him, however, he spoke cockney like a Londoner. Nobody—least of all Nicholas Cathgar—noticed. His eyes were transfixed on the vision. She looked, he thought with incredulity, rather smug.

"Is he dead?"

"I suspect not, by those oaths."

"Good. Grandfather was always very specific about that. I almost *never* shoot to kill. Unless it is an animal, of course."

"How encouraging." Nicholas's tone was dry, though the curves had indeed now appeared upon his startlingly masculine lips.

Tessie did not remove her eyes from his face, a fact he noted with fatalistic calm. But she did address her victim. "If you move, I am very much afraid I shall have to shoot you again." This to Mr. Grange, who was now stifling his oaths and approaching Miss Tessie cautiously from the floor. She reloaded—Nicholas noted her skill with fleeting admiration—then calmly approached him, a serious look upon her piquant features.

"I shot his leg, for I think it very unsporting to shoot from the back. But you will agree it was necessary."

"Oh, undoubtedly."

Mr. Grange apparently did not, for he eyed Miss Tessie with a cold stare that made her suddenly aware of the inadequacy of her garments, despite the darkness of the barn and the fire now almost at its embers.

"Are any of them likely to return? I watched them leave from behind the hale bales. They are strewn upon the footpath."

"What, the men?" Nicholas wouldn't have been surprised.

She considered him gravely. "No, for that would have been a foolish waste of ammunition. I meant the hay bales."

"Ah."

Nick, concealing a grin, considered that this was probably the single most diverting conversation of his four and thirty years. He would have prolonged the discussion, but all the while he had been grappling with his bonds, and though his wrists were now raw, he found himself free at last.

"I am not certain. There were a good dozen fellows here tonight, maybe more. Shall we leave, dear delight?"

Tessie ignored the "dear delight," for it made her heart beat quite unconscionably when she was holding a pistol. Besides, the man was a rogue to speak to her that way without a by-your-leave! So she depressed his presumption by speaking rather severely, though in truth she was horribly worried about his wound.

"No, for you have lost blood."

" 'Struth, woman, we are not going to sit here like trussed chickens till dawn!"

"No, for you are no longer trussed, my lord. Possibly, however, like chickens." In spite of herself, Tessie smiled impishly. Joseph, she knew, could not be far away.

There was a grim silence. "Give me the gun."

"No, for you are bleeding. Not at all up to a fight."

"And naturally, *you* would be?"

"But of course, for I have the advantage of the pistol."

The twinkle now *definitely* lit Nick's deep, sapphire-blue eyes. It was too dark for Tessie to notice.

"Shall we call the authorities?"

"There is a magistrate in Stipend. It is a half hour from here."

"Then we shall ride there at once."

"Oh, we *will,* will we?" Nicholas wondered quite where he had lost the plot. It was his custom to be the one making decisions. But then, time-honored custom seemed to have deserted him completely. He therefore meekly prepared himself for a half-hour ride in the moonlight with an unchaperoned lady of quality clad in naught but her nightshift. Strangely, bizarrely, he was tempted. Even the novelty of being ordered about would have been amusing had he not been about to faint. The wound must have been worse than he thought. He paled just as the broad-set, rather burly villain reentered.

Quick as a flash, Tessie whirled around, but the man called Fagan, his customary smile wiped from his face, advanced toward her menacingly.

Then Nicholas disgraced himself utterly by dropping to the floor in a dead swoon. Tessie, distracted, turned to him. Mr. Grange grabbed at her ankles—neat and excellently well turned despite her boots—so that she tripped over her billowing white nightgown. In seconds, it was *Tessie* who was on the hay-strewn floor, her precious pistol shaken from her hand.

There was a loud report, then a yelp from Fagan, for the gun had fired clean through his boot and doubtless shattered his ankle, if his colorful curses were anything to judge by.

Tessie should have run then, for Grange looked likely to murder her, injure or not. Fagan was too self-absorbed to be any further obstacle. But Tessie did *not* run. She picked up her pistol, though she had naught to reload it with—and dropped to Nick's side.

"Are you dead?"

There was no welcoming answer.

"My lord! You *must* wake up!"

Again no answer, so Miss Hampstead ripped open the greatcoat and put a hand on the tattered shirt. It was stained with blood. She could feel it warm and sticky, though the barn was too dim to see the red.

She leaned over to look at the dark, angular face. Long lashes fluttered over those disdainful eyes, but in his neck there was a pulse. Tessie uncertainly extended her hand, for she wanted to be sure. Everything was so damnably shadowed, it was hard to tell. Suddenly it really mattered. More, even, than Hampstead Oaks and Grandfather's bequest, it mattered. Fagan was crawling toward her, and Grange was muttering something about a dagger, but she cared naught for this.

Her hand rested on the neck. It was warm and pulsed quite noticeably. For a strangled moment Miss Tessie felt herself blush.

"Wake up, will you?"

There was a long silence in which Nicholas's features became etched in Miss Tessie's consciousness. It seemed as if she had known him forever, a lifetime, not a moment, a mere few hours, indeed only a *half* hour if one counted their exchanges and not the lifetimes in between. He was undoubtedly exasperating, disturbing, odiously annoying, but Tessie knew if he did not live to insult her horribly, just one last time, all the Granges in the world could do their worst. It simply would not matter. Nothing, she supposed, would.

"Wake up, dammit! There is a room full of villains!"

"How appealing. Yes, definitely an inducement." The voice was a murmur, but audible enough.

"You are alive! I knew it!" The triumph in Tessie's voice was unmistakable. The murmur, now, was stronger.

"I believe it is customary, in such instances, to kiss the victim." Lazy blue eyes opened below her, amazingly—bizarrely—quizzing.

Tessie caught her breath, spellbound, despite Fagan's approach. Now it was *her* pulse she felt. She ignored it.

"You are lost to all propriety, my lord."

"And you are not, my little hoyden?"

"Not if I can help it." How curious that her heart should burst with a sudden flutter of extraordinary lightheartedness at a time like this. She supposed it was the triumph, really, of knowing that Nicholas's bored indifference—so skillfully feigned—was merely skin deep.

She continued. "But we are about to be killed, so I suggest we leave. Can you move?"

"I believe so."

"Watch out!"

Nicholas sat up and grasped Fagan's hand. It held a long sliver of a blade. It looked distinctly unwholesome. Fagan lunged, but Nick was swift, pushing both the blade and Fagan's wrist above him. Then it was a contest to the death, for if Fagan's wrist dropped any closer, the blade would have pierced Nick most horribly. Tessie did not dwell on the point, for Grange's hands twisted around her ankles. He sought to trip her again, knowing that this time, her pistol was empty.

Drawing every bit of strength she could, she wriggled herself free and brought her boots down hard—crunching, cracking, crisply hard—down, down on Grange's elegantly gloved hands. The doeskin was too fine and too thin to withstand such calculated onslaught. Consequently, the Monsieur le Duc screamed such as would have woken bedlam and very likely roused some of the midnight occupants of the taproom.

There was a clatter of steel upon cobbles and Fagan's

blade dropped just inches from Nicholas's abundantly endowed head. Fagan scrabbled to fetch it, but Tessie was swifter, kicking the glint of metal far out of sight.

Then, miraculously, there was Joseph and the moonlight prisoner entering through the stalls, and she watched with satisfaction as they bound Mr. Grange efficiently while he screamed about fingers and curses and horrible oaths that were patently unsuitable for maidenly ears. When they approached Fagan, she begged them to beware, for his pockets were plentiful and he seemed to favor the blade. Joseph, no longer surprised by the wench's bloodthirsty knowledge of such unmaidenly facts, merely nodded and frisked Fagan thoroughly. He withdrew an ivory-handled dagger and another of those lethal little blades that was clearly not honorably intended. Then it was a matter of finding sufficient rope for Fagan, for he was bulkier than Grange, and there had been only one coil.

"Here!" There was a loud rip in the darkness. Then another, and another. "Take these." Miss Tessie's voluminous nightrail was being torn to shreds. Oh, she was still perfectly respectable if one disregarded the boot-clad ankles and the glimpses of flesh one could just catch below her knees—*if* one was sitting in the correct position. Nicholas, on the floor, most certainly was—his eyes were not above gleaming, despite some evident pain.

Miss Hampstead hardly noticed, for having provided ropes, she now used the remainder of her linen strips for his lordship's wounds.

"I believe I can manage, little Miss Nobody."

"Oh, do stop calling me that ridiculous name!" This, in a hiss, for Tessie was fearful some of the Luddites would return.

"You are right. Under the circumstances, I believe I shall revert, once more, to Charity."

"Wrong again, for this is not charity, this is payment. I always pay my debts."

"What a strange female, to be sure. How terribly odd! And what debts are you repaying, if I may be so bold as to ask?"

"Oh, the dinner tab, for I lost not a sovereign over it and I believe it must have been prodigiously expensive despite the cod's eye. . . ."

". . .which is a delicacy . . ."

". . . a revolting one . . . now, where was I?"

"Payment, I believe. Ouch!" Nicholas flinched.

"Did that hurt?"

"Damnably, but since I've already disgraced myself by swooning, I shall make no complaint."

"How heroic. No, this should not take much longer. Try to relax."

"Perhaps if you were to kiss me . . . medicinal purposes . . ."

"I believe I have paid my shot, my lord. The cost of dinner and access to the posting house. We are quits now."

"Oh, do you think so?" Nick's eyes were limpid, and his tone was so low, it was almost a murmur, but it held both a threat and a promise that made Tessie shiver, whether from delight or from sheer apprehension, she could not say.

Seven

How infuriating that Nicholas should not allow the matter to rest but should challenge her further still! She rolled up the remainder of her makeshift bandages and refused to be drawn. But when he asked again, his voice provocative and infuriatingly low, she answered him.

"Quits? Indeed. *Quite* quits. And kisses, my lord, are not for ladies. They are for tavern wenches."

"How instructive. I might never have known, else. Direct me immediately, if you please, to a tavern wench with hair as black as tar."

"There are any number of them, I believe."

"What a broad education you have, most curious. Do these wenches also have lips as ripe as berries?"

"My lord!"

"I shock you? Good God, you blush!"

"Only because you are—"

"A sadly rag-mannered rogue. Yes. You repeat yourself. Did I mention limbs? Do those tavern wenches have long, long legs that seem to go on forever. . . ?"

Tessie felt guilty again. Other young ladies, no matter *how* desperate, did *not* scramble down trees in nightgowns, then proceed to rip even those inadequate coverings to shreds. If she had shown a smidgen of sense, she would have stripped the revolting Grange of his neckerchief, for it was still neatly bound about his throat in a passable imitation of Brummell's famous "waterfall."

Still, she would not admit as much to Nick, who seemed bent on shamelessly regarding those tantalizing glimpses of forbidden knees.

"Stop staring, if you please. If I can't rely on your natural decorum, then think on this. If the moon changes, you will go squint."

"Ah, but in *such* a cause!"

Tessie severely admonished herself not to smile at the rogue. Instead, she smoothed down what little skirts, if she could call them such, she had, and frowned.

"Unfair! Ripping the length of my nightgown was a severe sacrifice to my dignity. You should not tease me about it. A gentleman wouldn't."

"But I am talking of *tavern* wenches. You seem such an expert upon the subject."

"Oh! You are the most odious, exasperating . . ."

"Children, children . . ."

The prisoner—or so Tessie thought of him—approached. Apparently, Joseph had released him after she'd run off toward the dim light of the barn. He now towered over Nicholas, who, despite coming around some moments before, was still lying upon the cold—and I daresay pungent—barn floor.

"I believe I owe a lump the size of a crow's egg to you, my lord."

"What the devil are you talking about?"

"I am talking about my good Joseph here, who coshed me over the head and very kindly gagged and bound me. Strictly *your* instructions, I am told."

"You are *not* Murray Higgins."

"No, and I rather think *you* are not either."

"My head hurts, I have lost blood. I rather think my heart too—" Here a swift look at Tessie, but she was gathering a horse blanket from one of the stalls.

"My sympathies." The prisoner grinned. "I assume

you are telling me you cannot make head or tail of the night's events."

"A most distressing confession. My usual omnipotence deserts me."

"It always does when there is a female involved."

"How sage. And you are . . . ?"

"Christopher Lambert."

"The name rings a bell. . . ."

"Oh, possibly. My illustrious bloodlines, I suppose. I am Atwater's third."

"Ah, yes. A hell-raiser, I recall."

"Not in your league, my lord."

Nicholas rose to his feet, grimaced a little in pain, then effected a mock bow. "Shall we remove to the inn? I rather think our little adventures are over for one night. *Joseph!"*

"Me lord?" However disrespectful Joseph might be in private, he was always perfectly subservient in public.

"Take my horse and ride off to Stipend, will you? I shall scribble you a note to the local magistrate. I fear, after my injury, the ride will be too taxing. Unless you can procure me a glass of blue ruin, of course."

"Which you won't, for nothing can be more injurious to my lord's health than scrambling his brains with alcohol." Miss Hampstead had returned with the blanket, which was now draped decorously—and voluminously—about her person.

"Revenge, Miss Nobody?" Nicholas smiled sweetly.

"No, common sense. Though if it goes hard with you not to drink, I daresay you deserve it."

"When I am well, you shall get what you deserve."

"I quake with fear."

Miss Tessie felt rather courageous as she said this, for in truth, the meaning behind his steadily emphasized words had not escaped her. Or, rather, the intent behind them, for she was maidenly enough not to know anything precisely of Nick's proposed methods.

Retrospectively, she blushed, glad of the concealing dark. Nicholas's eyes were too observant—and damnably overbearing—by far. Now, however, he concerned himself with the work of the moment, his velvety tones becoming crisp and starkly efficient.

"Joseph, hop on that horse and go! Those bonds will not hold for long."

"Fortunately, you seem to have incapacitated both quite admirably, Miss . . . Good God, I cannot keep calling you Miss Nobody, and Charity Evans sticks in my gullet! You *must* have a name?"

"Yes, but I need not reveal it."

"Beggin' pardon, miss . . ."

"Yes, Joseph?" Tessie smiled upon the valet with utter sweetness. Nick was fascinated as he watched her pink lips part, revealing perfectly straight little white teeth that sent his grizzled old servant into a spin.

"*Must* I go now? Oi'd raver stay, yer ken. The fun is just begginin' like. Those nobs might bleedin' ransack yer chamber 'gin."

"I fancy they will not, however. Go, Joseph!"

"Aye, miss." Without a word to his master he began to turn on his heel.

Lord Nicholas Cathgar, with a faint hint of amusement playing around his mouth, drew him back. When he spoke, it was with that slight drawl that Tessie detested.

"Since when, my good man, did you start taking orders from anyone other than my illustrious self?"

Joseph blushed to the tips of his ears. "Since wot the little mistress got a rare bleedin' 'ead on 'er shoulders she 'as, gov."

"Elegantly put. You are dismissed, Joseph."

"Aye, me lord." Joseph grinned a little ruefully, doffed his cap, and scampered out into the mists. The last Tessie heard was the piebald horse neighing a little before settling into a simply spanking great pace.

"You have forgotten the note to the magistrate."

"So I have. It shall have to be the blue ruin, then, and the innkeeper's best stallion."

"I believe I may offer assistance here, having no small interest in the outcome of tonight's endeavors."

"Ah, Christopher. Almost I had forgotten you." Nicholas's tone was dry.

"How flattering! But I collect your wits are wondering."

"Indeed."

"Then may I offer you my compliments and my assurance to see to the matter myself. The fat one is of no consequence, but Grange we *must* have. And the skinny one. Margate, I think he is called. But Grange is the ringleader. He has his bony fingers in too many pies by half."

"Fortunately, judging by the crunch I was gratified to hear, they are now really rather mangled fingers. I believe you speak, chiefly, of the *French* pies, or should I say soufflés?"

Lambert smiled. "Chiefly. With rumors of Napoleon such as they are . . ."

"Indeed. Am I to understand that you, too, were sent by the Foreign Office?"

Christopher Lambert grinned. "Circuitously, yes. I am an envoy direct from the great man himself. Lord Castlereigh is my second cousin once removed, or some such thing. But apparently, lines were crossed somewhere. *Two* impostors are really rather overkill. Classic."

"So it seems. Convey my compliments to the minister."

"I shall. And now, good people, I must fly. Dawn must not be far, and I must needs find that valiant little valet of yours. Does he shine one's hessians, one wonders, as well as he delivers a flush hit? The mind boggles."

Lord Cathgar nodded.

"He does. And you can eat your heart out, Lambert, the man is mine. Apart from his impertinence, he is perfection itself."

Then, without further words, and certainly without a glance at the prisoners, who were sullying the air with language unfit for the gutter, he tucked Miss Hampstead's hand—the one not holding the pistol—into the sleeve of his greatcoat and strode, at last, from the barn.

"I shall sleep in your chamber tonight."

"Over my dead body, little Miss Nobody."

"Well, it just might be if I do not, Lord Cathgar."

"Nick."

"Lord Cathgar."

Tessie regarded his lordship quellingly. Her scrape was quite bad enough not to commit the further social solecism of calling him by his given name. In the light of the events of the evening, she knew her scruples were ridiculous, but old habits died hard, and she was, after all, still a lady.

"I shall not die tonight, Miss Nobody. I am like a cat. I have nine lives."

"And you've probably used up eight! You are still bleeding."

"It is a trifle. I loathe women who fuss."

"Then you shall loathe me at your leisure. You may need to be leeched."

"You minx! You *want* me to suffer!"

Tessie suppressed a bloodthirsty grin.

"Not at all. I am merely informing you of your options."

"Wait till I start informing you of *your* options."

"You will need to be fully recovered to do that, so I rest my case. I shall spend the night in your chamber."

"Joseph . . ."

"Joseph is at Stipend. He may relieve me when he returns."

"I am not an invalid!"

"No, but your walk is unsteady, and you have fainted once this evening."

"I shall never live that down." The words were faintly rueful.

"I, too, am not a tattletale, Lord Cathgar."

They stopped walking for a moment and turned to face each other in the gentle moonlight. There was no sign of the rabble that had furtively disbanded earlier. Trudging home, one shouldn't wonder, or drinking ale in the tavern, or warming some wench's bed . . . neither Tessie nor Lord Cathgar knew or cared. They were staring at each other.

Then, in response to the smallest constriction of Tessie's throat, Nicholas had her in his arms, and his lips, at last, were crushing down upon her own. When he was done, Tessie had no more to say, a state of affairs Nick apparently found most satisfactory.

". . . So you see," he continued in a conversational tone, just as if they had never digressed from their topic, "you *shall* be safer, Miss . . . Evans . . . in your own bed."

"Did I tell you my chamber has been ransacked?"

"For your forty-two gold sovereigns?"

"Indeed. And my virtue."

"But that, I collect, remains intact."

"Yes, by dint of shinning down an apple tree with a loaded pistol."

"You are a remarkable woman, Miss . . . will you not trust me with your name?"

"No, I will not."

"Miss Nobody, then."

Tessie shrugged. Her lips were still warm from his kiss.

She ached to confide to him, yet, perversely, could not do so.

His eyes shuttered once more. "We are at the entrance. I shall be perfectly well."

"You are pale. I shall attend you. At least till Joseph returns."

"And then? What then, my little charmer?"

"Then I shall disappear, Lord Cathgar, and I shall not darken your path again."

"How dramatic! But rest assured, little one, *I* shall darken *your* path."

"Maybe."

"How noncommittal!"

"Merely prosaic. You should not make promises while you are feverish."

"I only ever propose marriage when I am feverish."

"Marriage!"

"What better way to scotch the impending scandal?"

"There must be hundreds. You are nonsensical, my lord."

"Nicholas. And it is you who are nonsensical. And compromised beyond redemption."

"Then I am an unsuitable candidate for countess, my lord."

"Go to your chamber, little one, while I am still being chivalrous."

"No!"

"Then beware of the consequences."

"Be certain I shall, my lord."

Tessie stepped into the warmth of the inn before Nicholas. There was no one in the taproom, but a fire burned in the grate, its embers still glowing a fiery red. Tessie wondered where the innkeeper's wife was, or who had her keys. She shivered for a moment at the thought, then smiled in relief at Nicholas, who was regarding her closely.

"Come, my lord, you are surely no worse a fate than some unknown thug entering my chamber. That, you must know, is why I was escaping this evening."

"What, feeling merciful, were you? Not put a bullet through his heart?"

Tessie did not allow her lips to twitch in an answering smile, though she felt a distinct gurgle welling up inside her.

"You are pleased to tease, but it is no funny thing, I assure you, having drunken men attempt one's chamber."

"I shall slay them for you."

"Now you are absurd again." But Tessie felt that traitorous gurgle of laughter rising up in her throat once more. She felt Nicholas unashamedly regarding her, and when he smiled, she felt a peculiar lightness of being that had little to do with slaying.

For once, they took the stairs in perfect harmony, though Tessie several times noticed Nicholas wince. Though the hallways were shadowed, she noticed strange hollows beneath his eyes that she attributed to pain.

"Is it much farther? You look not at all the thing."

"How salutary. I set such store by my good looks."

"They are still good, in a raffish sort of way." Then Tessie bit her tongue and colored ferociously, for of all the bold, unmaidenly comments she had made that evening, this one must surely have put her beyond the pale. Nicholas, however, merely looked faintly amused, so she was encouraged to continue.

"Not that I know anything of men, my lord, or—"

"Now you disappoint me. You must surely have a vast knowledge of my fellow creatures to draw comparisons?"

"Only Mr. Dobbins, sir, and I do not think I shall be committing any maidenly offense to admit you look better."

"On the contrary. The offense would have been if you'd admitted the reverse. Ah, here we are. Miss Nobody, you are going to have to draw the key from my person. I am afraid my arm is rather stiff. . . ."

Tessie regarded him sharply. Clearly, the pain was greater than he was admitting to, for his brows were furrowed and he had momentarily stopped his teasing tone. She nodded, anxious for him.

"Where is it?"

"In my pocket."

Miss Hampstead, quite unused to rifling through gentlemen's pockets, nodded nonetheless. She felt about his capacious greatcoat, but he shook his head, dark hair just lingering on his shoulders.

"No, not that one, my waistcoat . . ."

Now it was Tessie's turn to pale, for reaching into his waistcoat was far too intimate for comfort. Nicholas was nothing like Grandfather Hampstead, whom she used to embrace regularly, or even Mr. Dobbins, whom she shrank from. Nicholas was . . . but no! She resolutely put from her mind what he was and searched him for the key, remembering that a male's anatomy was quite different from her own and blushing like a schoolgirl as her fingers accidentally touched hard muscles through the workaday cambric and patched rags he effected.

"Ah! Here it is!" The relief was tangible in her tones as she extracted the key. Nicholas's face was perfectly inscrutable as she busied herself with the lock and finally, finally, opened the door. It was well oiled and swung open easily, just as though it were not made from solid oak and trimmed with brass and filigreed lead.

"Come on in as I light the candles."

Nicholas nodded, and casually slid the greatcoat from his back. What he wished for now, above all else, was a soothing bath and a bottle of brandy, but he was not an unreasonable man, so he made do with the claret sent up on a silver tray and tried to forget about the execrable attire he was wearing.

Tessie turned her back modestly so that he could climb under the covers as she lit all twenty-nine candles of the inn's second finest candelabrum. The finest, she noted, was almost spent, the flames having eaten most of the wax down to the wicks. Evidently, Nicholas—or the innkeeper—had not expected him to spend most of the evening outside.

Fortunately, fires were burning in both the grates, though the logs needed tending. Tessie was glad of this chore, for it concealed her burning cheeks as she contemplated, again, the enormity of her actions. She had practically forced herself into his chamber, and very likely he had no need of her at all! Worse, in all likelihood she had merely confirmed his opinion that she was a brazen, managing female . . . and as for his *offer!* She must truly be sunk beyond reproach for him to have deemed such a thing necessary.

Well, she would nurse him until Joseph came back, then disappear on the morning's stage. He had no direction and no name, so even if he *did* have the inclination to follow her, he could not. Tessie did not know whether to be glad or to be sorry. She swallowed a great big stupid, unbidden lump in her throat and stoked at a log so fiercely that flames leaped from the grate and scattered in bright sparks over the heavy rug she was kneeling upon.

"Great good gun, do not, I beg you, incinerate us." This from the shadow in the bed. Despite a definite edge of fatigue, she could also detect laughter. Her mouth twitched as she extinguished the rogue sparks. She might never see him again on the morrow, but tonight—at least till Joseph came back—tonight he was hers.

She wondered how it came to be that she so craved his company. It was, after all, only a few hours since she had first made his acquaintance. Only a few hours since he had disdained her jellies, condemned her dress, and muttered several disparaging remarks about her hoydenish behavior. Only a few moments since he had kissed her.

She avoided looking at the centerpiece of the room, the great bed curtained in faded velvet. Old, but evidently clean, with a hot brick heating in the hearth. She supposed she should tuck it beneath Nicholas's feet, but her famous courage seemed to have failed her, so she rearranged the tinderboxes, then fussed around the tepid washing water set majestically on a gilded table edged with mythical creatures.

"Leave it, doubtless it is cold."

"Lukewarm. I could heat it up. . . ."

"Leave it."

"There is some fruit. . . ." The occasional table was laden with a large china bowl filled with Spanish oranges, mandarins, and some small golden apples.

"I am not hungry."

"Would you—"

"What I would *like,* little Miss Nobody, is a sight of something more than your very starched linen. Doubtless backs are all the rage, but I find I prefer your face."

Tessie set down an apple and was surprised to find her fingers shaking.

"No!"

"No?"

"No. I must go. . . ." She regarded once more the great oak door. She must leave, she knew, before there was no turning back. She had the faintest of suspicions that Lord Nicholas Cathgar was not a man to be trifled with. He would marry her out of hand if she compromised herself utterly. And she did not want that—not for her, and not for him. She wanted to be Miss Theresa Hampstead again, of impeccable name and lineage. She wanted no charades, no marriages of calm convenience, no bitter-sweet temptations . . . no regrets. Her fingers touched her pistol. She would need it if the thugs below stairs had been patient. . . .

Eight

"Put that thing away!"

"It is *my* pistol, sir!"

"A damnably stupid toy for a female!"

"You did not complain earlier."

"No, for I must have temporarily lost my wits. Put it down and come back here. I want to look at you."

Tessie remembered his kiss, and hardened her resolve.

"I am going. Joseph shall be here shortly. It is not a long ride to Stipend. . . ."

"Over my dead body! You are here now, and here you shall stay, and damn with the consequences."

"I cannot . . ."

"I feel faint."

Tessie, finally, turned around and looked up. The man was sitting, and though he in no way looked faint, he *did* look bloody, his shirt stained brown and clinging tightly to his person.

She regarded him severely. "You are funning me, sir. A shabby trick, for which you deserve to be deserted mercilessly. Or perhaps I should offer you a restorative, like I did poor Lord Christopher?"

"God's brew! What did your conniving little brain offer *him?"*

"Cod liver oil, and as it was purely in your service that I did it, I should thank you to be more grateful!"

"Come up here, little infant, and I shall show you grateful."

"Now you are talking fustian besides taking great liberties. But I *shall* step up, for I need to look at your wounds."

Nicholas instantly lay back upon his sheets. He would be loath to admit it to the infant, but he did have the devil of a headache and felt as weak as a kitten due undoubtedly to the wound he had incurred. Still, he had suffered worse during the abroad, and then there had been no beauty in a bedraggled nightrail to offer him succor. On the whole, he felt rather smug.

He heard some rustling and opened his eyes. Sat up. His head spun, but he ignored it. He glared. He frowned. He bellowed.

"What in *tarnation* are you doing?"

The smugness had quite vanished from his fine aquiline features.

"I am trying to make myself respectable, sir."

"Respectable? In a mud-stained garment several sizes too large for you, and one, I might add, that almost certainly *smells?"*

"It was good enough for *you."* Tessie, who delighted in feathered bonnets and frivolous muffs, buttoned each tawny button with methodical decision. It was not, she knew, the most flattering garment she'd ever worn, but it would certainly dull Lord Cathgar's ardor. Now, *that,* after all, was what she wanted.

Or was it? She eyed those teasing lips with decided disfavor, for they caused her resolution to fade like melted snow. Her reputation, she knew, was already in shreds, but the voluminous coat protected her virtue. She may be improper, but she was *not* impure.

"I was impersonating a Luddite."

"And *I* am hiding from your view the sight of my ripped nightrail. A very serviceable coat, I find."

"I shall have Joseph burn it. It did not serve its purpose for me, and it does not serve its purpose for you either."

"Why ever not?"

"I have no notion why not, for it is truly hideous, but I find I still desire you."

"My lord!"

"Climb up and box my ears."

"I am not so green as that. I shall wait until you are asleep before I touch your wounds."

"Very well, though I must warn you I believe I have reopened the wound, for it aches damnably and . . . yes . . . see here . . . it is bleeding again."

Tessie eyed him suspiciously. But because she found she truly *did* care, she fetched a single taper from the washstand and drew it up close.

"Stand on the bed stair. You can't see from down there."

Tessie obeyed, taking care with the flame. The quietness of the room, coupled with their closeness, disturbed her. It was too intimate, somehow . . .

"See here? This patch is red rather than brown."

He was right! Forgetting her shyness, she set down the candle close to the bedstead and touched him gently.

"I am going to have to remove your shirt. Or, at least, cut it open. Is there a knife?"

Nicholas nodded. "I shaved earlier. Look near the washstand, doubtless Joseph did *something* with it."

It took Tessie not a moment to find what she was seeking, and to draw up the tub of tepid water and a fresh towel.

"It will hurt, but I will be gentle."

"Are there no end to your talents, little one?"

"I cannot draw, I can sing, but only indifferently, and I am—was—the despair of my dance master."

"How mortifying! I loathe young ladies who draw and sing, but I see I shall have to take you in hand with respect to dancing. My wife, you see, must be permanently in my arms."

"But I am not you wife, my lord."

"A mere technicality. You shall be just as soon as I can leave this damnable place and procure a special license. Ow!"

"It pulls as I tear off the cloth. Very soon it will be feeling better. I wish I had some of Finchie's powder. . . . It is said to be a great balm, though its color is vile and the application often stings."

"Then I am glad you did not think to carry it with your pistol."

"No, a great oversight, though I am at a loss to know how I am to carry both ammunition and a vial . . . oh! You are teasing me again!"

"Only a little, and you shall have your revenge, for that hurts damnably."

"Bother! I was trying to be gentle!"

"Ouch!"

"Sorry, I could not see, this light . . ."

"Step up closer, then."

"But it is . . . indelicate . . ."

"Good God, you are missish, O brave of heart!"

"Yes, for though you may think me highly improper . . ."

"I do . . ."

"I am *perfectly* proper, only I can't help tumbling into horrible scrapes . . ."

"From which I shall no doubt have to rescue you a dozen times . . ."

"No!"

"No?"

"No! For I am not so poor a person as to entrap you into marriage."

"And *I* am not so poor a person as to ruin your reputation, then leave you on the shelf."

"You have done no such thing. . . ."

"Step up closer. I can't argue with the top of your head."

"I forgot my nightcap!"

"Indeed, and very fetching you look too."

"I should have remembered. . . ."

"Yes, and your forty-two gold sovereigns, too, but you were in a hurry. A pardonable offense under the circumstances. Now, climb up here before I throw you up!"

"You would open all your wounds."

"Yes, so spare me the pain, if you please."

"Oh, very well."

Tessie climbed up gingerly and immediately averted her eyes. His chest, though covered in blood, was excessively masculine, peculiarly tempting, and damnably interesting, with muscles she never knew existed, giving it a contour she had somehow not expected. Or, perhaps, not permitted the odd wayward thought to guess at . . .

"Where does it ache?"

"Everywhere, confound it."

"Can I help?"

Again the sudden spark of mischief that Tessie found more dangerous than a positive *troop* of Luddites.

"Perhaps if you stroke me just here . . ."

"You take liberties, sir!"

"Tell me your name."

"No!"

"Then I shall take a great deal more!"

"You tricked me up onto this great lumbering big bed. I do believe there is nothing wrong with you at all!"

"And *I* do believe I was right. You are, despite your . . . unusual accomplishments, as green as a goose."

"Which, I infer, means a complete innocent, however rag-manneredly you wish to put it. I'd rather be innocent than jaded, so I thank you, my lord, for the ill-turned compliment."

"Ah, wits as well as beauty. Too bad my bed is not a place I traditionally reserve for semantics."

Tessie opened her mouth, then shut it again. She had nearly, very nearly, fallen into his trap. But she was not so green as he thought, and she would *not* ask him what he traditionally reserved his bed for.

Nicholas, accurately reading her bluster, then blush, then tongue-biting silence, chuckled.

"Very wise, little chicken. Safer, I think, not to ask."

"Safer to depart your chamber immediately!" Tessie sounded cross, for she hated being on the wrong end of a quarrel. And he did pique her so!

"Too late. I *did* try to tell you that!"

"Yes, but that was when I thought you might be dying."

"And now?"

"Now I think you are shamming it, and I feel very ill used."

"The blood is real, and I do feel faint. . . ."

"Yes, and I feel like the Princess Esterhazy!"

"Take off that revolting coat and tell me your name."

"No."

"Oh, for heaven's sake, I can't get a special license for Miss Nobody!"

Tessie, recalled to her primary troubles, grew suddenly somber.

"That is just what I might be."

"Nonsense, you might be minus forty-two gold sovereigns, but I would wager my rather considerable fortune you are nonetheless a lady!"

"One of dubious character, however. Recollect that in the space of twenty-four hours I have traveled unchaperoned, I have disgraced myself utterly by shooting two people, my attire makes me seem like a . . . like a . . ."

"Lightskirt?"

"Yes, though it is shocking of you to say so . . ."

"And of you to know of such matters . . ."

"My point exactly! I am simply not respectable! Look at me now . . ."

"I am." The voice was like velvet, and his unspeaking, outstretched arms seemed like heaven, but Tessie, very virtuously, resisted.

"You are ridiculous! But you prove my point. No gentleman would look at a lady in that rakish fashion."

"When you are my wife, I shall always look at you so. Unless I am glaring at you, of course."

"I am not going to be your wife."

"How much do you want to wager?"

"Nothing, for I have lost my sovereigns and can be sure of no more until I see my man of business."

"Who is?"

"Sly, but I am up to snuff. You shall not know from me, sir."

"Why in the world are you so stubborn?"

"It is my besetting sin; Grandfather always said so."

"He was right. And I shall marry plain Miss Charity Evans."

"The banns will not be binding."

"Am I such an antidote? I am acclaimed most eligible in some circles."

"You are not precisely an antidote, but you are arrogant and overbearing, and a shade uncivil . . ."

Nicholas ignored her. "Why can you not tell me who you are? Trust me."

"You said you did not want to be bored by my tale."

"Well, that was before you saved my life and I had the faintest inkling what a devilish fine shot you are!"

"A fine shot is no recommendation for marriage, my lord. And I told you. Saving your life was payment of the tab."

"Extravagant payment."

"Indeed, but then I was horribly hungry and sadly in need of a chamber. I do not deceive myself that I should have succeeded in either had you not intervened."

"True, but it took little effort on my part."

"Yes, it is a shocking thing what rank and a haughty demeanor can achieve."

Nicholas grinned, but those subtle marks of pain were back. Tessie noted it instantly, for his brows furrowed, and there was telltale moisture upon his brow.

"I am sorry it hurts."

"So am I."

"Try sleeping. If there was some laudanum somewhere . . ."

"There is. Joseph always carries it. For . . . emergencies."

"For acting the spy, you mean."

"For acting government's agent, Madame Sharp-Tongue."

Tessie grinned, for he was obviously nettled.

"I shall get some, then. And a cotton shirt. You will feel better clean."

She slid down from the bed, glad of something to do other than fall under the spell of those mesmerizing eyes and the sheer lines of his body, hardly decent under the bedclothes.

The laudanum helped, for though Nick would not admit it, the wound was starting to cause him some concern. It was a mere scratch by dueling standards, but it ached nonetheless, and his head felt like lead. He wiped away some of the perspiration and shut his eyes for a fraction of a second, noting that Miss Tessie had drawn up a chair, regrettably out of reach, but that her precious pistol was nowhere to be seen. She was not, then, going to abscond. He closed his eyes just for a fraction of a second. Tessie climbed up the bed stairs. Yes, he was sleeping. She was relieved and yet, curiously, disappointed.

* * *

Dawn dappled the room with faint shades of light. The candles were well burned now, but it was possible to see perfectly well in the morning shadows. A knock, rather hearty, woke Tessie from her dreams with a start. She hoped it was neither the innkeeper nor his detestable wife. It was too early for that, surely?

"Joseph?"

"Aye, mistress, back from Stipend, and with a jolly tale to tell." His words were whispered but loud enough for Tessie to hear perfectly. She fumbled with the large key and opened the door, still resplendent in her borrowed plumes.

Joseph, entering, eyed her shrewdly.

"Dosed 'im with laudanum, did yer?"

Tessie shut the door. "How did you know?"

"If yer be all tricked out in that them togs, 'is lor'ship must be right weary."

"I had nothing else, only my ripped nightrail."

"Aye. My point precisely."

"Oh!"

Joseph grinned. "Now save yer blushes, lassie. 'Is lor'ship is a right good gun, if a bit . . ."

"High-handed?"

"Yes. Took a right likin' to yer, 'e did."

Tessie brightened. "Did he? I thought he thought me a shimble-shamble hoyden."

"Then he is a fool, 'e is, not lettin' on . . . but I should not be jawin' with yer with 'is lordship wounded. Is it bad, then?"

"I don't know. He says it is a scratch, but the wound seems deep and I have no restorative powder. . . ."

"Did 'e take his laudanum gently, or did yer force it down 'im?"

"Joseph, I am a lady. I don't force."

Joseph grinned. “Aye,” he agreed blankly, but Tessie was not fooled. She tried to suppress a grin, but failed. “If you must know, he took the stuff meekly.”

Joseph sobered a little. “Then ’e is in a worse way than I feared.”

“I think he had a fever. I wiped his forehead several times but hesitated to call for help. One does not want talk hereabouts.”

“No, there will be enough blabberheads in the mornin’, when the barn is swept clean.”

“Shall they suspect?”

“No, for what gentry mort goes a jaunterin’ about up to mischief?”

“Ask Lord Cathgar.”

“Oi ’aye, but ’e just laughs. Right infuriatin’ ’e be.”

“But you love him.”

“Now, don’t yer go tellin’ *’im* any such tales.”

Tessie laughed. “I won’t. He is far too complacent as it is!”

Joseph walked up to the bed.

“Like as not ’e will do, missy. You did a fine job with the bandaging, and there ain’t no seepin’ that oi can tell.”

“There was, and I had no liniment, but I cleaned quite thoroughly . . .”

“Oh, yer did, did yer?” Joseph afforded her a sideways glance that held the whisper of a smile.

Miss Hampstead, remembering her unsuitable garment, and worse, the unsuitable night spent in a man’s—albeit mostly unconscious—company, blushed.

“E’ll marry yer right an tight, e’ will. ’E may be a ’ard ’ead, but ’e’s a gentleman born.”

“Joseph, don’t put such thoughts in his head again! For your information—and I don’t usually gossip with servants, but you seem a very superior sort—I have already refused him.”

“ ’E took it meekly, did ’e?”

"No, you rascal, he did not. But when he's recovered, he will see that I am perfectly right. I must go now."

" 'E will 'ave my 'ide if I let yer go."

"Then you shall tell him you did at pistol point." With that, Tessie picked up the pistol, still nonchalantly lying upon the occasional table, and smiled sweetly. She aimed it, rather considerately, at his lapel. If she shot, it would not be at his heart.

"You are mad!"

"Maybe a little. Au revoir, Joseph. Take good care of your master."

With a nod, she was gone.

Nine

It was two days since Tessie had returned to her room, recovered what was left of her possessions, and changed into a respectable gown. It was a pearly mauve, not fashionable, but presentable nonetheless.

The grimy pink she discarded, along with the ruins of her nightrail and several laboriously written notes to Lord Cathgar. None, it seemed, could express the half of what she wanted to say, so she satisfied herself by calling up a hansom cab and referring the tab to his person.

Not, she knew, either prudent or virtuous, but she had no choice, with not a feather to fly with until she drew her pin money off Markham's, the family banker.

She was fortunate that the innkeeper, remembering his tactical error of the day before, maintained his bowing and scraping demeanor all the while through her morning chocolate and cinnamon buns. It was he who vouchsafed for her to the hansom cab driver, indicating slyly that she was "under my lord's protection." She valiantly refrained from arguing the point, considering that since her reputation was in shreds, there was little to be gained.

London was bustling with traffic, with hackneys, with great crested carriages and market carts loaded full with fruit and breads. Despite her situation, it was exciting, for she had missed her first Season and consequently not seen the great buildings, the museums, the tower, for oh, *such* a long time. The cobbles resounded with the sound of hooves as matched bays and regal chestnuts drew phaetons and more cumbersome barouches.

"Where to, missy?"

But Tessie had no idea, no respectable address, and no maidservant. She hesitated as a cart of oranges nearly collided into the hansom cab. It was too late for the lawyers, so she murmured the only respectable name she could think of: The Colonnade. Thus it was that on the morning after her great adventure, Miss Theresa Hampstead, unchaperoned, checked into a hotel. Prudently, she did not tell the porter that she was the granddaughter to a viscount. In her faded dimity, he probably would have laughed.

Mr. Devonshire, when she was finally ushered into his presence, appeared grave. Theresa could not help but feel shabby in her olive half mourning, sprigged, as it was, in Mantua silk with only a whisper of white rosettes at the hems and sleeves. She had procured it from Madame Fanchon's, a half block from the Colonnade, after presenting herself at the banker's.

The gown had been the only item, ready made, that had fitted her. Madame Fanchon usually only made to order, but in this instance she had been lucky. Lady Pendergast had canceled at the last moment. Grown, according to the loquacious seamstress, "too fat."

Still, save for the prospect of wandering through the Pantheon Bazaar unescorted, Miss Hampstead had had no alternative. If only Mr. Dobbins had not made off with her valise!

But she could not lament what she could not change, so she held out her hand to Mr. Devonshire and afforded him one of her calm smiles.

"Please excuse my attire, sir, my journey was more arduous than I expected."

The lawyer waved away her excuses. In truth, she looked perfectly presentable to him, but he knew nothing of stylish modes. He fixed, therefore, on the second half of her utterance.

"I am sorry the journey was arduous. It was not one you should have undertaken! I would have made the trip myself; you must know that."

"But I don't, Mr. Devonshire." Tessie hesitated, then, annoyed by feeling at such a disadvantage, continued firmly.

"Despite repeated correspondence to your office, I have not had the courtesy of a return word. Believe me, had matters not been . . . desperate, I should not have undertaken this troublesome venture for all the world."

There was a pause as Mr. Devonshire polished a lens.

"Or at least," Tessie more truthfully amended, "I might not have done it in so shimble-shamble a way."

Again, there was that grave nod of silvery-white hair. She wondered if she had seen a glimmer of disapproval in his eyes. But no, his voice was gentle.

"Do take a seat, my dear. I shall ring for a fortifying cup of tea."

Miss Hampstead had little desire for tea, but her natural good manners caused her to thank him most politely as she drew off her gloves and reached into her reticule.

To her profound horror, she was feeling vaporish. This was a foible she positively despised in other females. How many times had she abhorred quite roundly the use of sal volatile and other loathsome restoratives! Now she rather wished her reticule held more than two handkerchiefs, her purse of replenished guineas, and her pistol. Since none of these items were of any use to her at that moment, she satisfied herself with tangling her ribbons into a knot.

Mr. Devonshire, watching her keenly through rather beetling white brows, was surprised. His dealings with the gentler sex—fortunately they had not been common—had always led, somehow, to several maudlin fits of the hysterics.

Miss Hampstead, though agitated, did not succumb to a fit of feminine whining—or worse yet, weeping. When she'd finished mangling the ribbons of her reticule, she seemed to regain a great deal of composure, for she sat becomingly upright upon her upholstered seat and contemplated fiercely the portrait of Sir Francis Drake upon the far wall.

Mr. Devonshire could not help experiencing a fleeting satisfaction. An excellent rendition it was, having been purchased from Lord Marlborough for the quite hideous sum of forty-five newly minted sovereigns. Drake was dressed all in black with a short white ruff and an elegant ruby gleaming upon his finger. Well executed, but the oils, though rich, were somber in tone. The lawyer found this tasteful, but Miss Hampstead, sad to say, found it only depressing.

There was something in Drake's dark hair and heroic stance that reminded her . . . but her mind wondered wickedly. She swallowed the ridiculous lump in her throat.

"I have been remiss, it appears, in not replying sooner to your letters. *Very* remiss, if it means you have traveled by stage."

Miss Hampstead said nothing, for it would be impolite to agree, though she had railed at him several times privately for this omission.

"You must know, my dear, that I have only late returned to London. I formed part of Lord Castlereigh's contingent in Vienna, and it has taken me some small while to catch up with a good deal of my clients. My foolish clerks held back some of my correspondence, you see, pending my return. I was greatly saddened by the

Viscount of Hampstead's death. I must offer you my condolences."

"Thank you."

"Ah, the tea. Set it there, Mary." He poured punctiliously and handed Tessie a steaming porcelain cup. Though the drink was far too sweet, it was strong and delightfully aromatic. Miss Hampstead drank deeply and found her hands were trembling less, a fact for which she could only be grateful.

"Mr. Devonshire, might we come straight to the point? I am loath to appear mercenary, but I find myself quite at a stand. There are rumors in the village that I have been left without a feather to fly with, and though I am convinced this is quite untrue and contrary to Grandfather's intent, I must ask you to clarify this."

"Yes, quite." Mr. Devonshire returned his spectacles to his nose and shuffled through some papers.

"I understood that I was my grandfather's heiress."

"And so you were, Miss Hampstead. Notwithstanding, of course, the title and the entailed land."

"Of course. That is to go to the fifth viscount, some distant cousin, I apprehend."

"Yes. He is proving difficult to trace, but doubtless he shall be found in due course. His father died in the colonies, so it is likely that he still resides in the Americas."

"But Hampstead Oaks?"

"That not being the principal seat of the viscount and thus not covered by the entail, it belongs to you."

"Oh!"

"However, I should mention that at present it is more of a burden than a boon. The capital invested to maintain it is all but gone, and you shall be reliant on the rents to maintain yourself. Not satisfactory, given the costs of running the estate."

"I don't understand. Hampstead Oaks is a thriving concern. Grandfather's irrigation schemes have proven most successful, the breeding programs and stables alone . . ."

Mr. Devonshire's face revealed he did not approve of young ladies, however respectable, knowing anything about breeding programs.

"Yes, well. All that is naturally true, but the investment was lost the night before his lordship's death."

"How so?"

"On a bet relating, I believe, to . . . but no! The exact details are rather irrelevant, are they not?"

"Are you saying Grandfather staked Hampstead Oaks on a card game?"

"Not a card game precisely, but the principle applies. And strictly speaking, it was not Hampstead Oaks he staked, but the principal of his capital. He drew on his banker on the morning of the seventeenth. Precisely, I believe, twenty hours before he died."

"He said nothing to me of it!"

"My dear girl, a gentleman, however well heeled, never speaks to his relatives of such things."

"Oh, but he did to me! I swear, half of Grandfather's fortune was acquired through some bet or the other."

"Yes, well, if it is any comfort to you, young lady, he fully expected to win it back on the night of the eighteenth. He boasted of it to Markham, the banker, who was shocked at having to disperse so large a sum."

"I should imagine he *was!* Poor Grandfather. He was so wise, so canny, yet when it came to a simple game of hazard . . ."

"He was a fool."

"You should not speak so of the dead."

"No, especially not of one who was a client of mine. However, I take leave to inform you, Miss Hampstead, that his lordship's actions were rash in the extreme."

"Well, of course they were! All gamblers are rash."

The lawyer adjusted his lenses and frowned. Tessie

could just see the hairs of his eyebrows raised above the rims.

His tone, when next he spoke, was more definitely disapproving. She could not tell whether it was of herself or of the late viscount. She did not suppose, really, that it mattered.

"You are remarkably sanguine, Miss Hampstead." From which reproving comment she gathered it would be more fitting to either swoon or succumb to hysterics. She did neither, though the room swam a little and she felt hot for such a mild day. She grimly ignored both discomforts.

"Sanguine? I have to be, Mr. Devonshire. I could wish it otherwise, but Grandfather lived by gentleman's rules. He gambled recklessly, but never so recklessly that he could not pay the stake."

"But the stake was too high! It was your inheritance he dallied with!"

"No, sir. It was *his* fortune he staked. If I had expectations, that is all that they were. Expectations. I am glad Grandfather settled his debt."

"Well, he did, at your expense, though of course, there is still your mother's annuity. . . ."

"I had forgotten that."

"Not surprising, as it is insignificant relative to the viscount's estate. I have the papers just underneath these . . . let me see. Ah, yes. You are to receive two thousand pounds a year. . . ."

"From my nineteenth birthday. I remember now. Grandfather spoke of it when Mama died."

"Yes, well, you will agree it is hardly a fortune. Even being cautious, you would need three thousand for a decent Season. I know several young ladies who spend double as much!"

"I don't intend being fashionable, Mr. Devonshire. I

could live on two thousand if only the rents could maintain the land. . . ."

"Nonsense, my dear. I have, on your behalf, requested the presence of Lord Alberkirky in my office at ten. I am certain that if I explain the circumstances . . ."

"Lord Alberkirky?"

"The gentleman to whom the wager was lost. I have made some inquiries on your behalf and find that there was no witness to any wager having taken place. That being the case, there is some legal question . . ."

Tessie choked on her scalding hot tea.

"Mr. Devonshire, I *forbid* you to go down this path!"

"You are overset, Miss Hampstead, you cannot quite understand . . . but here, have a nibble on these macaroons. I believe they are wonderfully tasty."

"I am certain that they are. But it is not macaroons I want, sir, but your assurance that—"

"Ah, that must be Lord Alberkirky. Early, it is not yet quite the hour, but I daresay it does not matter. Do sit down again, Miss Hampstead, it does not do to be bobbing up and down like a cork . . . ah, your lordship!"

This as a rather gangly gentleman of, Miss Hampstead guessed, around four and twenty, was ushered into the room.

"Lord Alberkirky, might I present to you . . ."

But Tessie was standing up again. In her most regal manner, she made Lord Alberkirky a curtsy and extended her hand,

"De-de-delighted to m-m-m-m-m-m . . . meet you."

Tessie could not help but smile. The gentleman reminded her almost exactly of the engaging young man of the curricle. So dashingly dressed she was hard-pressed not to laugh, for his boots shone like mirrors and his waist was so nipped in, she was certain he must have had difficulty breathing. Still, who was she, in her drab olive merino, to comment on a collar that was starched far too stiff, or on an attempt at the waterfall that would have had her grandfather in whoops?

No, Lord Alberkirky evidently aspired to be a gentleman of the first stare, and it would be unkind to view him as anything otherwise.

"I am sure you cannot *possibly* be delighted, if you know the reasons for your summons to these rooms."

"B-but, then, I had no-no-no n-n-n-notion, Miss Hampstead, of . . . of . . ."

"Yes?"

"H-how *pretty* y-you are!"

"Well! It is very kind of you to say so, sir, but I take leave to tell you that *that* is Spanish coin! I am held to be tolerable, at best, though a little too frivolous to be pleasing. And though dark hair is currently rather modish, my curls are perfectly unmanageable and the despair of my abigail. Indeed, she frequently tells me to keep it all well tucked under a bonnet."

"N-n-no! That is, I am certain—certain that if they were *not* all tucked up, they would be p-p-p-pretty."

"There you go, then!" Mr. Devonshire sounded suddenly hearty and indulgent. "Lord Alberkirky, please meet Miss Hampstead."

Miss Hampstead retrieved her gloves from the desk.

"I am pleased to meet you, Lord Alberkirky. My felicitations. It must have been quite an extraordinary wager to have so high a stake."

"Indeed, yes, Miss—Miss—Miss Hamp-Hamp . . ."

"Hampstead."

"Thank you." Lord Alberkirky smiled shyly.

"Well, as to that . . ." Mr. Devonshire grew brisk again.

"Lord Alberkirky, I have corresponded with you on this matter. You know my views and I am prepared to test them in the courts if need be."

"N-n-n-no need, Mr. Devonshire. Miss Hampstead

c-can draw funds off my account. And by the b-b-bye, the wager was all legal, you know!"

"Then you merely regard me as an object of pity!"

"Nonsense, Miss Hampstead, you are overwrought. I am sure Lord Alberkirky is showing all the proper feeling—"

"Well, *I* think the suggestion is most improper! And, Lord Alberkirky, might I say, since this is *my* business, that I have no intention of pursuing any matter in the courts whatsoever. You won the wager fair and square. Let us leave matters as they stand."

"Young lady, you cannot know what you say! Just think . . ."

"I *always* think. If Grandfather had wished to challenge the matter, he would have done so at the time. He would not have boasted in the clubs that he would win the whole of it back the following day."

"But, Miss Hampstead, he *would* have!" Lord Alberkirky sounded anguished. "I have the most damnable luck! Never won so m-m-m-much in all of my life, I haven't. *B-b-bound* to lose it the next night . . . all the c-c-clubs were *b-betting* on it."

Lord Alberkirky blinked at the length of his sentence and the exertion of it all. He was amazingly likable despite looking like a small boy caught with half a plum pie in his hands.

There was a moment's silence. Tessie would have giggled if the matter were not so serious.

"Very likely you *would* have lost, my lord, for Grandfather almost always recouped his excesses. But he died. That fact is unanswerable. Therefore, my good sir, possibly in spite of yourself you have won fair and square."

"What is this nonsense?" Mr. Devonshire frowned. "Pay her no heed, Lord Alberkirky. I shall call on you tomorrow, perhaps, to settle the matter."

Lord Alberkirky nodded doubtfully.

"You shall do no such thing! If you think I will have Lord Alberkirky—who I am sure is a very decent young gentleman—fund me into society, you are far out! There is no reason for me to accept gifts from him—any help must be construed as such. I cannot do it!"

"By George, she is r-r-r-right, sir! I will dashed well b-b-b-b-be compromising her if sh-sh-she draws off my b-b-b-banker."

"Not if the money is rightfully hers."

"But it *isn't,* Mr. Devonshire. You told me so but half an hour since!"

"Yes, but technically speaking . . ."

"I do not wish to speak technically, Mr. Devonshire." Tessie drew on her gloves. Her hands were trembling again, and the need for sal volatile seemed greater than ever, but she refused to acknowledge any of this.

"Farewell, Lord Alberkirky. Mr. Devonshire, you must pardon me, I am very tired. If you need me to sign any papers, you shall find me at the Colonnade on Upper Wimpole Street. Good day to you both."

"Stop!"

Tessie sighed. "What is it, my lord?"

"Mmmmm . . . mmmm."

Lord Alberkirky, in great agitation, fumbled with his neckerchief.

Tessie regarded him with patience.

"What I mean to-to—what I mean to say is . . ."

"Yes?" The patterns of the carpet seemed to be swimming in swirls above Tessie's head. She steadied herself and focused on the uppermost corners of dear Lord Alberkirky's stammering lips. They were framed by the whisper of a blond moustache.

"Marry m-m-m-me, Miss Ham-Ham-Ham . . ."

"Well, well, what an outstanding outcome to this little interview." Mr. Devonshire rang his golden bell once more. It tinkled in Tessie's ears as she heard champagne called for in a hearty tone.

"I don't deny I had hoped for something of this sort . . . such a sweet little slip of a thing, excellent lineage, you know, mother was . . ."

Lord Alberkirky, already severely tested, looked bewildered under this sudden barrage.

Miss Hampstead, herself entirely ignored by the august gentleman before them, could hardly blame him. Mr. Devonshire, it seemed, was in an expansive mood, quite relieved to have settled the matter so expeditiously.

Marry Lord Alberkirky! Tessie almost laughed aloud. The contrast between him and Nicholas Cathgar could not have been greater. And, though she could not now, in all conscience, encourage Lord Cathgar, neither could she engage herself to anyone else. Not the least a charming—but excessively foolish—greenhorn who was hardly out of short coats. The idea was ludicrous.

"No!"

"No?" Lord Alberkirky looked anxious again.

"No, Lord Alberkirky, I am afraid we should not suit. I am by far too managing."

Mr. Devonshire waved away the tray of champagne just as it was placed on an occasional table to his right. He looked suddenly most grave, all his jocularity fleeing.

"Miss Hampstead, if you refuse this most . . . most . . . *generous* offer, I shall have to withdraw my stewardship of your affairs . . ."

"Very well, I shall seek someone else. Lord Alberkirky, you are very handsome indeed to have made this offer. But I am very much afraid your mother should not like the match at all."

"N-n-n-no . . ."

"There, you see. I have saved you a good deal of trouble and doubtless a scolding."

"Yes, but . . ."

"There are no buts about it, I am perfectly firm on the matter." But Tessie did not feel firm. She was shaking, and despised herself for such weakness.

"May I have the folder with my affairs?"

"If you are determined on this course, I shall, of course, continue to represent you despite my reservations."

"Thank you, sir." For once, Tessie was humble. Both men, she knew, were trying to be kind.

"Matters are not good, but neither are they entirely hopeless. There are still two debts of honor to be recovered and . . . let me see . . ."

The spectacles went on again. "Yes, the stables are still intact . . ."

"But the horses need feed. . . ."

"Sell them." Two voices this time, and nary a stutter between them.

Tessie nodded. "I shall."

"Now the debts . . . hmmm . . . the Duke of Portland. Not good news, I am afraid."

"Why ever not?"

"The man is notorious for his debts. Never pays them. Or not on time, at all events. Don't know how he gets away with it."

"Royal blood. Mmmm . . . Mama says if it wasn't s-s-s-s-so, he would never be received."

"I shall sue him in the courts!"

". . . and drag Miss Ham—Hampstead's name through *The Tatler* and *The M-M-M-Morning Post?*"

"If that is what it takes."

"Gentlemen." Tessie had had quite enough of being talked about as though she did not exist. "I believe *I* shall decide, thank you. The second debt?"

Mr. Devonshire shuffled some papers. "The sum of . . . let me see . . . oh! Yes! Now, *this* is more suitable. Oh, indeed."

Tessie felt herself relax. It was terribly difficult to think of oneself as an heiress, then a pauper, then a lady of substance again in the space of a single interview. Also, to be proposed to . . . though the proposal—her second in as many days—bore no resemblance to that of her childish dreams. . . .

"Yes, the sum owing is ten thousand pounds. Not much, my dear, but sufficient to see you through the next six months . . . if I invest this carefully. . . ." Mr. Devonshire muttered a little under his breath and wrote down several figures in a large ledger blotted all over with ink. "Yes, I believe here will be some little capital to invest and Lord Cathgar always pays his debts. . . ."

"Beg pardon?"

"What, m'dear?" Mr. Devonshire did not look up.

"Did you say Lord Cathgar?"

"Yes, yes, nephew to old Sir John . . ."

"Lord *Nicholas* Cathgar?"

"Yes, indeed. There is only one. As I was saying . . ."

But Tessie did not hear. She was too busy concentrating on not swooning like a regular flibbertigibbet. Oblivious to their stares, she fumbled with her reticule, executed some kind of curtsy, and begged both men's pardons.

"You know my direction, Mr. Devonshire. I shall doubtless seek another interview with you tomorrow. You will forgive me now, I hope." Then, concentrating fiercely on the tassels, she stepped across the Axminster carpet.

Lord Alberkirky muttered some protest, but she was too tired to listen. Right past Sir Francis Drake she trod, down two flights of imposing stairs and out, at last, into daylight.

Her life had never been in such dizzy disorder, and this, despite all of her best efforts. Grandfather, invested with a wicked sense of the ridiculous, would probably have chuckled. Tessie, after a vigorous ride in a hackney cab, could hardly share his sentiments. She was never closer to those loathsome tears she despised.

Ten

In Grosvenor Square, Nicholas was reading *The Gazette* with a faint twist to his lips. There was much on the upcoming nuptials of Lady Larissa Ashleigh to Captain Marcus Harding of the seventh dragoons, he late having served with great honor in the Peninsula. There was precious little, however, about the recent midland uprisings, or of the attempted assassination of his royal highness. He supposed he should be grateful. He frowned.

He sipped his tea. He frowned. "Amesbury!"

"My lord?"

"Take this confection to the kitchens and bring me a port."

"Aye, my lord." He frowned.

Amesbury opened the curtains. Nick frowned again. But Amesbury expected no less. Nick was in a black mood, blacker than his doting staff had ever known.

The port was poured. Another frown.

"Will that be all, my lord?"

"Has the mail been delivered?"

"Not since an hour ago, when you last asked, my lord."

"Tell me when it has. Ah, Joseph!" A slight lightening of the features as his valet strode in.

"Parding yer lor'ship, but yer should not be drinkin' that muck on an empty stomach."

"That *muck,* as you put it, Joseph, was brewed in France in the last century."

"Then it is old and will curdle yer spirits."

"My spirits are already curdled."

"Aye, me lord, that is as plain as a pikestaff."

Amesbury made a stiff bow and departed, relieved. Really, there was no dealing with Lord Cathgar in such a mood! He would never dare address his lordship in terms of such familiarity! But then, the little valet had fought with him in the last campaign. Doubtless that accounted for matters. The door shut, and Joseph continued.

"Oi 'ave taken the liberty of puttin' out yer black velvet with the sapphire pin. . . ."

"Stow it, Joseph, I am not going out."

"The Dowager Countess of Cathgar arrives tonight, me lor'."

"You devil! I should dismiss you at once."

"Very likely, me lor'." Joseph drew out some top boots that sparkled like a very mirror. He eyed them complacently.

"My lady will want to inspect your wounds."

"And *I* want to inspect your back. *After* it has been thoroughly whipped."

Joseph grinned. "Will it be the velvet, then, me lor'?"

"Oh, God rot it, I suppose so. Anything better than Mama fussing with a hot posset!" And in this manner was his lordship, the great Nicholas Cathgar, coaxed from his solitude.

He was disappointed to find, however, that the dowager countess, whose robust disposition he always underestimated, was *not* safely tucked up and asleep when he arrived home several hours later. He had spent fruitless hours in his club, watching the great grandfather clock tick by, being rude to sundry very good friends, and generally feeling like a bear with a sore head.

How ever he could have let that little slip of a thing vanish into thin air he could not imagine. He vowed never to touch laudanum again if it could have so addled his wits. His wound hurt damnably, but the more so because they reminded him of her—the mischievous face framed in dark curls, the cheeky, insouciant smile, the unsure part of her, budding into shy womanhood, and, naturally, of course, the outright courage.

No one—*no one* had seen or heard of her, and he felt like a fool asking after someone whose name he did not know and whose kin he could not cite. Yes, he had suffered several sidelong glances from his peers, oh, countless quips about quivered hearts, until he needed a bout at Gentleman Jack's to release all his energy. Unfortunately, no one would be so unsporting as to spar with a wounded man, so he was denied even that tame outlet. And now, here was his mama, resplendent in court dress and emerald-studded tiara, waiting up for him with a calm patience. It was enough to make a man scream.

"Mama! I thought you would have been in bed hours ago."

"Nonsense, Nicholas! You know there was a supper party at Carlton House! And I do wish you would have attended, for I swear yours would have been the most handsome face present!"

"Oh, Mama! You are cutting a wheedle with me!"

"Indeed not, for poor Prinny grows fatter by the day, and I despair of any of the dukes, for Cumberland becomes as plump as a hothouse turnip. . . ."

"Mama! Have a care he does not hear you say that!"

"Well, he has, for I told it to him to his face."

In spite of his black mood, Nicholas laughed. "Well, what did he say?"

"He made a very improper advance, with which I shall not sully your ears. . . ."

"He did *not!*"

"Indeed, he did, for though I have aged, I have aged, if I say so myself, most gracefully." The dowager duchess preened herself slightly and smiled a self-satisfied kind of smile. "Now, the poor Countess of Froversham . . ."

Nicholas sighed. The Countess of Froversham and his dear mama had always been arch rivals. It was said that if one wore emeralds, the other wore diamonds. If one acquired a lapdog, the other would acquire a pug. And so it went on. If his mama had warmed to her pet theme, it would be a long night. Nicholas shifted one booted foot and winced.

"Sit down, Nick. I hope your fool of a valet rubbed basilicum powder into those wounds?"

"How did you know . . ."

"Oh, don't be ridiculous, Nicholas, you know I know everything."

"Sometimes I believe you do."

"Well, of *course* you do. You *know* I am the nosiest, most inquisitive, prying old harridan in all of London!"

"Mama, I *do* believe you are proud of it!"

"Yes, well, at my age, there are fewer diversions than there used to be. I daresay if that handsome devil *Rutherford* were still alive . . ."

"I thought he was."

"No! Popped his cork on the hunting field. *Most* inconvenient!"

"For you or for the hunt?"

"Now, that would be saying, my dear Nicholas! And I am shocked at the low direction of your thoughts!"

"What a whopper. Nothing shocks you, Mama!"

The dowager countess smiled. "Precious little, my son. Precious little. And now may I take a look at those wounds?"

"No, you may not!"

"Yes, Joseph told me you were tetchy!"

"Joseph talks too much by far."

"Indeed, I tend to agree with you on that point, for he praises you to the point of positive tedium."

"Does he? I cannot say why, for I do not make good company, I fear."

"Yes, I surmised that. Amesbury is tiptoeing about the house in a more stealthy manner than usual."

"Good God! Does he think I shall eat him?"

"Very possibly, for you *do* have a tiresome temper. Now, am I to see those wounds or not?"

"Not."

"You are very like your father when you glare at me like that. Now, *he* was a handsome rogue. . . ."

"You should not talk of him like that!"

The dowager countess ignored her son utterly. "But self-willed, opinionated . . ."

"Arrogant?" A hint of sarcasm in Nicholas's tone.

"Oh, yes, indeed. Thank you. Arrogant, high-handed . . ."

"Mama. Are you cataloguing my sins or his?"

"Mmm . . . witty, and quick, too. Spill the beans, Nick, or we will be here all night. And much as I positively *adore* this glittering tiara, it is heavy on my head."

"Take it off, then."

"No, for it requires my dresser. Hideous amount of pins. But we digress, my son."

"Is there no stopping you?"

"I think not, though one can never be certain. One of those earthquakes, perhaps, or a house fire possibly . . ."

"Maybe I should just take the tinderbox and set my house ablaze."

"Easier to just tell me the truth. Besides, I like all your Axminsters. Such *superior* carpets. It would be a shame."

"Mama, you are a bully. But maybe, this once, you can help . . ."

So Lord Nicholas Cathgar, after pouring himself a *very* strong drink—and his mama, for punishment, a watered-down version—finally succumbed. He spoke, at last, and at length, of a certain Miss Nobody.

"But, Nicholas, she must be staying *somewhere!*"

"True, but she has no funds, if you recall."

"Maybe you should wait. She will probably send the tab for some posting house or other to your account."

"Like she did the hansom cab?"

"Exactly."

"I think not. She is a dear little hoyden, but she has strict notions of propriety. She will not borrow a farthing from me if she can help it."

"Then why the hansom cab?"

"I would say she calculated that it was a fair exchange for my life. That, and the tab for dinner."

"What an extraordinary girl!"

"Yes, and I want you to find her for me."

"Me?"

"Oh, don't look so innocent, Mama, you know everything. A whiff here, a scandal there . . ."

"Indeed, but I have so little to go on! Family in Wiltshire, you say?"

"Yes, she let slip something of the sort, but it is all supposition. She was wearing half mourning, if that signifies to anything?"

"Well, of *course* it does, Nick! No self-respecting female would don half mourning if she was not in half mourning! Gracious, all those poor, drab colors—I still shudder to think on it. I loved your papa dearly, but I did *not* enjoy my period of mourning for him! There is nothing original one can do with blacks and browns. Even when one gets to the puces and olives . . ."

"Mama, I have no wish to talk of fashion!"

"And *that* is why you will never find your lady! I say, if she was in half mourning, there was a death of a near relative. Maybe six months ago. In Wiltshire . . . mmmm . . . I will make inquiries."

"Thank you. You might be eccentric, but you are a great good gun!"

"Which is no way to talk to your mama, but I will be lenient. Nick?"

"Yes?"

"What will you do with this paragon when you finally find her?"

"I will wring her neck."

The Dowager Countess of Cathgar chuckled. "If ought of your tale is true, it is more like *your* neck that will be wrung! I have a mind to meet this girl."

"Very funny! Now, if you will be kind enough to leave me to my port—"

"Without question—here, have mine." The dowager duchess watched as her oldest and dearest gulped several sips of the disgusting stuff he had served her.

Then she chuckled outright, ignoring his roar of fury as she made her stately exit. Later, when the tiara was finally prized from her head, her brow became thoughtful. Extremely thoughtful indeed.

The idea of dunning Lord Cathgar was ludicrous. If she approached him, he would simply wed her out of hand as he had threatened to do. But were those not the words of a delirious man, one faint from blood wounds, one hardly capable of making rational choices?

Perhaps he no longer was so intent on marriage. Perhaps he was even now thanking heaven for his lucky escape. Worse, if he was, would he not think she was deliberately seeking him out? And would it not compound all of her scrapes together if she approached him, unattended, at his London residence? Tessie rather thought it would as she contemplated her warm chocolate and watched the smoke curl in slivery wisps from the cup.

But she needed to make a decision. Either the estate must be sold—that way she could maintain a small competence—or she must find some means of supplementing its meager income until it became self-sustaining again. That was by far the best option, since it meant the tenants and dependents could remain on the estate, a no small consideration being that most had been born and raised there, and certainly none had other resources to sustain them. Tessie had been brought up haphazardly but not without moral principle. Grandfather Hampstead would have expected her to find some solution. He had often enough himself when hamstrung with debts. And always, except for the occasion of his death, he had come right. Tessie must, too.

But how? She could not apply to Portland, who was debt ridden himself—no point in that. But Cathgar? It was not as if she were asking for charity. The money was hers by right. Just as she did not question poor Lord Alberkirky's claim to *her* principal. That was the way of things, peculiar or not. Truly, Lord Cathgar must be approached. He simply must be. Then, if she were frugal, she might be able to keep the estates rolling over until summer. Until then she would refrain from making any kind of debut into London society.

Well, without funds she could not, of course. And though bloodlines were important, she could not think anyone would wish to take up or sponsor a penniless orphan. The beau monde, then, was probably now permanently out of the question.

That said, there was no reason she could think of not to procure for herself a job. Respectable, of course, not opera dancing or any such thing, but perhaps a milliner's model. She had seen some at Hetty Martin's, and they all looked very fetching in their feathered confections, smiling here, smiling there, encouraging all manner of rash purchases. Yes, she thought she could do something of the sort, if only someone would take her on!

But in the meanwhile there was the wretched business of Lord Cathgar's ten thousand pounds. She scribbled a letter at the serpentine-fronted writing table provided for her comfort. It sounded too stiff, so she began again on more familiar terms. Then, confounded by her own annoying blushes and the manner in which her hand trembled, she threw the letter at the ink pot, causing its contents to spill onto the two blank wafers she had left.

She could have cried in frustration but did not. Instead, she dusted down her gown, shook out her hair, brushed her locks vigorously in the manner of her dresser, twisted the whole of it up in a tight top-not, and marched out of the room, famous reticule and all, prepared for battle.

It did not once occur to her through this whole process that she should leave the matter in the able hands of Mr. Devonshire. She had been doing *that,* after all, for a whole six months or more. The fact that a teeny traitorous voice urged her to see Lord Nicholas Cathgar one last time was most irrelevant. *Most.* She quashed it as firmly as she trod on the red carpets, soft with pile.

She ignored the curious eyes as she made her way down the marble staircase of the Colonnade. A gentleman with eyes far too admiring for his own good made her a low bow. She ignored him, hardly noticing, but she herself, unchaperoned, did not go unnoticed. Indeed, she raised several eyebrows in her plain half mourning as she trailed down the stairs, lost in thought. Fortunately, it was too early for the fashionable to take their promenades, and too late to be trapped by the men of business, who would take breakfast in the front salons. But still, she was noticed.

Calling a hack was less of a problem than giving him directions. As she tucked in her muff—for it was passing cold—she realized with a guilty look at the driver that she had no idea where on earth Nick lived. But if *she* had no idea, it transpired that she was in the minority, for half of London did. It was a short drive to the Mayfair address, much too short to collect her thoughts and her wits. She paid off the driver with scrupulous exactness and looked up at the great edifice that was Cathgar House. It was splendid, ice white with huge colonnades and marble pillars. It was so high, Tessie had to crane her neck back to catch a glimpse of the roof. When she did, great Gothic gargoyles seemed to glare out into the sunshine.

Then there was a bright polished knocker hung from an elaborate paneled oak door. To reach this, she realized, she would have to take at least a dozen steps up highly polished slate. She almost jumped back into the hack, but the horses were already trit-trotting off, and there seemed little else to do but push ahead with her original plan.

Only, in the broad light of cold day, it did not seem much of a plan at all. Tessie tossed her head. Lord Cathgar was simply her debtor. He could not *eat* her, after all. The fact that he could *kiss* her she refused to contemplate. Such thoughts were simply for ninnyhammers.

Eleven

It was the second footman's pleasure to receive Miss Hampstead. Had she not knocked with such imperiousness, he doubted he would have admitted her, for she was far different from the kind of morning caller to which he was accustomed.

As he later apologetically confided in Amesbury, he did indeed note her inadequate gown and unfashionable boots, not to mention the absence of a chaperone. Amesbury rather quellingly announced he should also have noticed that young ladies do not call on gentlemen, and that the hour was not so sufficiently advanced as to permit morning callers.

To which, abashed, the second footman had nothing to say. They all waited, now, in anticipation of a roar from Nicholas's study, where he was busy with accounts. He had been uncommonly moody lately, a fad that was not lost on his long-suffering staff, who permitted only their affection for him to stop a rash of sudden resignations.

All except the French chef, that is, who'd resigned the day before amid a bitter tirade of bluster and a perfectly incomprehensible dialogue that the rest of the staff preferred untranslated. So what, after all, if he forgot to compliment the lightness of the soufflé, or if he should send back a dish of the finest crème brûlée? But then, of course, there was no accounting for the French.

Now Miss Hampstead, cold in the third best reception

chamber, shivered a little and contemplated her fate. A perfectly lovely ormolu clock ticked loudly upon an escritoire of sycamore marquetry, but Tessie was too nervous to admire either. Rather, she watched the hands of the clock, feeling more and more apprehensive and ill at ease. If she could have found her way through the rabbit warren of rooms without being stopped by a servant, she would probably have simply slipped away. But she knew she was being foolish, so she fingered her pistol in her reticule, bit her nails through her satin-fingered gloves, read and reread Lord Cathgar's hastily scrawled note of hand, and waited.

Finally, finally, the door opened. She expected, wide-eyed with sudden fright, the earl himself. It wasn't. Rather, it was the butler. Tessie noticed at once his perfectly sumptuous livery, emblazoned with all types of braiding. She swallowed but managed to smile at him quite civilly.

He bowed back, and directed her to follow. Nervously, she patted down her skirts and trailed behind him, past a corridor full of portraits, past a hall decorated in the classical style, with marble statues of Venus and Andromeda . . . past several antechambers and a large breakfast room, hung in azure silks. Then it was up a fluted stairway carved in mahogany, and down yet another corridor, silent, for the soft pile of the carpet cushioned her steps. Here and there she caught a glimpse of a maidservant or a footman, but by and large the house was empty.

Tessie felt severe misgivings, for it felt like she was being drawn into the lion's den, and for the life of her she felt there was no escape. It had not occurred to her that Cathgar would receive her anywhere other than in a respectable receiving room. But then, of course, she knew so little about Cathgar. . . .

"Miss Charity Evans, my lord." Tessie had used this

name so that Cathgar would recognize her and allow her admittance. She felt abashed, though, to still be clinging to the obvious falsehood.

"Enter." The butler withdrew, allowing space for Tessie to step forward. She did, clutching at Mr. Devonshire's papers and trembling in sudden nervous anticipation.

The room smelled earthy, of pines from the fire and oak from the paneling. Sandalwood, too, and subtle scents of snuff . . . there were great, wide volumes on shelves, and leather-bound books scattered on reeded mahogany tables. Then, of course, there was Nick. He was holding a crystal glass, and its contents shimmered under the light of a thousand candles. Or so, indeed, it seemed to Tessie.

Of course, he was impeccable in morning coat of jade green, with a whisper of emeralds about his throat, and fine lawn breeches that clung to his calf muscles like glue. . . . Tessie could hardly bear to look. And she, in her horrible olive, clutching dunning papers! Oh, it was too dreadful to even contemplate!

He said nothing, just stared at her for a long while, until it seemed to her that she was no larger than a mite or a beetle. She did not notice the spark of happiness or the blaze of sudden excitement in those ridiculously blue eyes. She was much too nervous for that, especially as his presence seemed to take up a room rather than the small balcony doorway behind him.

"Little Miss Nobody, I see."

"I wish you would stop calling me that!"

"And *I* wish for many things I daresay I cannot have. Or not easily."

Tessie noticed the scar above his temple and the silver just flecking the glorious dark hair. Those eyebrows were arched, as usual. And she wondered what they portended.

Nicholas waited, arms folded, for his little love to speak. He thought, after all the agonies he had endured, it was the least he could do.

Miss Hampstead said nothing, she just clutched the papers a bit harder and wondered rather futilely whether it was too late to escape.

At length, Nick, still loath to be the one to break the interesting silence, compromised by ringing a bell. Almost instantly a servant appeared, so Tessie was obliged to conclude the worst—Lord Cathgar had curious servants, and any conversation she might conduct in private would doubtless be overheard.

The servant, to give him credit, had a wooden face that evinced no such curiosity, but then, that was *always* the mark of a superior footman. She sighed, not audibly, but sufficient for Nicholas to notice.

"Tea, Rutherford."

"Tea, my lord?" Rutherford nearly disgraced himself by spluttering. Tea was not usually his master's preferred drink.

"Tea." The answer was firm. "And some of those little cakes Mrs. Guthrie bakes."

"Very good, my lord." The servant bowed, but his eyes lingered for an instant upon Miss Hampstead. Once again Tessie felt shabby in her makeshift olive.

"Take a seat, my dear."

"I'd rather stand, my lord. This is not a social call."

"How very disappointing. And intriguing. You shall not mind if I own myself intrigued?"

"You must please yourself, my lord."

"How very obliging. Possibly, I shall. Certainly, I believe I deserve to after the trick you served me!"

Nicholas advanced toward her, his intention quite clear. He set his crystal down on the library table, causing Tessie's heart to beat most erratically. When he was but inches from pulling her into his arms, however, Tessie turned her back, her eyes wild with . . . she knew not what.

"That was *not* a trick, my lord! I waited until Joseph returned, just as I said I would."

Nick swiveled her toward him. Her gloved hands pushed him back, though her heart still beat most traitorously.

He captured those silk-soft hands, retreating from their impetuous foray on his waistcoat. Papers crinkled against his starched shirt, his muscled stomach.

Miss Hampstead pulled then, but his grip was quite fierce. He stepped closer, so Tessie had to look up, to glare at him.

He laughed, though his eyes grew dark.

"I thought I said I had other plans for you?"

"Yes, but those were not *my* plans, my lord!"

She felt her hands released.

"Is your heart engaged elsewhere?"

"No, but . . ."

"Then you can have no possible excuse for behaving like a hoyden and not consenting to a proper conclusion."

"I was saving your life, my lord."

"True." His lips quirked. "But in a most hoydenish fashion!"

"That is *my* concern. I trust you are fully recovered?"

"Alas, no! Would you like to inspect my wounds?"

"Certainly not!" Tessie snapped. The temptation confronting her was large, and her temper was frayed. She realized she had to ask Nicholas—yes, she still persisted in thinking of him as that, however deplorably improper—for the ten thousand pounds, or she would lose her nerve.

"Lord Cathgar . . ."

"Nicholas. And it is churlish to refuse to see the outcome of your ministrations."

"Churlish but ladylike, for a change. You may think me beyond redemption, but I am not, I assure you!"

"I think no such thing. . . . Ah, the tea tray. You are dismissed, Rutherford."

Rutherford bowed.

"And shut that door!"

The door shut behind them.

"This is not proper, my lord."

"You should have thought of that before calling on me, unchaperoned, at this hour. One of these days you will get yourself into trouble, my girl."

"I feel I already *am* in trouble."

"How true. So you might as well relax, forget your remarkably stuffy notions of propriety given your propensity for scrapes, and sit down."

"I would rather stand, thank you."

"Suit yourself. But I shall sit. Though I am undoubtedly restored to my remarkable good looks, I am still rather weak."

"I am sorry for that. Have you consulted a doctor?" Tessie weakened as Nick hoped she would. He grinned.

"Joseph had a sorry old sawbones in. Sent him packing."

Tessie's eyes could not help a sudden twinkle. "Then doubtless you are restored to perfect health, and I shall waste no more sympathy on you."

"Ah, I have committed a strategic error, I see."

"Indeed."

Nicholas remained standing. "Are you not going to honor me with your name?"

"I shall, but only because it relates to the business I have with you. You must read nothing into my relenting."

"I shall not. I shall be extremely obedient."

Tessie eyed him suspiciously. "I find that hard to believe, my lord!"

Nicholas tried his very best not to grin. So he regarded the teapot for some moments, until Tessie found herself surprised by his silence. He was a hard man to read. And it did not help that he was standing so devilishly close to her, or that his emeralds glittered so brilliantly, so enticingly. . . . She shut her eyes.

"If you do that again, I shall kiss you, I give you fair warning."

Her eyes opened swifter than she could ever have dreamed possible.

"I shall either slap or shoot you, so be warned yourself."

"Little minx. I tremble in fear. And you are not carrying your famous reticule."

"Botheration! I must have left it below stairs."

"Good, I am safe, then. Or relatively so. I am not mindful of having a bullet wound added to my other pains."

"You forget I can slap you."

"Do I? You underestimate my memory. And my ability to retaliate."

"You would not slap a woman!"

"No, I have other, more subtle weapons."

Tessie blushed, for he was looking at her most meaningfully, and the color could not help rising to her cheeks. Oh, she had forgotten how infuriating he could be!

"Your name, if you please."

"It is Theresa Hampstead. Of the Wiltshire branch."

Nick regarded her musingly. Hampstead . . . there was something he recalled about the name, it rang curious bells, but he was not sure why. He focused on the second part of her speech.

"Did you say the Wiltshire branch?"

Tessie nodded.

"Now, *why* am I not surprised?"

"Beg pardon?"

"Oh, it is nothing, only I bemoan the fact that I have a remarkably omniscient mama . . ."

"What?"

"Hush, you look confused. Have a cupcake."

"I have not come for cupcakes."

"More fool you, for they are perfectly delicious and I recall that you have a rather large appetite. . . ."

"Do you not wish to know why I have called on you?"

"No, for I am sure it was for some positively odious reason. You have not allowed me to take even the smallest liberty . . ."

"You are funning. And, for your information, it *is* for an odious reason that I have called!"

"Now you interest me, Miss . . . Theresa."

"Tessie."

"Thank you. Tessie."

"No! I mean I am not ever called Theresa. My friends call me Tessie. *You* are to call me Miss Hampstead."

"I am suitably chastened. But I challenge you, *Miss* Hampstead, to deny we are friends. Hush, don't bother to do so, for there is more between us than mere strangers." He stepped closer, so that his mouth was tantalizingly close to her own. "You feel it, Tessie, I know you do."

"Oh, you will hate what I have come here for!"

"Have you just been married?"

"No . . ."

"Then I shall not hate it. Have your tea. You will need it while I inscribe your name, at last, on this." He opened a bureau drawer inlaid meticulously with mottled amboyna wood.

"What is that?"

"It is a special license for us to be married."

"You really mean it, don't you?"

"I always mean what I say. You have saved my life at the great expense of your reputation. You shall marry me before there are any scurrilous rumors floating about."

"And we shall live happily ever after?"

"I doubt that." Blue eyes blazed, suddenly, in amusement. He was not deceived that marriage would be meek and harmonious. With Tessie it would be like walking the plank into ever-increasing danger, but he was glad of it.

Tessie, less attuned to his thoughts than she should have been, heard his funning words bleakly.

He didn't *want* to marry her, why should he? Doubtless he had a thousand eligible belles fawning at his feet for the privilege. He felt obliged, which was kind, and very possibly noble, but not at all, at all, at all what she wanted. But neither did she want to reward his kindness by dunning him. She drew in a breath and flung the papers in the fire.

He stopped her by staying her arm and catching a charred sheet just as it was about to ignite. He blew on the blackened edges.

"What is this?"

"It is nothing. Let it burn!"

"A curious nothing that you have been clutching more closely than your pistol! I must, if you please, see this nothing."

"No!"

"You intrigue me now enormously." Nick flicked some ash off his sleeve and reached for the second paper, burning merrily in the grate. He singed his fingers a little, which caused Tessie to alternately chuckle and look upset, a situation he found mollifying.

"If you hadn't been such a chucklehead as to throw those things in the fire, I would not have had to retrieve them!"

"You would never have burned your fingers, my lord, if you had just let be. Does it hurt very much?"

"The very devil!"

"Then you must pour some of your Madeira over it. Cold liquid will help."

"Oh, no, you don't! That was smuggled out of France, if you please!"

"Then your fingers shall ache and very likely blister."

"You look uncannily pleased, little madam!"

"Well, you would be well served, for you have no right to scrutinize my private papers!"

"I do if they burn in *my* grate. Let me see . . ."

Tessie made a dive for him but tripped over her troublesome skirts and landed in a tumble at his feet.

"Good, a woman who knows her place. Now, let me read—"

"No!"

"Good gracious, woman, stop being such a pelterhead! I only want to know what dastardly words can be penned in there! Or can they possibly be love letters dedicated to the arch of my brow, or to the scar at my temple?"

"None of those, my lord. I fear your consequence is quite large enough."

"Oh, you slay me. I shall make you eat those words, lady wife!"

"I am *not* your lady wife!"

"No, but you shall be just as soon as I can get you to a dressmaker. My consequence simply does not allow me to wed a young lady dressed in that vile shade of green."

"Olive, my lord."

"Olive, then. A particularly dreary color." He helped her up with a touch as light as silk. Tessie snatched her hands back and ignored the sudden arching of his brow.

"It is all Madame Fanchon could whistle up upon such short notice!"

"Then we shall take our custom elsewhere. I would like to see you in pinks and silvers, maybe a touch of turquoise . . . the glimmer of gold, possibly, and pearl buttons . . . but I digress from the point."

For an instant, Tessie was so tempted, it seemed like a physical pain. Nicholas Cathgar was so exactly like the type of person she could fall in love with, it seemed heresy not to do so. This despite his deplorable manners and his insistence on snatching things that did not belong to him . . .

"You have a very strange idea of fashion, my lord! Turquoise and golds are *not* the colors of half mourning!"

He grinned, an endearing twinkle lighting up the severe blue of his eyes.

"My bride, my dear, shall in no way be mourning! It would be a blight on my manhood I simply could not tolerate!"

"Fustian! Your consequence is quite large enough for me to wear sackcloth and ashes!"

"Which I must implore you not to do, for kissing a sack, while novel, must nevertheless be somewhat depressing." The seriousness returned to his eyes. "Hush, don't argue for once, little Tessie. For whom do you mourn?"

"My grandfather. He was the Viscount of Hampstead and the dearest, nicest man. . . ."

"Indeed. I was on terms with him. His death was tragic, but it must be put behind you. No one in society will look askance at the Countess of Cathgar dressing as she pleased."

"You mean as her *husband* pleases."

"Indeed, no! If she were to dress as her *husband* pleased, she would wear nothing but nightrail—preferably torn to the knees—all evening long."

"Now you are being absurd! And all this is academic, my lord, for I shall not marry you."

"We do not suit?"

"We do, I believe, but for your high-handedness . . ."

"Then?"

"Then I am not what I had thought. It changes everything."

"What had you thought yourself?"

"My grandfather's heiress. It was for that reason I traveled so precipitously to London."

"For that reason you traveled as Miss Charity Evans?"

"Yes, for I thought I could drop that persona and slip easily into my new one—that of Miss Theresa Hampstead, heiress—without anyone being any the wiser."

"Silly! Don't you realize that head of hair would be recognized, or the clarity of those eyes? Or that haughty stare, for that matter . . ."

"It is not haughty!"

"Yes, it is . . . and if you go about shooting people, you are bound to be noticed!"

"I do *not* go about shooting people . . . or not in the ordinary way. I did not shoot Mr. Dobbins, and he was odious enough to deserve it!"

"What did you do to him?"

"I bit him and kicked a little . . ."

Nicholas laughed. "If I didn't want to crush him to pulp, I might feel a little sorry for him!"

"Well, spare your sorry, for he stole my valise and left me with nothing but a drab mauve gown. . . ."

"Then I shall kill him undoubtedly if ever our paths cross."

Tessie laughed, but she was holding her breath again, a habit she seemed destined to adopt in this rakish man's presence. It almost felt like he was about to kiss her again, but he did not. The papers, still crushed in his hands, crinkled a little. Tessie noticed a black, charred end float idly to the floor.

"I wish you would give me back my property."

"I wish so, too, but alas, my besetting sin is curiosity. You shall have them back after they are read."

"You are a beast!"

The beast eyed her quizzically and grinned.

Twelve

He smoothed out the papers and scrutinized them carefully. Then he drew out a quizzing glass from his desk and stared at one of the charred pages longer than seemed strictly necessary. Tessie said nothing, squirming at her ridiculous plan to extort money from him.

"Good gracious, what a singular female you are! You are actually dunning me!"

"I *was* actually dunning you. If you had let the wretched papers burn, you would know nothing of it."

"But I didn't, did I?"

"No, for as I believe I have repeatedly told you, you are rag-mannered and never, simply *never* do anything to oblige me!"

"Oh, I wouldn't say *that,* my dear. It is really far too tempting a prospect to contradict you. I recall once or twice when I have *indeed* obliged you . . . ah, yes! The telltale color in your cheeks! You really are very modest for the little spitfire you purport to be. Maybe it is because your weapon is safely out of harm's reach. At least I hope it is!"

Then, rather negligently, Nick leaned forward and drew poor Tessie into his arms. She regarded this as supremely unfair, for it is very hard to stick to one's resolve to be noble when the beneficiary of all this self-sacrifice is being so disobliging as to kiss one's nose.

Tessie slapped him.

"You little vixen! That stung!"

"I warned you, my lord."

"So you did." The voice was a trifle cold as he regarded her. Tessie wanted to weep, but instead, she stiffened her shoulders and turned on her heel.

"Just one moment!"

She stopped.

"I owe you a sum of money, I believe."

"It is void, my lord. I believe I made that clear."

"And *I* believe I am a gentleman. A gentleman always pays his debts."

"Then why was this one never paid?"

For a half second, Tessie thought she had gone too far. Then she noticed the fingers, arrested at his neckerchief, relax. The grim expression altered subtly. For some reason, *she* breathed easier, too.

"I am sorry. I should not have—"

"No, by all means Miss Hamptead. Chastise me. You are perfectly correct."

"I am *not* chastising you!"

"No, that sort of activity can become tedious, can it not?" He gestured to his cheek, though the redness had long faded.

"It is my damnable temper. I am sorry about that too."

"Oh, dismiss it entirely from your mind. I am sure my mama would conspire with you to say I was most deserving of it!"

"Well, you were . . ."

"*Such* contrition!" The mocking laughter returned. Better, Tessie thought, than that truly bone-chilling coldness. She smiled, but he was striding across to his desk. He opened a locked drawer, pulled out a box fashioned in leather, and beckoned her to sit.

"Now, Miss Hampstead, to business. I did not, as you point out, pay the debt on time because I have lately dismissed my man of business and have had great difficulty finding a reliable replacement. I did, at last, on Tuesday, but my desk is piling up with bits and pieces that will take us to Christmas to wade through. The note must have been one of them. How much, precisely, do I owe?"

"Do you not know?"

"No, for the sheet has burned at the crucial figure. Most distressing, is it not? So tell me, how much do I owe?"

Tessie skirted around the question and finally helped herself to an iced cupcake. She was hungry, after only her morning chocolate!

"You owe me ten pounds."

"You lie, Miss Hampstead." Blue eyes gazed directly into nutbrown. He pushed her into the seat beside his desk.

"Ten pounds is a fortune, my lord."

"Ten pounds will buy you a gaudy bauble. I do not deal in baubles."

Tessie swallowed. "And *I* was mad to come here! It is just that . . . oh! I do *not* wish to become a watering pot!"

"What an inestimable relief! I do *not* think I could tolerate tears upon my very fine Axminster carpets. Did you notice them?"

"Yes, they are very fine, like everything else in this . . . home."

"I am glad that they please you." Nicholas caught a tear that was about to offend his precious carpets. Tessie tried her very best not to startle to his touch. Her efforts were wasted, however, for he trailed a gloved finger right down her face, almost to her lips. Then she *really* wanted to cry, for he was horribly comforting and maddeningly impossible to resist, though all her principles cried out against succumbing. She pushed his hand away ungratefully and rubbed crossly at her face.

"I am probably all blotchy."

"Very likely, for my sisters say tears are fatal to the complexion!"

For an instant Tessie was diverted.

"You have sisters?"

"Oh, dozens of them! They bully me frightfully. It is a great trial."

"I'll bet they cosset you rotten!"

He grinned. "I was the baby, you see, and a rare uproar it was, for Mama had been trying for the succession for positively eons!"

"No wonder you are spoiled!"

"I am *not* spoiled, hellion! Tell me at once how much I owe."

"No, for though you are overbearing and wickedly tempting—yes, I own myself tempted, and it would serve you right if I relented—I do *not* think I should cadge money off you like a . . . like a . . ."

"Like a street urchin?" he put in helpfully.

"Street urchins ask only a penny."

"And you ask?"

"I am not saying."

"This grows tedious. It is a small matter for me to find out. Perhaps I shall just notify my banker that you may draw whatever you like."

"You are negligent, my lord. I could be a thief."

"A singularly pretty thief."

"Nonsense, for I know perfectly well that you must have . . . vast experience of beautiful women."

"Yes, indeed."

Tessie's heart sank at his careless agreement. He smiled.

"All of them would be perfectly wild for the banker's draft I've just promised you!"

"You are being completely nonsensical. I wish you would be serious. I must take my leave."

"Not until you finish those cupcakes."

"There are a dozen on that plate!"

"You need filling. What did you have for breakfast?"

"Only chocolate. I was nervous. . . ."

"Oh, nervous, were you?"

"Yes. It is not every day I dun peers of the realm!"

"Well, you are making a hash of it. Tell me, for goodness' sake, what I owe!"

"Ten thousand pounds!" Tessie glared at him, choked on her cupcake, and coughed.

"Oh, is that all? What a pother over nothing. Here, I'll make it over to you now. Doubtless my new man of business will be reminding me of it when I see him."

"Ten thousand pounds is not nothing, my lord!"

"It is when considered in the light of a dowry."

"It is not a dowry, my lord! I will have you know, I intend to turn it to good use!"

"Another of Madame Fanchon's gloomy gowns?"

"Don't be absurd. I have an estate to maintain. I can do so for a six-month on that!"

"And then?"

"That is *my* business, my lord!"

"And yet, curiously, my business, too." Blue eyes searched her face.

In a rush, Tessie defied him.

"You are so certain you can coerce me into a marriage! Well, you shan't. My reputation is not worth salvaging, my lord. I am *never* going to make a court appearance or appear in the ballrooms of the Duchess of Doncaster or Lady Aberfeldy or their like. Perhaps, if I were not penniless, wedding you might have made some marvelous difference. But I *am* penniless and I *am* unchaperoned, and I *am* having a private interview with you in a closed library in a most improper manner! Society cannot forgive that, they won't."

"They shall if I send a note to *The Gazette*."

"Well, you won't! I won't have you acting the martyr when I am perfectly able to stand on my own two feet!"

"You are *not* perfectly able to stand on your own two feet! I have seen you trip over your hems—"

"Oh, how literal you choose to be, but you shall see!"

"What shall I see?"

"You shall see me make an honest living."

"As a companion? Governess?"

"Good Lord, no! I would make a shocking companion—my terrible temper, you understand—and as for a governess! The very thought makes me laugh."

"I like to see you laugh. It brings the bloom back to your cheeks."

"Now you are saying I am like a washed-out rag, in the usual way."

"Well, you are, in all those drab gowns, and with your pale skin and dark lashes casting shadows across your countenance—"

Tessie was indignant. "Well! If you want to trade insults . . ."

"I do not. Tell me why you won't make a good governess? Your answers intrigue me."

"Don't you have someplace to go, my lord? I am sure all this must be a shocking bore."

"I will tell you swiftly when I am bored. Go on."

"I would make a nightmare of a governess because I would very likely encourage the pupils to play truant, like I did. And I would spill the watercolors, teach them to poach trout from the lakes. . . . I would never get the job. No references. I could forge them, but Grandfather always says these things come back to haunt you."

Nicholas's mouth trembled, but he managed to retain a straight face through this tangled explanation. "How sage. And so?"

"And so?"

"Yes. Tell me what would be a preferable alternative to marriage with me."

"Oh! Well, not necessarily *preferable,* for it must be great good fun to have people bowing and scraping and kowtowing to your every word. . . ."

"I do not notice *you* doing such!"

"No, but then, Grandfather always says I am a contrary female. But you noted how the innkeeper jumped to your commands, where he merely turned up his nose at mine."

"Yes, well, you did look like you'd stepped backward from a hay cart!"

"Unfair! I was wearing a perfectly respectable traveling gown before Oliver Dobbins mussed it up! And the innkeeper, whatever you may say, did treat you royally and ensure the fire was lit and the sheets aired. . . ."

"True. So tell me this plan that is not preferable to marriage with me." Nicholas Cathgar's eyes twinkled.

Tessie refused to look at them. Rather, she fiddled with her fingers.

"Not preferable, but a good deal more sensible. I may not be able to draw or dance, but I can sew. I am remarkably good at it, actually, though Grandfather always used my samplers to clean his guns."

"I am amazed you did not shoot him!"

"No, for they are silly kickshaws, but the finer work, the beading on poplins and gauzes, even on jaconets, I always hid up in the attics. I would have been as mad as fire if he had used those."

"Oh, undoubtedly. So what are you going to do? Set up shop?"

Tessie eyed him suspiciously. "You are funning me! I daresay you think I don't know what sort of sum I would need for such an enterprise!"

"Oh, no, you sadly underestimate me, madam! Nothing, you know—especially in the more manly line—would astonish me!"

Tessie grinned. "Grandfather always said I had a good head for finances and a perfectly rotten one for the softer arts."

"I delight in hearing the viscount's utterances—always so judicious—but I suppose it is your pleasure that I die of suspense?"

Tessie looked severe. She did not want to smile at his sarcasm—it might encourage such frivolous behavior in the future. She closed her mind to the fact that there *was* no future.

"Now you are talking nonsense again. But I did think I could put my skills to good use. . . ."

"Undoubtedly. There must be a way. . . ." Nicholas murmured this quietly, and the wicked gleam returned to a sapphire-blue eye. He took Tessie's hand and kissed her palm, but she withdrew it immediately, a troubled frown upon her brow.

"If you do not behave with decorum, I shall be forced to leave."

"You have vanished once without trace. Do not, I pray you, do so a second time. I shall, with reluctance, forbear to kiss you."

"Good. For if you compromise me any further, you might get all noble again. Very inconvenient."

"I apologize. Now, are you going to tell me your plan, or am I going to shake you till your teeth rattle?"

"They will not rattle. All my teeth, thankfully, are my own. But I will satisfy your curiosity and tell you what I mean to do. I am going to—no, don't look shocked—I am going to trim ladies' bonnets. You know, create subtle effects with ermine and gauze and peacock feathers. . . . Don't gape, my lord, it is very bad form."

"Yes, added to my undoubted crime, I am going to supplement my income by becoming a milliner's model! My abigail once told me—she is frightfully chatty, you know—that you can make a fortune on Bond Street selling hats."

Tessie took a breath and smiled radiantly at Nicholas. The notion had only just crystallized in her mind, but it seemed to her to be rather perfect. Her ten thousand pounds could be sent home to make improvements on the estate and supply the tenants. With any luck, the land could be self-sufficient, carefully managed, in six months.

He smiled as he scribbled his note of hand. "Novel, if idiotic. I look forward to viewing your progress."

"You shan't, for gentlemen are not permitted to such establishments."

"And a very good thing too."

Tessie did not raise her brows at this cryptic comment. She merely reviewed his note and remarked that the sum was incorrect.

"No, for if you compound it with interest, you will find I have made the calculation perfectly."

"It is apparently an extortionate interest rate."

"Your grandfather was as shrewd as they come."

"Very well, I shall accept your word. And your note. You have been most obliging over this matter, my lord."

"I am *always* most obliging."

Tessie chuckled. Now that the interview she'd dreaded was over, she felt singularly relieved. Tomorrow's worries—that of finding an employer—were not upon her today. Today she held in her hand a sum that would satisfy her bankers and buy her a sherbet at Gunthers. She could not, she supposed, ask for more.

"Will you come to me for help if you need it?"

"No, for we have no claim of kinship. Are the Luddites arrested?"

"All but one. But they have Grange—he went up before the magistrate at Stipend and is currently awaiting trial. If we have stopped his activities, it was worth the wound. I fear I might have another scar, though, to mar my comely countenance."

Tessie wanted to ask how he acquired the other, but for once she was silent. He was staring at her strangely, so that her pulses raced again, and she nearly—very nearly—disgraced herself by flinging herself into his arms.

"The Prince of Wales wishes to convey his compliments to you."

"Pardon?"

"He has been apprised of your no small role in the affair."

"It was a foolish role! Oh, you should not have said a thing!"

"I did not, though it seems the same could not be said of Lord Christopher Lambert. It appears, dear delight, that you have stolen his heart, too."

"I have not stolen your heart, my lord."

"No?" Nick looked whimsical for a moment but did not pursue or contradict the matter. Tessie, holding her breath again, told herself not to be such a clodpole. Of course she had not stolen his heart. How could she, when she had acted foolishly, churlishly, hoydenishly . . . oh, she could think of dozens of uncomplimentary phrases!

"He is holding a ball at Carlton House. He would like you to attend."

"I cannot, my lord, I am not yet out."

"Perhaps the occasion can rectify that. Queen Charlotte will be attending. His highness might present you to her himself."

"No! I have not a thing to wear and I doubt that he—or the queen—could wish to consort with milliners' models."

Nick's eyes twinkled. *"Au contraire,* but I shall spare your blushes. Further, I have a mind to have you safely wed before you make any curtsies to his highness. His reputation, sadly, is more ruinous than your own."

"Let us not argue the matter again, my lord. You have had my answer."

"But, sadly, I do not accept it. I always get my own way, Tessie."

"Not with me, you don't!"

Nick's eyes narrowed. "Is that a challenge? I am singularly fond of challenges!"

"You lost to Grandfather!"

"All the more reason to repair my losses."

"You are bullying me!"

"Nonsense! I am merely being forceful. I happen to want to wed you, Tessie, and I will."

"You can't without my consent."

"I will make you consent."

"How?"

"How?" Nicholas took two paces forward and pulled Tessie into his arms. He was too quick for her to struggle, and he pinned her hands against his chest so she could not move. Tessie opened her mouth to protest, though she was trembling so much she could hardly do more than murmur. Besides, his mouth was upon hers before she could think of anything sobering or witty to say. And, oh, it was so, so luxurious! He was gentle, but just firm enough to stop any nonsensical protest.

Soon Tessie was not protesting in the least but losing herself deep in the jade green of his morning coat, until he pushed her from him so that he could kiss her lashes, her temple, her throat . . . but she wanted his warmth again, so she drew her fingers up his starched white shirt, silky thin against his skin.

"You appear to convince rather easily."

The voice from above was lazy and amused. He pushed her from him, teasing.

Tessie's throat constricted. Oh! However could she

have let matters get to such a stand? Now she could add "wanton" to her rapidly compounding list of sins, and what was more, if she did not extricate herself soon, she would lose all her resolve. She would simply melt and give in to Lord Cathgar's very pleasurable demands. It would be no hardship marrying him, more like an absurd dream come true.

She would do it, if only she were convinced that the dream would not turn into a nightmare for either of them. She rather thought it would when Nick finally did meet someone he wanted to marry . . . someone who was not troublesome and meddlesome, who was not inclined to be trigger happy, who behaved with fashionable decorum . . . who was beautiful . . . oh, the list went on, and Tessie's hands flew to her mouth in horror at what she had done, was doing. . . . She could not permit a few moments of wicked pleasure to cloud her judgment.

Grandfather Hampstead had always taught her to think with her head, not her silly, wayward heart. She *must* convince Nicholas to alter course. If she did not, he would live to regret his reckless chivalry. Tessie did not think she could ever live with herself—or him—if he did.

But how in the world to convince him? After her enthusiastic response, he appeared more determined than ever, the arches of his brows testament to a certain smug satisfaction. He seemed so certain she was going to meekly do his bidding.

It was clear, despite her note of hand, that he did not take her plans seriously. If she became a milliner's model, heaven and earth would not then allow her to become a countess. He was not so stupid not to realize this, yet still he persisted with the confounded notion that she was to be his wife.

Something had to be done to shatter his composure once and for all. He needed to know, as she did, that a marriage between them could not take place. Tessie bit her lip at the irony of finally loving when it was quite impossible. She would be viewed by the world—viewed by him, with time—as no more than a fortune hunter. She could not, somehow, bear that.

She swallowed, and lunged a sword into his heart. It hurt more surely than as if it had been her own. "You are not the *only* eligible offer I have had, my lord."

"But the only one you are going to accept." The words were faintly possessive. Tessie ignored the sudden hope that he really *did* want to marry her—for herself, not simply as a means out of an impossible scrape. She took a deep breath and threw caution to the winds.

"My lord, your offer was kind but misguided. Understand that I am grateful for the ten thousand pounds, but I shall not wed you. You hardly know me, nor I you."

"That can be rectified."

"No, it cannot. You forget the other offer."

Nicholas's eyes narrowed, his mind suddenly keen and alert. "Good God, if I didn't know any better, I would say that that puppy Christopher Lambert beat me to the post!"

"This is not a race, my lord! And I doubt whether the dose of cod liver oil endeared me to him quite as much as you think! No, indeed . . ."

"Then, who . . ."

"Another peer of the realm, Nick. Someone kind . . . and gentle . . ." Tessie guiltily ignored poor Lord Alberkirky's stammer, and his patent relief at being freed from her obvious clutches. She suspected, though, that nothing would deter Nick from his course but this. He was used, sadly, to getting his own way. Several sisters had not cured him of this fault. If he decided for whatever insane reasons—all of them hopelessly wrong, of course—to marry her, then marry her he would, unless he had very strong provocation to the contrary.

It appeared the absent Lord Alberkirky was provocation enough. Tessie felt a great pain at her triumph.

Lord Cathgar turned his back and picked up his drink. Tessie waited in silence.

"So! I am a fool. You did not *need* all my knight-errant behavior." A wry, self-deprecating smile as some of the Madeira was tossed from his glass into the fire. It blazed dangerously for a moment, then settled.

He continued, his voice light but unmistakably brittle. "Doubtless your reputation shall be spared by someone far more suitable than myself. I am relieved. You have spared me much trouble, though I rather wish, when I asked you upon two occasions earlier whether your heart was engaged, you had told me the truth."

The lightness in his tone changed, suddenly, to become as hard as granite, and though an elegant back was turned to the window, Tessie could hear the grinding of clenched teeth, see the smooth lines of his gloves fold into a tight white ball. She would have run to him then but for the fact that it was not his heart but his ego that was engaged. He would recover, and one day he would—might, if ever their paths crossed again—thank her for it.

Tessie wondered if they would ever meet again. The cupcakes looked miserable on their silver dish.

"Good-bye Nick. You have been very, very kind."

If her heart ached more than she either liked or owned, it was her own silly fault.

Nicholas strode back to her and tilted her chin in his hand. For an instant—for a glorious instant—she thought she might be kissed again. But she was not. The Earl of Cathgar merely touched her cheek, and regretfully rang for Amesbury.

Amesbury, closing the door behind the earl, did not seem to notice Miss Hampstead's tear-filled eyes or hesitant walk as she followed him through the maze of passages and hallways. He could not know that she was memorizing every last feature of the gracious establishment, or reflecting on the unlikelihood of ever seeing good Lord Nick again. The sunshine, when the second footman opened the great oak door, flooded across the steps and into her eyes.

Thirteen

"Nicholas Cathgar, did I hear you right?"

"Yes, you did, Mama."

"Then you are a fool."

"Yes, for falling in love with a scheming little hussy!"

"Did she tell you she was betrothed before or after you persisted in your bullying?"

"I did not bully!"

"Of course you did. You always do when you don't get your own way. And how, pray, is she scheming? I collect that if she had accepted your offer, she might be placed in that category!"

"Mother, if you have nothing useful to say, do pray leave me to the sanctuary of my library!"

"The sanctuary of your precious Madeira, you mean. Not on your life, my son. I have a mind to meet this girl."

"To what purpose? She is probably happily cooing at some aging marquis . . ."

"Nonsense and tommyrot!"

"What do you know of the matter?"

"I am a female. I know how females think. They do *not* prefer aging marquis to godlike earls."

"I am not godlike."

"Ho, ho! Indeed, not! But you *are* blindingly good-looking despite your battle scar, and you would be a fool if you did not own it!"

"Perhaps she is not moved by good looks."

"A sensible chit, then, for I already see the silver peeping through your splendid head of hair. You shall doubtless be as white-haired as your father before you."

"How comforting."

"Indeed, for he was a wickedly handsome fellow, but I digress. . . ."

"Indeed you do." But the twinkle was back in Nicholas's eye. He could be very indulgent with his mama, whom he loved dearly, despite their frequent tête-à-têtes.

The Countess of Cathgar smiled and dug deep into her reticule for a sugarplum. "*What* did you say she was going to do? Draperies or some . . ."

"Millinery. She is going to become a milliner's model."

"There you go, then! I knew it was all a hum!"

"Mother, must you talk in riddles?"

"Nicholas, I declare I have never known your wits to be so addled! If she had such a scheme, she could not be betrothed to any peer. Not even a baron would permit such an outrage!"

"You don't know Tessie. I doubt if she has ever waited for permission in her life! She tumbles into scrapes like I—"

"—dip into the bottles of French port your father laid down. A very bad habit. We must try to cure you both. I wonder which milliner she will be likely to approach?"

"Bond Street, I think she said. What does it matter?"

"I would prefer, Nicholas, that your future wife is above reproach!"

"Good God! Then don't, I pray you, look to Tessie!"

"Well, I shall, for I have taken an unaccountable liking to this little lady. We shall deal famously together, for if there is one thing I cannot tolerate, it is a milk-and-water miss. I have always had the liveliest dread you might wed such a one, for there are times, Nick, when you are most preposterously stuffy."

Nicholas ignored this last admonition, his attention, at last, arrested.

"What are you going to do?"

"I am going to buy myself bonnets, Nick! It is high time my wardrobe was refurbished. Yes, I shall purchase myself several. And crimson feathers, I think. Oh, yes, indeed."

"Doubtless you shall be sending the reckoning on to me?"

Despite an incipient headache, Lord Cathgar's thinking was still clear. "But naturally! It is a small price, my dear son, to pay. And *I* shall have the satisfaction of being in turbans and tippets—I do hope they sell those glorious swansdown tippets—for the remainder of the season."

"Doubtless a strong inducement!"

"But naturally! I am so delighted Miss Hampstead did not decide to become a baker, or . . . or . . ."

"Blacksmith?" Nicholas provided helpfully.

His mama rewarded him with a peal of laughter at such an outrageous suggestion.

"Oh, you are absurd! But she shows great good sense, the little one, to think of hats. Hats are always so delightful."

"And costly."

"Tut, tut, Nicholas! Remove, if you please, that frown from your countenance. I swear, you grow more like your father each day."

"You fell in love with my father."

"Indeed, but that is no reason to gloat. Now, *do* be a good boy and call me up a coach. And you might as well send a notice into *The Gazette.* If that girl does not marry you within a fortnight, I shall eat every damn bonnet that I procure!"

The Earl of Cathgar was still chuckling over this unlikely image when his beloved mother, inclined to think his answer might be biting, disappeared from the room.

It was not fifteen minutes later, however, that she could be viewed from the gallery window. She was being helped into a crested carriage and was wearing the most hideous muff Nick had ever laid eyes upon. When she glanced upward, her eyes danced with youthful mischief. Nick, caught in the act of staring, could only bow ruefully and wave.

Milliners, Tessie learned very quickly, were a breed apart. She was treated reverentially upon her arrival at Millicent Dorsom's fashionable enterprise. Indeed, she was seated upon a velvet chair and treated to a chorus of compliments regarding her height, her build, and, naturally, her abundant but curly shock of dark hair. It was quickly agreed that she was sadly—sadly—in need of a bonnet, for her own, though fashionable, was lackluster and needed the enhancement of several ostrich plumes, or possibly even a quilling of blond about the edge.

Tessie wholeheartedly agreed but went on to explain that she had precious little money for quilling, never mind plumes, though indeed, Miss Dorsom's was famous enough. This compliment fell on deaf ears, for the smiles quickly froze on the faces of her listeners.

"No money? Then why, pray, are you here? We do not extend credit, except, of course, to a few of our more *select* young ladies. . . ."

"No, no, it is not credit I want!" Tessie could not help smiling at the notion. "No, I would like very much, Miss Dorsom, to apply for a post with you. I know it is unusual, but I assure you I would apply myself most diligently, and I am not unskilled, you must understand, with a needle. I have trimmed many of my own bonnets—some with gros de Naples, which is hideously expensive, but it was worth the risk, for they came up perfectly. . . ."

"My *dear,*" Miss Dorsom herself twittered, "we cannot

possibly hire you! Why, we are overstaffed as it is, and what with the Prince Regent canceling the royal regatta at Clyde, we are positively having hats returned! Yes, I do assure you, it is mortifying! Petra here has no wage but only her board paid, and even *that,* I tell you, is a hardship. Now, if you were to be interested in another line of work . . ."

"Like what?" Tessie, determined to be positive, clutched eagerly at this crumb.

The girl called Petra laughed. "She 'as the looks for it, proper lady an all."

"Yes, and excellent lines, though a trifle on the voluptuous side . . ."

"No gennelman has ever complained about *that.* . . ."

A series of friendly chortles followed this incomprehensible dialogue. Tessie, looking around her at the hats, felt uncomfortable.

"Are you talking of my being a milliner's model? That would suit me perfectly! I am quite accomplished at hemming silks and net, but if you thought I could learn . . ."

Again the twitter of high-pitched giggles and a couple of whispers behind large bolts of milliner's lace. Tessie started to feel annoyed.

"I *am* a trifle clumsy but . . ."

The annoying chuckles deepened. Tessie had to school herself not to lose her famous temper. "I don't see what is funny about my proposal. I will naturally prove myself before you need feel obliged to pay me. . . ."

Miss Dorsom looked at her little circle of stitchers. They all had an assortment of kerseymere, velvet, and sarcenets on their laps, half-finished bonnets and tippets and bandeau with feathers. No one, however, seemed to be in any hurry to sew, though some intricate beading caught Tessie's interested eye.

"Deary," Miss Dorsom said. "We are not talking about high pokes or cambric biggins. We are talking about . . .

gentlemen, and their singular preferences for . . . novelty."

Tessie understood at last! "You mean you are all . . ."

"Not all . . . some of us. The pretty ones." Again the laughter and the sly glances here and there.

Tessie thought rather irreverently that it was then unlikely that Miss Dorsom was impure, for she was as ugly as she was twittery. But she sobered up sharply when Miss Dorsom set down her stitchery and pointed a long, manicured fingernail in her face. Her polished accent slipped a little with every breath she took. "You 'ave the makings, lass. If you are interested, you may 'ave the room upstairs and full board. Two hours in the mornin' beautifying and the afternoon's yer own. Can't say better'n that. Terms of 'alf an' 'alf, of course. Only fair with lodgin' an' all."

Tessie did not dare ask what the evenings were for. She was not as green as Nick accused her of being.

"I am not interested in that kind of work."

"Oh, la di da, ain't yer?" Miss Dorsom's smile faded. She directed her attention at an opera hood lined in moss silk and ornamented with lilies of the valley. Her needle flew in and out with perfect precision. "Well, ye'll find many a lady 'ard on 'er luck wot 'as taken that road, and none complainin'—or none of my ken. If you change yer mind, come back. If not, you can let yourself out by the back—there, the bell is tinkling—hush—oh, *dear* Lady Salisbury, what a *pleasant* surprise, how *wonderful* you look in that white tiffany tunic—dear, dear, is that a lozenge front I detect? Yes, I see you must be employing Paris designers, how naughty of you, though naturally you must look your best. Now, you have come about bonnets, have you not? And, oh, what a *delicious* sampling I have for you. Yes . . . saved especially. Oh, you must see what we have prepared for you. Elsie, fetch the Ionian cork bonnet. Ma'am, it is a dream . . . composed of twelve thousand—twelve thousand, mark you—pieces of Ionian cork. We've arranged the pieces in the same manner as mosaic gems . . . oh, *do* sit down . . ."

The milliners had dropped everything—beads scattered all over the shiny parquet flooring—as if on cue. Tessie could see bonnets of all sorts—silk and straw, the velvet gypsy, the Spanish hats of satin, all appearing as if by magic, practically from nowhere. The woman named Elsie modeled upon her head an enormous cork confection lined in strawberry satin. There was a twittering again, but this time all over *dear* Lady Salisbury and her plentiful purse. Tessie, forgotten, slipped past Petra and the other ladies.

She had come up a marble stairway with banisters curled and gilded in gold. The back way was slate, and covered largely in grime. Tessie grimaced. It would be better, she thought, at someone more reputable. Madame Fanchon's perhaps. She, surely, was everything that was respectable! Tessie refused to let her spirits sink. Further, she refused defeat.

Madame Fanchon's was not a milliner precisely, but she *was* a premiere seamstress. Tessie was a trifle disappointed, for she was certain the wages of a novice seamstress would not match that of a milliner's model, but she was game nonetheless. She only needed, after all, to keep herself for a six month.

Tessie had no qualms about applying for a post, for though she had never fashioned any gowns before, she was positive she could set her mind to stitching up mantles at the very least. Indeed, when she was younger, she had fashioned for herself a blue levantine pelisse edged with blond floss silk of which she had been most proud. It was sitting up in the attics, out of the way of Grandfather Hampstead and his pistol cloths, but was doubtless still as good as new. Tessie sighed for it a little, for though she knew she was being foolish, she did *so* love fashion!

Madame Fanchon could surely use an extra pair of hands—she'd purchased her present drab olive from her and could see at once how busy she was.

It was a considerable walk to Madame Fanchon's, for Tessie did not think she could spare the money for a hack. She meant to start as she intended to go on. She would not whittle away at her precious ten thousand pounds while there was still life in her feet and the morning, though mild, was not as cold as it might have been. Her toes might curl up in her half boots, but they would not actually freeze. She comforted herself with this thought as she walked past a vendor selling hot apples off a charcoal stove. She shook her head at the baker, calling out, "Hot loaves," and selling rolls at two a penny. No, indeed. She ignored steadfastly the fact that she was hungry, and her mouth watered from the warm, freshly baked smell.

She scolded herself and walked on, wishing for her cape and muff, another black mark chalked up against Oliver Dobbins. A young man, not dissimilar, tried to stop her course, but Tessie scowled blackly and uttered such a vile epithet that he was startled. Miss Hampstead took advantage of this opportunity by calling, "Thief" and running, with her skirts slightly above her ankles, across the road. She did not stop traffic precisely, but she caused a great deal of reining in of carriage horses and muttered oaths from ostlers. She was hardly aware of it, lost in her thoughts.

Unfortunately, she was contemplating her forthcoming interview to such a degree that she noticed neither one of the newfangled gaslamp posts that proudly blocked her way, nor the eel-pie hawker who shouted his wares. It was in such a shrill tone, too, that it was a testament to the serious nature of her thoughts that she heard him not at all. Crash! She smacked straight into his basket and knocked her head against the lamppost.

Her bonnet was knocked almost off her head, for the

ribbons loosened in the turmoil. The hawker was furious, shouting all kinds of threats and demanding an outrageous compensation for such a small calamity. Just as Tessie was despairing, alternately apologizing and fussing with her bonnet and smiling at the vendor and wishing, most prodigiously, for one of his flattened pies, a familiar face appeared before her, mumbling, apologetic, and sweetly sincere.

"M-M-M-miss Hampstead. De-de-delighted to see you again. May I h-h-h-help?"

"Yes, you may! You may pay for all the bleedin' pies what the young lady squashed. No eyes in 'er 'ead, I say!"

Lord Alberkirky ignored the man but dug into his morning coat of smart purple stripes to reveal a shining sovereign.

"There y-y-you are, m-m-man. Stop h-h-hounding the lady. Very uncouth."

The vendor stopped his grumbling and bit into the coin. It must have satisfied him, for he dropped the basket—Lord Alberkirky had evidently paid handsomely for the privilege of owning *all* the damaged pies—and took off at a trot. He was no slow coach, that one. As he later regaled his mates, " 'E was not loikely to 'ang about for the downy cove to come to 'is senses, 'e wasn't. It was up and off 'e was, with no further murmurin', for 'oo," he asked, "up an' pays a guinea when a common coach-weel would be regular right and tight?"

Tessie was not, of course, privy to this jubilation, but she *was* privy to Lord Alberkirky's kind ministrations as he made a rather incongruous bow regardless of the curious onlookers and the basket that stood between them.

"Thank you. I don't know how I came to be so clumsy!"

"As to that, i-i-i-it was the villain's fault. He stepped forward on your gown just as you were passing. I—I—

I—I happened to see it, you s-s-s-see, from my chaise." Tessie looked up and noticed that a barouche, headed by a team of four matched bays, was circling the area.

"Is that yours?"

"Yes, I leaped out wh-wh-when I saw your dis-distress. The d-d-d-driver could not let them stand."

Tessie hid a smile. "No, indeed. Lord Alberkirky, it appears I am once more in your debt. You are a very kind person indeed."

With which compliment, Lord Alberkirky started stammering more than ever, and Tessie was positive she could see a hint of youthful color rising to his cheeks. Not that she could make out much of his cheeks, really, for they were hidden away under a collar of quite preposterous proportions. This was compounded by a neckerchief of striped poplin tied in the style of the great Beau Brummell, further obscuring any possible vision Tessie might have acquired of his chin. Upon his person were a great deal of fobs and seals, and Miss Hampstead noticed that several portions of his close-fitting morning coat sported pads.

She did not mind in the least, for his good nature more than compensated for these minor deficiencies. Besides, not *all* men could look perfect. Nicholas Cathgar—and why she should be thinking of him at a horrible time like this she could not say—was merely the notable exception. She would have been horrified to know that the notable exception was even now bearing down upon her from across Great Grosvenor Street on the right.

She did *not* know, however, so she salvaged the steaming eel pies and offered them to Lord Alberkirky, who looked quite bewildered at the offering.

"No, no, Miss Hampstead, I ate at B-b-b-b-Boodles. Very fine dishes they have there, if you must know, with a fine Bordeaux too . . . y-y-yes, by all means t-t-t-take them. . . ."

Tessie tucked the basket under her arm. It did not compliment her ribboned reticule, still containing naught but her pistol, the handkerchiefs, and the oddment of pennies and ha'pennies that she'd permitted herself after banking Lord Cathgar's fabulous sum. Nevertheless, the basket exuded the most mouth-watering smell, especially since some of the pastry had yielded to the inner filling, so that great whiffs of the warm, aromatic eel could be detected blocks away.

She rather thought that when she had rid herself of the kind ministrations of Lord Alberkirky, she would partake of lunch. Madame Fanchon, with whom she had no appointment, could surely wait.

"Allow m-m-m-m-me to g-g-give you a r-r-ride."

"No, indeed. I can walk. Truly."

"I would s-s-s-s-so like to. See, my horses are restless. Y-you would be doing me a f-f-favor."

"Tarradiddles, Lord Alberkirky! Your fine horses do not need *me* to be aired! They are in high fettle already, though I fancy the front left is faltering just a little. Perhaps if you were to adjust the harness a fraction?"

"By criminey, you are right! V-v-v-very perceptive for a female, if I m-m-m-might s-s-say so!"

"I own a stable of high steppers myself. At least, I used to. Mr. Devonshire is organizing their sale."

"All because of me! I f-f-feel f-f-f-frightful, Miss Hampstead."

"No need. You have been very kind. And now, dear sir, I must go."

"Y-y-y-you *must* step into my chaise! I insist! That basket is heavy, and it is n-n-not fitting for y-y-y-you to walk! Certainly not in Bond Street!"

"It is not fitting for me to step into your chaise either."

"It is i-i-if I have asked you to m-m-m-marry me!"

Tessie smiled. "You are splitting hairs, Lord Alberkirky!"

A shadow fell across the cobbles. Tessie could not account for it, but her heart began beating quite wildly.

When the basket was wrested from her hand, a pair of ice-white gloves closed upon its handle, she looked up. The Earl of Cathgar was not smiling, but he *did* bow infinitesimally.

Tessie curtsied, though she thought she would rather faint.

Nicholas smiled, a curious, unreadable twist curving his masculine lips.

Fourteen

"We meet again, Miss Hampstead."

"It appears we do, Lord Cathgar."

"And in the very heart of Bond Street. Remarkable."

"Not for a milliner's model!"

"Indeed, I am forgetting."

Lord Alberkirky looked from Tessie to Lord Cathgar with puzzlement.

Tessie collected her wits. "Lord Alberkirky, are you acquainted with Lord Nicholas Cathgar?"

The penny dropped with Lord Alberkirky. Lord Cathgar—a coxcomb if ever he had seen one—was the man who owed Miss Hampstead ten thousand pounds!

"Y-y-you!" he exclaimed indignantly.

"Yes, it is I." The arches of Nicholas's brow rose dramatically, and his imperious voice held a cold interrogative. If Tessie knew no better, she would have said that the two gentlemen looked like cockerels at a bantam fight.

Lord Alberkirky, for no real reason that he was aware, felt himself bristle. He felt suddenly rather overdressed in the garments his valet had taken such trouble over. It was maddening, for Lord Cathgar wore only the plainest of frock coats, deep velvety blue, with an ice-white waistcoat matched by a neckerchief of the identical white. It sparkled infinitesimally with sapphires but bore none of the flamboyant pins that Lord Alberkirky effected. Certainly, the ensemble was not striped as Lord Alberkirky's was, in purple, with a canary-yellow underlay. His gloves, fashioned from kid, were merely white rather than the modish yellow-cream Lord Alberkirky proudly sported.

Lord Alberkirky tried vainly to remember that he was tricked out to the very height of fashion, but failed dismally. Lord Cathgar put him to the shade, and for the life of him he could not imagine why. He therefore committed the unusual social solecism of broaching finances in the presence of a lady.

"You owe Miss Hampstead ten thousand p-p-pounds!"

Tessie nearly dropped her reticule in embarrassment.

"Hush . . ." she implored. Lord Alberkirky ignored her.

Lord Cathgar's eyebrows now nearly touched the sky. Or so it seemed to Tessie.

"Are you, my good man, her *banker?"*

"No, I am not, as you are p-p-p-perfectly well aware! But I h-h-h-have asked her f-f-f-f-for her hand in m-m-m-m-marriage!"

"Indeed?" Lord Cathgar's voice was excessively low. "Now you interest me greatly." White gloves clenched across the handle of a silver tipped cane. He spoke with his usual irony, but Tessie noticed a certain tension in his body and across those broad, unpadded shoulders. She wondered whether it was anger or indifference that caused him to turn from her, so that he was facing Lord Alberkirky directly.

Anger, she thought, for his tone was provocative if not downright insulting.

"Well, I d-d-d-don't see why I sh-sh—*should* interest you so!"

"Oh, it is not you, my good man, but your . . . eh . . . *betrothed* who interests me."

Tessie's hands flew to her mouth. She prayed Lord Alberkirky would not divulge the fact that his suit had been rejected. *Let* Lord Cathgar think her engaged! It was what she wanted, was it not? She rubbed a stupid tear that threatened to ruin the ribbons of her bonnet and smiled blindingly at Lord Alberkirky. He was so surprised, he nearly stepped back onto the bustling London road.

Lord Cathgar prevented this calamity by lifting his cane and providing a temporary barrier. Lord Alberkirky, staring at the ebony stick with its wicked silver tip, stuttered something quite inaudible. Nicholas, the devil in him, asked him to repeat his words.

"Sh-sh-sh-she is *not* my betrothed."

"Ah, rejected you, did she?" Nick attempted to sound sympathetic but failed dismally. His cane returned to the ground, but not before his blue eyes turned from Lord Alberkirky's and raked poor Tessie's instead. Mortified, she glared at his gleaming hessians, refusing, for once, to be drawn. Nick sighed loudly and, oblivious to the infelicitous surroundings, drew a pinch of snuff.

Lord Alberkirky, catching a whiff on the morning breeze, wished he dared ask for the blend. Instead, he drew himself up straight, shuffled a little with his commodious cravat, swallowed once or twice, and took up Miss Hampstead's cause. After all, it was the least that he considered he owed her after accidentally winning her fortune. He did not answer the more pressing question of whether she had or had not rejected him. Tessie could only breathe a sigh of relief and pray that her paper-thin deception could prevail.

"Y-y-y-you still owe her ten thousand golden canaries!"

"My dear man, *do* go consult your tailor or some such thing! You *must* have some business that is actually your *own?*"

Tessie eyed the two gentlemen with misgiving. Lord Alberkirky looked brimful of indignation, his starched collar seeming two inches higher, if possible.

"This *is* my business C-C-C-Cathgar! I have made it s-s-s-so! By George, if Miss Hampstead is too delicate a l-l-l-lady to broach the subject, I shall do so for her!"

Tessie and the earl spoke at once, but Lord Cathgar, sad to say, prevailed, whether from the force of his voice or from the justice of his comments, one cannot be certain.

"How *fascinating* that Miss Hampstead has such a champion. But it appears that she is *not* as delicate as you indicate."

Tessie squirmed as laughing eyes sought her own. He was amused, dammit! She did not know whether to laugh with him or to simply shoot him. Probably both. Lord Alberkirky, oblivious to the tension he was creating, continued his challenge manfully.

"Are you insulting Miss Hampstead? B-b-by George, in the absence of any m-m-m-male relatives, I should challenge you for that!"

Lord Cathgar did not break the gaze that was turning Tessie's knees to trembling jelly beneath her prim petticoats of plain white cambric. Rather, he grinned quirkishly at her but raised his voice for Lord Alberkirky's edification.

"My, my! Quite pugnacious, isn't he? You appear to have discovered yet another conquest, Miss Hampstead. Take care you do not leave a veritable trail of broken hearts across the length of England!"

Tessie ignored this sarcasm but informed Lord Alberkirky that Lord Cathgar's debts of honor had already been settled.

"Oh! B-b-b-beg pardon, Cathgar! I had no notion . . ."

"No, indeed. How could you?" Cathgar smiled, his tone nonchalantly forgiving. Tessie thought he looked mighty pleased with himself and felt some not inconsiderable misgiving. He gently touched her waist, urging her subtly forward against the stream of hawkers and their wares.

"Shall we walk on, or shall we just allow all these spectators to enjoy our elegant discourse?"

Lord Alberkirky remembered his tiger, no doubt relishing the ribbons of his well-matched team. "M-m-m-my cattle are just t-t-t-tooling the block. . . ."

"Ah, very good. Then we will not keep you."

Poor Lord Alberkirky looked confused. He made a bow to Tessie. "If you are cer-cer-cer-certain . . ."

"Yes, I am certain. Thank you, Lord Alberkirky. For everything."

The gentleman impulsively took her hand. "You will not reconsider . . . I mean, m-m-mama would c-c-come round . . ."

"No. I thank you all the same." Tessie glanced at Lord Cathgar. She hoped he had not understood the content of this last inquiry. He was regarding her with a quizzical light in his eye that made her rather nervous, and her heart plummeted to the bottom of her kidskin boots. If he had understood, then he would know that she had told him only a half-truth about Lord Alberkirky's proposal—she had indeed been honored with an offer, but that offer had never, never, never at any time been accepted.

Fortunately, he did not appear to have heard a thing, for he waited patiently for Tessie to complete her curtsy, then transferred the basket of squashed eel pies to his right hand. Tessie stole a glance at him. His expression was too bland to read, but she fancied she detected his lips twitching. How provoking! He was laughing at her!

It was he who should have looked comical, with all those pies, but instead he looked imposing, and regal, and . . . . damnably attractive. Tessie felt her resolve weaken as he marched her off Bond Street and into Upper Grosvenor, where a splendid crested chaise, enameled in a powder blue, awaited the earl's pleasure.

He nodded to the coachman, who instantly leaped down from his perch seat, opened the sapphire-paneled door, and waited primly as Nicholas helped Tessie to ascend. Only when the door was shut and the reins taken up once more did he speak.

"Tuck a carriage blanket around your feet. You look frozen."

"I am merely chilled."

"And so you should be! This weather is not fit for a young lady with neither muff nor pelisse! I can't conceive what you might be thinking of, for don't say you can't spare some of my ten thousand pounds for a wrap at least!"

In spite of herself, Tessie bristled. "It is not *your* ten thousand pounds, it is *mine!* And I am saving it for Hampstead Oaks."

"Very noble, but your tenants will have no cause to thank you if you should drop dead from an inflammation of the lungs! And while I am scolding—which invariably I seem to do with you—a young lady has no cause to walk up Bond Street alone."

Tessie scowled, but Nick continued. "You are lucky that that *abominable* gown does not do your features any credit. If you were recognized, it would be a scandal."

"It is *not* abominable! It is merely the color that is unfortunate, though I am sure these rosettes are perfectly acceptable. . . ."

"They are not, though I am no arbiter of ladies' fashion."

"There you go, then!"

"I do, however, know," Nick continued ruthlessly, "that spangles are currently more modish."

Tessie opened her mouth to dispute the claim, then shut it again wisely. Nicholas, as usual, was perfectly right. And doubtless he had every cause to know every detail of ladies' fashion. The thought was not comforting.

"Good God, you are silent!"

"Only till I can think of a scathing enough reply. And you may start haranguing me, my lord. You forget that I am *not* a young lady, I am a milliner's apprentice." Tessie hesitated a moment, for the aroma of the pies was driving her crazy in the warm carriage. The earl smiled lazily.

"Those are *my* pies."

"Which you will share with me, for I have had a damnable morning and missed my breakfast."

"Very well, though if you are talking of conduct, I might mention it is perfectly reprehensible of you to be kidnapping me in this manner!"

"I am not kidnapping you, merely enhancing your already tarnished reputation. Which milliner have you acquired employment with?"

Tessie had the grace to blush. "None, for Millicent Dorsom was a sad disappointment, but I have hopes. . . ."

"Good God, you did not apply to Millicent Dorsom, did you?"

"Yes, I did, though why—"

"My poor, green girl. What did she say?"

Tessie lowered her eyes to the carriage floor. It was apparent that his lordship already *knew* what Miss Dorsom might have suggested, for he was calling her green again.

"You might have warned me!"

"And have you snap my head off for meddling? I told you millinery was a damn foolish idea!"

"How was I to know Miss Dorsom's was not respectable? Indeed, how do *you* know?"

Lord Cathgar's eyes lit up with laughter. "What a singularly unladylike question! Not at all the thing to ask an unmarried gentleman with . . . a kindly disposition!"

"Oh!" Tessie felt mortified. Both with herself and with Lord Cathgar's careless answer. It was foolish, but she could not help thinking of the likes of Petra or Elsie wrapping their arms about his chest . . . no, she would not allow her imagination to wonder further than that.

"Very wise. Alter the direction of your thoughts. Much more *comme il faut!*"

"Oh! You are a beast!"

Nick grinned. "I like to see you blush. And I have this overwhelming urge to kiss you again, which I shall manfully suppress and offer you some of these revolting pies."

"They are not revolting, merely squashed."

"Yes, I saw the accident occur. It is fortunate, is it not, that I was driving in that vicinity at precisely that moment?"

Tessie thought so, for her heart, foolishly, was singing. She made no comment, however, preferring to remove her gloves and choose an enormous eel pie filled with steaming potatoes and other unidentifiable vegetables. She took a bite, then another, ignoring the fact that she was ruining her precious olive morning dress by dripping slivers of eel upon her lap. Nicholas drew out his kerchief and aided her, his touch coming as much as a shock as ever. Tessie would have protested, but her mouth was full and she was not so far beyond redemption that she would open it thus. So he had the infinite pleasure of scooping hot eel from her skirts as she licked her fingers with the greatest of satisfaction.

"When we are married, I shall order up eel pie as a matter of course. Doubtless my chefs shall resign, but as they do so regularly anyway, it shan't make a smidgen of difference."

Tessie decided to take the path of least resistance. For the purpose of this delightful, well-sprung carriage ride, she would let him think what he willed. Then, when he set her down at the Colonnade, she would simply disappear. A cowardly tactic, she knew, but possibly the only one that would work. And if she did not act quickly, she knew she would no longer have the will to act at all. The temptation set before her was far too irresistible.

If it were not for the fact that she persisted in her belief that Cathgar was merely being a combination of head-strong and chivalrous, she would doubtless have melted, unresisting, into his arms a long time since.

So in answer to this blatant statement of fact, she smiled demurely, fluttered those luxurious eyelashes of hers, and bit into some pastry.

"If you must know, ordinarily I hate eel. I was merely hungry."

"Ah, an admission at last! It is not so very pleasurable to be little more than a maidservant, now, is it?"

"I can cope with it, my lord, if it is to save Hampstead Oaks."

"Bravely spoken, but stop 'my-lording' me. All claim to such formality must surely have ceased when you insisted on coming to my bed."

"You rogue! You know I came only because you were injured and helpless as a baby."

"Oh, helpless, was I? You have high standards, my Miss Nobody. I shall have to exert myself more in the future. Think what a scandal it would be if the Earl of Cathgar was known to be helpless in bed!"

"I am sure nobody would say any such thing, my lord. And you are taking liberties again."

"The pot calling the kettle black, for which is worse, taking liberties or telling whopping great tarradiddles?"

"I did not—"

"Yes, you did, unless there is some *other* peer who has had the great misfortune of proposing to you?"

For a moment, Tessie nearly lied, but she could think of no one who would be in the least likely to back up such a tale, so she clammed her mouth shut and said nothing instead.

"Ah, I have scored a point. How perfectly pleasurable!

Now, don't be so glum. I have only to go home and ponder why you should feed me such a lot of unadulterated nonsense, and the riddle will be solved. It is not my evil scar, perchance?"

"Don't be ridiculous! It is a very . . . *noble* scar."

Nick's mouth twisted. "That is not what I hear whispered behind fans. I once made a young lady swoon from the very sight."

"Then she must have been a very silly female indeed."

"Ah, but you do not know its history. I acquired it, evidently, in a duel. I believe I was cast as the villain."

"More likely in service to king and country."

"You have faith, little Miss Nobody." Nick was surprisingly touched. Not so much because she had unwittingly guessed the truth of it, but because she believed in him. Heaven knew, he was not a fool; he had heard all the worst of the rumors. He had just never cared sufficiently to put the record straight.

Or perhaps, quixotically, he did not wish to set the record straight. His rakish reputation was a natural cover for the more clandestine services he delivered to the realm. He preferred, for the moment, to keep it that way.

"Yes, I have faith, for I know that despite your deplorably arrogant ways, you risk your life for what you believe in. It is commendable."

"A compliment, by God! If Joseph hadn't drunk the last of my carriage champagne, I swear I would open a bottle now!"

"Very likely you drank it yourself, my lord, and have forgotten."

"Ah, I am cast down again. You temper your compliments with faint moues of disapproval."

"I am not disapproving, though doubtless I should be, for I am sure you can get very drunk indeed, and Grandfather, who used to drink at least two clarets upon an evening, always said—"

The earl groaned. "Is there no silencing you?"

"No, for there is nothing more dismal than a carriage trip undertaken in perfect silence. Now, where was I?"

"I can't remember."

"Of course you can! I remember myself! Grandfather Hampstead always said there was no shame in holding one's drink—indeed, he insisted I learn to drink fortified wines at a young age, for he never held with orgeats or some of those vile syrups concocted for the young—but he did say there is no more foolish-looking sight than a man dead drunk, and though I have never actually *seen* any gentleman in such a predicament, though very nearly, when Uncle Hester . . . but, oh! I digress."

"Indeed you do, you awful child. Now I don't know whether to pursue the intriguing issue of your drinking fortified wines, or the matter of your poor inebriated relative."

"Neither, I think, for they are both tedious. I can't think why I introduced such idiotish topics."

Nick grinned. "Good! Now, upon the subject of your marrying me . . ."

Tessie's luminous expression vanished. "The subject is closed."

"Do you deny you wish it wasn't?"

"No, though it is beastly of you to pray upon my honesty."

"I don't recall your being strictly honest with me the last time we met."

Tessie colored. "I *had* received a proposal of marriage!"

"Yes, from a peer of the realm. Lord Alberkirky is undoubtedly that. What he *isn't,* however, is your affianced."

"I didn't actually say he was."

"You led me to believe he was."

"Your mistake."

"I shall be more careful in the future. Is there any reason, Tessie, why you are being so damnably stubborn and intractable?"

Tessie tilted her chin. "Despite the name I chose for myself, I am not a charity basket, Lord Cathgar."

"Good gracious, I should hope not! I despise the things!" The earl took a deep breath, choosing his words carefully, trying his utmost to be reasonable and logical and, above all, convincing. It was hard with Tessie so close, in disarray yet again, her bonnet all askew, sublimely licking her fingers of the eel pie and turning her large, impossibly curling lashes toward him.

Not flirtatious this time, but attentive. Her eyes, below, seemed enormous. She was awaiting his reply breathlessly again, and he knew, for some momentous reason, his happiness depended upon getting the correct sequence of words out. His mama, if she'd seen him as tongue-tied as a schoolboy, would have laughed out loud.

Fifteen

The moment lengthened as Nicholas tried to figure out the peculiarities of the female brain. Particularly *this* female, who was as unlike most other females as he could imagine. He began slowly, taking care to be cool, collected, and logical, as he was positive Miss Theresa Hampstead of Hampstead Oaks would wish.

"You are not a charity basket, Tessie, but you *are* a gently bred female with a damnable line of bad luck behind you, some of it caused by *my* unwitting interventions. You should be married, and I am fortuitously at hand." He found it hard to keep the irony from his tone, but Tessie was too sensitive not to hear it.

Her heart ached. Oh, if only he had said he loved and adored her! But all this cold reason! She knew what he said was perfectly true, and that there were thousands of such marriages made for much lesser reasons every day, but it was not what she wanted!

Worse, she was convinced it was not what he wanted either, despite this temporary persistence of his. If she had not saved his life, doubtless he would not feel so strongly or be so obligated. It was a debt of honor to him, no more. But it was more to her, and she did not want him to regret paying that debt every day and forever.

"I make my *own* scandal broth, my lord. No one forced me to venture to London unchaperoned, but I did. Just that circumstance puts me beyond the pale, and I think you know it. Disregard, if you please, the whole little episode of me in your bedchamber. It should never have happened, and, indeed, if you will be so good as to hold your tongue, it will never be known. That is all you have to concern yourself about. The rest was of my own making, and I shall pay the price as my grandfather did before me."

"Bravely spoken, O Mistress Pride." Nick's words were hollow, even to his own ears. "There is no convincing you, then? Not if I throw these confounded pies through the window and grab you in my arms?"

Tessie thought that might make all the difference, but she shook her head resolutely. She did not like being called Mistress Pride! But she refused to wrangle with him, so the remainder of the carriage ride was undertaken in silence, until they rounded the corner and Nicholas indicated for the horses to halt. They did so beside a huge crested barouche, where several of the fine team were grazing idly from hay bales. The coachman, resting beside the team, seemed to recognize Nick, but then, as Tessie knew, half of London did!

"Where are we? This is not the Colonnade!"

"Indeed, no. It is Madame Fanchon's. See, just behind you?"

Tessie peered through the window and did indeed see the familiar steps leading up to the elegant establishment.

"I thought I would save those half boots of yours. You were intending . . ."

"Oh, yes. But . . . oh, how I look! And my gown is ruined. I cannot possibly . . ."

"I'll buy you a new gown."

"You are determined to compromise me. You shall do no such thing! Only, can you help me with my bonnet?"

Nick forbore to utter any of the epithets he would have liked to, for now he was condemned to touching her for the sole purpose of losing her again. He only hoped that the countess of Cathgar—whose carriage, painted in regal purples, now blocked his own—could work a miracle. As Tessie held still patiently while he fumbled with the ribbons like a fool rather than the experienced rake that he was, he had never felt more in *need* of an appropriate word.

"Wish me luck, my lord."

"I do."

"And thank you."

"It is a pleasure. What about your eel pies?"

"Oh, you may eat them!"

Thus recovering both her poise and her spirits, little Miss Tessie made her descent.

In a private parlor draped all in crimson, Madame Fanchon's fingers flew through her work. It was not that she needed to anymore, for she was the Season's premier seamstress. As such, she could command any price she chose, and she had minions by the dozen to do the intricate beadwork she was currently engaged in. But sewing gave her time to think, and under the gaze of her patroness, she surely needed that time.

She snipped off a thread of blond silk and nodded crisply, at last meeting the gaze of the Countess of Cathgar.

"Indeed, madam, if such a one were to ever approach me . . ." She frowned as a tinkling bell disturbed her. "What is it, Elsie? Her ladyship is just choosing between the riding dress and the broderie Anglaise. . . ."

"She is here!" The rich voice held a note of triumph and ill-suppressed excitement.

Madame Fanchon rolled her eyes and smiled apologetically at the countess. "Who, Elsie, is here?" She rolled her Rs ever so slightly, in the manner of the French.

"The lady Madam is searching for! She answers the case exactly. Dark hair, curls . . ." She peeped around at the countess. "Oh, a havoc of curls, your ladyship! And she wants to speak to Madame Fanchon!"

"There are many who wish to speak to me, Elsie." The famous seamstress dropped the intricate bodice of lace and pearls and gazed inquiringly at her employee. She did not like being disturbed, especially as it seemed likely, to her experienced eye, that the countess would select both garments. But not if her train of thought was disturbed thus!

"But, madam!" Elsie's voice rose a little. "It is not gowns she wants, but work!"

The countess's interest deepened to the point of setting down her fan. Madame Fanchon, seeing her moment lost, recovered swiftly.

"Then by all means show her in, Elsie. And close the door after you, if you please. One would not care for her ladyship to catch a draft!"

It was not a draft her ladyship caught, but her breath. She had not expected such a beautiful face, or such a wistful smile beneath that tangle of curls. Now these she *had* expected, for they featured a good many times in Nicholas's rather graphic descriptions. And where was that famous reticule? she wondered. Ah, there it was, clasped firmly in the left hand, daintily gloved in matching olive. Oh, it was a shame. Olive was such a dreary color, to be sure!

"Madam, I interrupt. I can wait. . . ."

Tessie, under the stern gaze of not one but *two* ladies quailed. It was clear that the white-haired lady seated on the Egyptian clawed chaise longue was someone of consequence. She languished behind a jeweled fan, but her eyes were alert. She wore more rings upon her mottled fingers than Tessie had ever seen in all of her life. Madame Fanchon, of course, she already knew by sight. A tall, thin lady, dressed all in black but for a broad splash of buttercup yellow peeping from an under dress of sarcenet.

"You require work?"

It was Madame Fanchon who asked the question, but it was the older lady who appeared most interested in her answer. Tessie, had she not been desperate, would have been confused.

"Yes, indeed. I am quite skilled at needlework, but have never before worked as a seamstress. If you would be so kind as to offer me a wage, I would gladly learn all you have to show me."

Madame Fanchon shrugged. The girl was pretty behaved enough, though she had stains upon her morning dress. If she knew no better, she would have said eel pie. She tried not to frown.

"You have no referees, then?"

"No, but . . ."

"All my seamstresses have referees, Miss . . ."

"Hampstead. My friends call me Tessie."

Madame Fanchon, a little regal, ignored her, though her eyes slid to Lady Cathgar. What the woman could want with the girl, she could not conceive! She had trouble written all over her face despite her demure countenance. But ask for her she had, as had Lady Polly Leister, the countess's sister-in-law—who, incidentally, had bought an ermine cape at the same time—and Lady Randolph Peters, the present earl's sister, had mentioned something of the kind again.

It was Lady Cathgar, seated with an enormous turban upon her imposing head, who broke the silence.

"My dear, is it work that you seek?"

Tessie curtsied low, for though she did not know the identity of the lady, she did know she had rank—all her demeanor suggested it. It would not have surprised Tessie, indeed, to find she was in the presence of one of the famous Almacks patronesses, or even a duchess.

"It is, though as to referees, I have none."

"Then why should this good lady employ you?"

Madame Fanchon smiled thinly. Elsie, gaping behind her, tittered. She was waved away.

"Because I am good! I am not idly boasting, ma'am, though I fear I have a propensity to do just that at times, but only when we are riding or fishing . . ."

"You are good at these activities?"

"Yes!" Tessie's eyes lit up. She nodded shyly.

"Excellent, but an extraordinary accomplishment for a seamstress. Even an *unreferenced* seamstress." Madame Fanchon's voice was dampening. The little chit was too exuberant by far and the countess seemed to have forgotten all about the riding habit and the blond silk.

Tessie's face fell. "I am sorry. I was so hoping . . ." She did not finish her sentence. It would be too humiliating to cry. *Damn* Cathgar! He was right. Securing respectable work was by no means as easy as she had imagined it. Perhaps she would have to return to Hampstead Oaks, after all, defeated, eating into her miserable ten thousand pounds, unable to assist the tenants . . . but no! She would speak out for herself. If she threw away her chances, at least she would have tried.

After all, as Grandfather always said, a person could only really fail if he has never tried. The trying is his salvation. A wise man, the viscount, if reckless.

"I was hoping, Madame Fanchon, that you would give me a chance. I'll not charge you for my first week's work. If it is satisfactory, I trust you will keep me on."

"And your board? Do you realize how expensive it is to house and feed—"

"I'll pay that myself." Tessie was firm, and she wondered why the lips of the regal lady were twitching.

She continued. "What is more, I shall fund the materials I require from my own purse. If the garment is not to your satisfaction, I shall bother you no more, and wear it myself!"

In the face of such defiance—wherein the countess's

lips were seen to twitch even more—Madame Fanchon tried a new tack.

"Perhaps one of the less established houses . . . Cordelia Wiltsham's may answer, she is always at sixes and sevens looking for seamstresses, though heaven knows why, her establishment does not do half the trade of mine, but I shall send her a note. . . ."

"No!" The countess intervened. Both ladies started a little under her gaze. Madame Fanchon wary, Tessie surprised but interested. She wondered again who the lady was and why she should interest herself in her case. She did not wonder long, though the turbaned head was surveying her from top to toe with a quizzing glass and it seemed like an eon before she gestured her to take up a yellow cushioned seat next to her.

"Madame Fanchon, thank you for your kind services once again. Have the riding habit and the blond silk wrapped, if you please, while I speak to the young lady. Oh! I think also a gown for the good lady—not drab, I cannot abide drab colors—perhaps a marigold. Do you like marigold, my dear? Or perhaps a sky blue. Oh, bother it, I'll take both, but please do not forget the bonnet and stockings and gloves. Accessories are so important. Oh! The underclothes too, though I don't mean to put you to the blush, my dear . . ."

Madame Fanchon, very much more pleased at the track her ladyship was now taking, murmured helpfully. "Handkerchiefs? A fan perhaps . . ."

The countess nodded. "Yes, yes, all the folderols . . . you know what I am after. . . ."

Madame Fanchon's eyes sparked a little. "Indeed I do . . . her measurements . . ." She surveyed Tessie shrewdly. I shall have to borrow a little from Lady Celia's collection. Lady Celia is a little more rotund, but a few tucks . . . yes, yes, we can do it . . . short notice . . ."

"I am sure you can manage, my good woman, that is

why we ladies of the *ton* all rely on you so." The countess knew just how to bring the fashionable Madame Fanchon under her thumb. It was a mere matter, she knew, of loosening the purse strings and referring to her influence in society.

"Indeed, yes . . . yes . . . I shall have the garments sent around today. . . ."

"Thank you. And now, if you would be so good as to allow us the use of this chamber . . ."

"Indeed, indeed . . ." Madame Fanchon curtsied her way out, a calculating gleam in her intelligent French eye. Something was afoot, but for the life of her, she knew not what.

The man called Tallows loitered behind a lamppost. When he was eyed by the watch, he produced a few old apples from his pocket and shouted his wares. But what really interested him was the front door of Madame Fanchon's. Sooner or later, he was sure, the little miss would come out. It was sheer luck, really, that he'd caught sight of Cathgar's crested carriage and decided to follow it. More luck that he should recognize the girl, for Grange's descriptions from Newgate had been graphic, if more uncomplimentary than was necessary.

Yes, he would seize the girl. He doubted not that Cathgar's heart was involved, and Cathgar deserved a punishing lesson. His eye still ached in its sockets. Tallows rubbed it and smiled sourly. No one gave him such a blow and didn't pay. Least of all Cathgar—and it was the earl, he knew, who'd been disguised as Higgins. He was a canny one, remarking that scar. And there had been rumors drifting, too . . . rumors all over Newgate that Lord Cathgar . . . meddled. Not just this time, but other times, too. The prince was still safe—some said it was

Cathgar who kept it that way. Tallows grunted. He *must* have the girl.

Besides, there might be money in it. Fresh Bank of England notes for the Luddite cause. That would make Grange stare!

Grange, who promised to escape Newgate, though how, Tallows could not tell. But it was not his business to question Monsieur le Duc. Powerful friends, he supposed. Perhaps he'd keep a few sovereigns aside for a tankard of ale. And a little cottage, with creepers and vines and a well full of clear water. Lurking under the lamppost, Tallows's mind drifted lazily, though his eyes never faltered from his goal. Seizing the wench was just what he needed. Tallows sneezed. It was a pity, he thought, about the fog.

"Do you *really* wish to be a seamstress?"

"I do, though if I had known references were so important, I would have written them myself!"

The countess chuckled. "Well, at least you are honest! I happen to be in desperate need of a seamstress. My son is going to be married shortly, and I have the task of outfitting his bride."

"Are you offering me work?"

"I am, though I fear there will be much of it. I live in the country, where there is not hide nor hair of a decent milliner even."

"I can make hats!"

"Can you? A lady of rare talent!"

"Yes, well, I have not made many—"

"How many? A dozen?"

Tessie's tongue licked her small, delicate teeth. She was about to tell an unqualified whopper, and she wondered whether that was wise.

"Oh, piles and piles of bonnets . . ."

The countess's eyebrows rose a fraction. "Truly?"

Tessie couldn't do it. She sighed. "No, only in my imagination. I daydream a lot, you know. Grandfather said it is a very bad habit, only I can't seem to help it. . . ." She brightened, unaware of the countess's sudden cough, choking back laughter.

"I have *trimmed* bonnets. Oh, most marvelously. That is why I am certain I could fashion them with a very little effort!"

"Excellent. You shall try your hand with them. I have several bolts of velvet gathering dust in the attics. I shall pay you a weekly wage and board."

Tessie bobbed up from her seat in ill-concealed excitement.

"You won't regret this, Madam. I am most excessively grateful, for there are some people, I am sorry to say, who didn't believe I could find honest employment anywhere, and just look at how wrong they have proven!"

The countess, who shrewdly inferred the mysterious "they" to be a "he," and she suspected she knew exactly *which* "he," merely nodded her head crisply.

"Some people are fools. Run along and see how Madame Fanchon is doing. Perhaps one of the ensembles is ready for you. I really do not think I can tolerate a trip into the country looking at that olive."

"No, indeed, it is sadly drab, but better than puce, do not you feel?"

"Oh, undoubtedly better than puce but still worse than my nerves can tolerate. So do go dress yourself in something more pleasing!"

"But I cannot afford . . ."

"The outfits are your starting gift."

"I cannot accept gifts!"

"Why ever not? I do all the time! It was only yesterday that Blanche Netherton gave me a most horrible potion for skin blemishes, though why she should when my skin, as everyone says, is quite perfect. . . ."

Tessie wanted to laugh, for the countess's skin could hardly be seen, she wore so much maquillage and paint. Still, she was apparently a dear old creature, so Tessie nodded patiently and listened politely to a long list of outrageous gifts the countess had recently received. These ranged from oranges "from that odious toady the duke of . . ." well, she wouldn't say, but she was positive he was angling for a lengthy house visit at her expense . . . to a box of "positively scrumptious sweetmeats from Emily Cowper," an apology, she thinks, for ignoring her at the Pendergast ball, though it is hardly surprising, for it was such a crush, it was a miracle anyone could be seen at all, and what with being jammed between a pilaster and Lady Rotherham's ostrich-feather confection—hideous, but there is no accounting for tastes—" The countess rambled on and on, leaving Tessie intrigued but perplexed and finally in no doubt that it was quite *comme il faut* to accept a gift or two.

"You are very generous, ma'am. I shall make you the finest gowns I can! You shan't be sorry!"

"Indeed, I am beginning to suspect not. Is it true that you carry a pistol in that reticule?"

Tessie swung around, astonished. "Who told you *that?*"

The countess, realizing at once that she had made a mistake, that she could not divulge a word of Nicholas Cathgar's communications to her without giving the game away, fanned herself calmly and improvised.

"I thought I saw the outline of a pistol through that material. Forgive me, I am prone to sudden fancies. Very worrying."

Tessie laughed. "I think you are merely shrewd, ma'am! There *is* a pistol in my reticule, though no one has ever suspected it before."

"Can you fire it?"

"Yes, of course. But I prefer not to, on account of my vile temper."

The countess grinned. "Very wise! Hotheaded, are you?"

"Yes, though I almost always regret it."

"I shall bear that in mind when we quarrel. Now, do be a dear and get ready. We have a long trip ahead of us, for I shall be returning to my country home."

"What shall I call you?"

Tessie, who had been wondering for some time who she was addressing, now looked shy.

The Countess of Cathgar, by contrast, looked devious. No good telling the chit her real name before she'd had any fun. No point lying, though, for lies were always so tedious. So she smiled regally and answered with a deliberate vagueness that was really unparalleled in its sublimity.

"Oh," she said, "just call me Countess."

Tessie, overawed, for once in her life obeyed.

Sixteen

Lady Cathgar's barouche was supreme. From its blinding purple exterior—Tessie privately thought it wonderful—to the soft squabs of pinks, lilacs, and, yes, alas, crimson—Tessie thought she was in heaven. There were foot warmers at every place, and the chaise was so well sprung, there were none of the nasty jostlings that she had become quite accustomed to. The barouche was fitted with elegant mother-of-pearl drawers containing everything from sticking plasters to elixirs of all descriptions, a feathered muff, a jewelry case, and veritable feast of bonbons, Lady Cathgar's passion.

The countess selected for herself a sugarplum, recommended the candied pears to Tessie, then sank back gracefully into her seat. The carriage driver, seated up front, could be heard humming a gay tune, the sense of which, Lady Cathgar informed Tessie, though it was unclear how she knew, was licentious. Tessie grinned, for she suspected that the countess, though terribly regal, was also highly improper.

A kindred spirit. She only hoped, now that it came to the crunch, that she could earn her keep. The gown in which she positively luxuriated was a soft yellow with a crossover bodice, high-necked but soft, to show her swanlike features to advantage. Her sleeves, excessively modish, were tied in three places by lemon ribbons, the same ribbons that adorned her rows and rows of hem flounces.

It was hard not to sigh with a deep satisfaction, especially now that her curls were imprisoned in a high poke bonnet of Cumberland straw. Oh, it was heavenly! Tessie tried not to peek at her precious kid slippers, magicked up by Madame Fanchon so as not to disgrace the ensemble with her horrible half boots.

Then there were the silk clocked stockings, finer than she had ever worn at Hampstead, and the ivory fan with its intricate Chinese design. If only Nick could have seen her! Then, of course, it would have been perfect. But she would school herself not to think of Lord Nicholas Cathgar—not now, or ever.

Not so for the vagrant Tallows, who was at this moment cursing Sir Nicholas roundly. He was cursing him for interfering with the Luddite schemes. He was cursing him for delivering the flush hit that he had, and, above all, he was cursing him for employing a carriage driver who tooled his horses at such a spanking rate.

Yes, no one had noticed one solitary apple hawker catching a ride on the small platform behind the barouche. Tallows, unremarked, was hanging on for all he was worth. His good eye—the one not clammed shut from bruising—was covered in the dust from the road. His clothes were splattered in mud as two oncoming chaises had liberally sprayed him with dirt from their wheels. Not a happy man, Tallows, but determined.

The Countess of Cathgar snored loudly. Tessie, wondering not for the first time where she was being taken, stared out at the countryside and thought of home. She gulped a little, for so much had changed since she was the darling of Hampstead Oaks, spoiled rotten by the villagers, forging a delightful—if irreverent—life with her grandfather. That she was an orphan had never particularly bothered her until then. Now, strangely, just as heaven had taken a helping hand, just as she was embarking on the post she wanted most, she felt in dreadful danger of crying. She sniffed instead, and brushed back her tears crossly.

Oh, if only she had not fallen in love with Lord Nicholas Cathgar! If only he were not so daring and spirited and damnably handsome! If only he did not devour her with his eyes and amuse her with his impudent smile. It ruined everything, for she could enjoy nothing without her thoughts creeping to him. Most trying!

She wondered if she would ever see him again and thought it unlikely, especially now that she was to be buried away in the country, sewing her life out. The countess seemed kind enough, but she owed her much. She would have to sew from dawn to dusk at the very least to ever repay her and earn her keep. A gloomy thought. She sniffed again.

"Here. Take my handkerchief."

An enormous specimen was dangled her way. Tessie would have chuckled were she not so much in the doldrums.

"I thought you were sleeping!"

"I never sleep in a chaise. I have a nervous disposition."

Tessie thought it wise and diplomatic to smile rather than point out the fact of her ladyship's snores.

The countess peered at her closely. "Yes, you want to tease me, do you not? I have a horrible son who does the same. Says I snore, impertinent rascal!"

Tessie blew her nose with the proffered handkerchief. It was embroidered all over with little crests in diaphanous blue, strangely delicate for the size of the kerchief and its owner. Also, vaguely, faintly, familiar. Tessie puzzled a little over the circumstance, then gave it up. The carriage was lumbering to a halt.

"Ah, here we are at last. The village of Chiswick. Are you acquainted with this part of the country?"

"No, not at all. Grandfather Hampstead traveled frequently to London but never further than Hampstead Oaks. He always said travel was an appalling waste of time!"

"Do you mean the late Viscount of Hampstead? Of the Wiltshire branch of Hampsteads?"

Tessie nodded.

The countess found her quizzing glass among a pelter of items she deemed essential to travel. "Yes, you have the look of him, though I daresay a lot prettier. I knew at once you were a lady born and bred. Always trust my instincts." With a satisfied harrumph, the quizzing glass disappeared once more.

Tessie did not say a thing. Now was *not,* she felt, a good time to mention her disgraced reputation, though the very fact that she had offered herself into service must have spoken volumes. Her color rose slightly, but the countess was still musing, unaware of her discomfort.

"I was acquainted with him in my youth. Older than I, of course. A bruising rider to hounds."

Tessie smiled. "Indeed. It was one of his passions."

"Gambling too, if I recall. Never *could* beat him at a game of whist, though I tried often and often. Lost a ruby pin to him."

"Was that yours, ma'am? I have it still. On a good night he used to toss all *sorts* of baubles my way. All quite unsuitable, of course. I wonder he thought I could use them, me not out and never venturing beyond the confines of our gates!"

"How stuffy that sounds! I have traveled all over the length and breadth of England and recommend it most highly. Oh, Italy, too, of course, and the usual places abroad. Very exciting it was before that damned Napoleon spoiled it all. Still, you can have no notion . . . but I ramble on as usual. For the moment, you shall discover the pleasures of Chiswick. There are several antiquities, and a stone church of interest. . . ."

"I doubt I shall have the time."

Tessie looked wistfully at the little shops, displaying such interesting wares as ribbons and gloves and candle wax. On the street corner there was a boot polisher and a chimney sweep with a scrubby youngster beside him . . . there was a blacksmith, a rag-and-bone shop, a saddler . . . she tried not to peer.

"Nonsense. You shall have plenty of time in the mornings, for I positively detest rising early, and you shall need my opinion before hemming up the ensembles."

Tessie, her mind at once on her task—which had, up to then, been extremely vague, owing to the countess's surprising reticence—plucked up the courage to ask a key question. It had chiefly been occupying her thoughts all through the countess's slumbers.

"How many gowns do you think is required?"

"Oh, *hundreds!*" The countess airily dismissed the question as Tessie's heart sank deep into her beautiful kid slippers.

It was not permitted to remain there long, however, for the countess suddenly began pointing animatedly to a forest of oak trees in the far distance. The village of Chiswick—such as Tessie had glimpsed—was already becoming a faint memory. The driver was setting an absolutely spanking pace. Tessie could tell from the clouds of dust arising on either side of the chaise, and from the rate at which Chiswick vanished into the distance. She had the most peculiar feeling that she heard several coughs from behind the chaise, and a muttered oath or two. But her attention was diverted by the countess, her sharp eyes alight with pleasure. "Not much farther now.

Those forests border with my estate. Look, they are opening the gates."

Tessie looked. The gates were made of heavy black iron worked in intricate patterns and attached by hinges to a huge, imposing stone wall. The gatekeeper doffed his cap as the carriage rolled through, then there was a great creaking as the gates shut, once more, behind them. Tessie grew more and more nervous as they drove on, through a singularly long tree-lined avenue, past a topiary garden—the countess pointed this out with pleasure—past several stone monuments and an enormous circular fountain until finally the chaise ground to a halt outside an enormous multiwindowed edifice that Tessie assumed to be the countess's ancestral home. She could hardly see the rough reddish-brown stone, for it was covered almost entirely by ivy and bramble-berry vines.

The countess waited for the steps to arrive, then dismounted first in a flurry of scarves and traveling blankets. Then it was Tessie's turn. Next to the house, she felt very small indeed. Especially as the housekeeper stood at the top off the grand steps with three housemaids and a footman in attendance. The countess seemed to think little of the matter, and raised her hands airily to them all, accepting their bows and curtsies as her due.

Presently, the carriage, relieved of its passengers, rumbled on slowly to the stables. There was no sign of any vagrant apple hawker. Tallows, lurking in the shadows of the oak trees, had made very certain of that.

Nicholas,

You may stop scouring London in a black study. Yes, I know you, my son! I have Miss Hampstead safe and secure at the country house. She is busily engaged in styling perfectly marvelous creations, and I won't have her disturbed for the world. Now, keep away, do, or she will doubtless get into a pelter and make a bolt for it again. Such a pother over nothing! Really, Nicholas, if you had just kissed her properly . . . she weeps when she thinks I don't notice. You are a positive monster engaging her feelings so . . . but stay away! I shall write when you are to return.

Your loving et cetera,
Stella, Countess of Cathgar

P.S. I am spending an enormous portion of your indecent fortune and am enjoying myself enormously.

The countess sealed her missive with a contented smile and a sinfully wasteful amount of sealing wax. Then, eyes alight with youthful laughter, she ventured off to find her prey.

"My dear, the poplin is coming along marvelously, but I think a few frills around the border might be de rigueur. . . ."

Tessie sighed. This was the tenth time that morning the pattern had changed. She was working with some splendid materials—oh, *heavenly* materials, scented with lavenders and exotic spices from the East—but her fingers ached despite the useful thimble her ladyship had bestowed upon her.

"Yes, my lady. The lady's measurements . . . I would not like the flounces to be too long, or the hem too short. . . ."

"No, indeed, though my son is such a rogue, I daresay he would not object in the least. . . ."

Tessie smiled. In spite of her woes, the countess's humor was infectious.

"Then we shall have to thwart him! I will add two inches for the flounces. Shall your future daughter-in-law be stopping by? It will be helpful to have her at hand for the measurements. . . ."

"No, alas! She is suffering from—" The countess's agile brain misgave her.

Tessie regarded her curiously.

"Consumption!" she announced with a satisfied smile.

"Consumption! Oh, my dear lady, you must be so concerned!"

"Alas, yes!" The countess drew out another of her voluminous handkerchiefs and sniffed. The sniff sounded curiously like a snort, for Tessie looked stricken and the countess was suffering huge paroxysms of laughter, but Miss Hampstead, pricking her finger yet again, remained in ignorance.

"Ouch!"

"Have a care. Those are wicked needles. Are you certain you can have the gown ready for this evening?"

"I believe so, though the beadwork I shall have to take up to my chamber. . . ."

"A pretty chamber?"

"Ever so! I did not know servants had such pleasant places."

"You are a very superior servant. Indeed, your bloodlines are equal to my own."

"But I am ruined and you are not."

"Possibly . . . have a sugarplum."

Tessie laughed.

"I shall grow as plump as a partridge! No, I thank you. What shall we do about the measurements, then?"

"Oh, measure the gowns against yourself. I am perfectly certain the young lady is about your size."

"Truly? I am a little thin for the average. . . ."

"So is she, though I mean to fatten her up!"

Tessie laughed. "She will not thank you for that. But if you are certain about her measurement . . . her height, for instance, is crucial. . . ."

"Oh, exactly your own." Tessie raised her brows a fraction.

"Are you certain? It seems odd, indeed, though naturally my form is not out of the common way. . . ."

The countess begged to differ, for Tessie, quite frankly, was utterly perfect and a positive *marvel* relative to some of the young ladies of Chiswick. Even in Bath, more fashionable than the local village, it was impossible to find ladies who were not breathless from lacing that was far too tight. Tessie needed no such help—it was obvious from the undergarments Madame Fanchon had so artfully provided. Also, from the great gulps of air that she frequently took—sometimes from sighing, sometimes from sheer youthful exuberance. No one even remotely laced could be so excessive in their breathing.

The countess lied with practiced aplomb. "Indeed, your form is not out of the ordinary way at all, which is most fortunate for us. Continue, if you please, to use yourself as a model in all things. The finer details we shall attend to closer to the wedding."

"When shall that be, ma'am?"

"Oh, it all depends. My son is hopelessly rag-mannered. He has to be schooled in the gentler arts before the marriage can take place."

Tessie regarded the countess curiously. "Indeed! If the lady is consumptive, as you say . . ."

But she got no further. With a great snort into her handkerchief, the countess took her leave, as abominably rag-mannered as her absent son. Bewildered, Miss Hampstead had no option but to carry on stitching.

The house, in the next few weeks, was positively beset with morning callers. Poor Tessie had not a moment to be bored, for she had no sooner finished the seams of an ermine mantle or a satin-trimmed pelisse frogged with lavender braid, when the butler was announcing another guest in stentorian tones.

Tessie always put her needlework away and made to leave the drawing room, where Lady Cathgar insisted she sit "on account of the light"—and, indeed, sunshine *did* stream into the first-floor room with its rows and rows of French windows, paneled here and there with colored glass—but the countess always stopped her.

"Oh, my dear," she would say, "you simply *must* meet Lady Halgrove, or Lady Ashleigh. . . ." The list seemed enormous, and each lady seemed to wish to place yet another order with her, so that Tessie felt quite sunk with the pressure brought to bear upon her shoulders.

Surprisingly, it was the countess who came to her rescue, frowning prodigiously on one particularly handsome lady with sapphire-blue eyes that seemed extraordinarily familiar, when she begged a new spencer of "lead-colored silk, fur trimmed, perhaps . . ."

Tessie smiled wanly, but the countess was outraged.

"Miss Hampstead cannot be expected to sew on the whim of my guests! As it is, she has her hands perfectly full sewing a trousseau for . . . for . . ." She looked about wildly, then brought out her great handkerchief yet again and began coughing so loudly that Tessie felt *she* might be consumptive. The lady in question, languid, drew forth some sal volatile, much to the countess's indignation.

"Take that hideous stuff away from me! You would be well served, Delia, if I banished you from the house!"

"Well, you won't, not before I first become acquainted with your newest houseguest! Do you ride, Miss Hampstead?"

"I do, but it is really not proper, and I have no habit. . . ."

"What nonsense is this?" The lovely lady smiled archly.

Tessie looked to the countess for help but received

none, she obviously seeing nothing extraordinary whatsoever in her seamstress dillydallying with the morning callers.

"I am not a houseguest, ma'am, but an employee."

"Oh, is that all? I shall not tear you away from your precious gowns long, but I *do* think I shall show you the sights of Chiswick! We have a haunted castle, you know. . . ."

Tessie did *not* know, but she soon did, for she was being dragged out of the house toward the stables with not the slightest consideration for the fact that her morning dress was far too short for a country ride, and that indeed, as she had protested, she had no suitable riding habit.

"Oh, pshaw!!" had come the merry response, and Tessie had warmed prodigiously to the lady despite the difference in their ages—ten years at the least—and, naturally, their stations in life.

"You shall have Bess. A genuine thoroughbred Arab. A little darling, though a demon if you can't ride. You *did* say you could, didn't you?"

Tessie nodded, her eyes shining, for Bess was *magnificent.* Better yet than anything the Hampstead Oaks stables had to offer. She would ride, for it might be the last time she ever had the opportunity. Besides, Lady Ashleigh, dressed all in blue velvet and looking very much the thing, seemed to expect her to. Neither lady waited for the requisite groom, both mounting with consummate ease and grins of sheer pleasure that cut straight across the social barriers that might have come between them.

"Race you to the downs!'

And Lady Ashleigh was gone. Tessie, her spirits soaring, flew after her, Bess as responsive to her touch as if they'd ridden together forever. Lady Ashleigh jumped a stream, so Tessie did the same, ignoring the great splashes of mud that ruined her delightful new morning gown of blue organdy cut high at the bodice and flowing in classical lines. The thrill of the chase was upon her, and by the time Lady Ashleigh had negotiated a topiary hedge, Tessie had caught up.

"By God, you are a bruising rider!"

It was hard for Miss Hampstead to look demure, little dimples peeping cheerfully from flushed cheeks.

"I learned when I was little. Not sidesaddle either."

"You don't mean . . ."

"Astride? Yes, shameful, isn't it? Just as well I am no longer a lady. My reputation would not stand the scandal!"

Lady Ashleigh frowned. "Tessie Hampstead, we have not known each other long, but I vow and declare if you talk such fustian again, I will rinse your mouth out!"

"What?" Tessie, not surprisingly, looked astonished.

"Don't gape, young lady! You know perfectly well you are as much a lady as I. As for your reputation . . ."

"It is in shreds."

"By becoming a seamstress?"

"Yes. That, and . . ."

"Oh, *do* tell me! I swear, if you clam up, I shall positively *die* from curiosity!"

"There is nothing to tell. I have behaved scandalously and must pay the price. It is not so very unusual in our circles. Come, let us find this church. I would rather be haunted by specters than by . . . sad memories."

"Are they so very sad? None . . . worthy of a fluttering heart or a clandestine smile?"

"You make me sound like a heroine from one of Walpole's romances!"

"Well, aren't you?"

"Certainly not! Wherever can you have conceived such a notion? I am very plain and ordinary, though I fall into the most fearful scrapes. . . ."

Lady Ashleigh laughed. "Then we are kindred spirits! But come, answer my question. In that dark and gloomy past of yours, is there not some shining knight lurking somewhere? I sense it!"

Tessie laughed. "Perhaps. But I have placed him in the gloomiest corner of my mind and am determined to forget all about him!"

"Why? If *I* had a knight—and, indeed, my dear Robert, though I love him dearly, is far too prosaic to be termed such—*I* should not merely pine over him and consign him to the dusty recesses of my mind!"

"You would if it was the best thing for *him*!"

"Nonsense! For how can *any* knight care to be treated thus? What good is a knight without a corresponding damsel in distress?"

"Perhaps I am the wrong damsel. Indeed, I am sure of it, for I cause nothing but trouble, and the only reason why the knight is offering for me is out of pigheadedness and pride!"

"Offering for you, is he?" For some reason, Lady Ashleigh brightened considerably on her russet-colored side saddle.

"Yes, but only . . ."

". . . out of pigheadedness and pride. Sounds about right. Most knights offer for those reasons, for they are too stupid to admit the truths staring at them in the face."

"Which are?"

"Which are, my dear Tessie—I shall call you that, for I am certain we shall be friends—that they are head over heels in love! Gentlemen just can't seem to admit to such thoughts. Well, not without a little prodding. The amount of times I had to prod dear Lord Ashleigh you would simply not credit! It is not in their makeup despite the delightful sonnets they make such fools of themselves over."

"Oh, you mean, like 'Ode to Tessie'?"

"I suspect so. How does that go?"

Miss Hampstead giggled. "I shan't tell you, but it contains about five stanzas devoted to the peculiar shade of my hair."

"Not by your knight? Oh, tell me not!"

Tessie sobered. "No, for I doubt he would write me so much as a line. He thinks I am a child, you see."

Lady Ashleigh's gaze became piercing. "Yet he has offered?"

"Only because . . ."

"He is stubborn and proud. You would not love him else, I swear. Beware, Tessie, that you are not tarred with the same brush."

Lady Ashleigh, possibly at her gentlest and most perceptive, gave Tessie a sweeping stare that again was tinged with that enormous sense of familiarity. Tessie wondered why this should be so, or, indeed, who Lady Ashleigh reminded her of so forcibly.

But she was not permitted to muse long. Bess, champing at the bit, was ready to forge the stream.

Behind her, to the right, she was watched. The man called Tallows had been very patient.

Seventeen

The church in Chiswick was all that Lady Ashleigh promised, minus the ghost. It was old, built in the sixteenth century, and boasted a crumbling tomb, and some impressive mosaics upon the stone floors. It was no longer habited, partly because of the ghost theory and partly because the current archbishop of the area preferred the more modern structure just east of the Great North Road.

The church, then, was a mere curiosity, its winding stone steps abandoned chiefly to dust, spiders, and the more intrepid sightseers of Chiswick.

Tessie, though cold, insisted on exploring the entire edifice, laughing as she mounted the steps ahead of Lady Ashleigh.

"But where is the ghost?"

"Perhaps it is too cold for him."

"Or her. I feel certain the ghost is a her."

"Then you should sew her a mantle to keep out the cold."

"I have enough to sew, thank you very much, for the countess's daughter-in-law."

"Ah, yes, the consumptive one!"

"I do not see why your eyes sparkle so mischievously, Lady Ashleigh! It cannot be pleasant to be so afflicted!"

"No, indeed. And *do* call me Delia. If you are going to scold, you cannot be forever ladyshipping me!"

"I am *not* scolding! I am merely . . ."

"Curious?"

"Yes, indeed, though I know it is none of my business. . . . Why *does* the lady need so many gowns? You can have no *notion* of how much has been ordered. . . ."

Lady Ashleigh swallowed a cough. "I am sure, if the countess has ordered them, they are very necessary. Shall we go?"

Tessie nodded. She felt reproved somehow. She was not to know that Lady Ashleigh's cough was actually a repressed giggle, or that if they remained a second longer, her ladyship might have done something dire.

Like spoiling everything and telling the little seamstress the truth. No, indeed. The truth, as everyone but Tessie knew, was for Lord Nicholas Cathgar to tell. Too bad he was still languishing in town. Now that her curiosity was satisfied, Delia had a good mind to write him a letter of her own.

They passed, along the way, an enormous common bustling with peddlers and gypsy caravans and cartloads of produce. Ordinarily, Tessie would have begged to stop, for she adored fairs, and this, clearly, was the beginning of one. But her high spirits had deserted her, and her pockets were to let besides. So she ignored the familiar bustle, and the stalls of fruit and gingerbread and cheeses, kicking in her heels instead, so that Delia had to race to catch her.

While Lady Ashleigh finally took her leave—with an indecorous wink that relieved Tessie's mind—Lord Nicholas Cathgar was not, as his sister had accused him, "languishing in town."

He was, in fact, purchasing, as a result of a tip from Lord Alberkirky—to whom he was now being more civil—a certain stable full of horses. The friskiest of these—a lively little chestnut called Pebbles—he transported to his own residence in London. For the balance of his time he was inspecting roofs, talking to bailiffs, and generally exciting a very large degree of interest in Hampstead Oaks.

Indeed, Tessie, returning, would have been quite astonished, for the village people, wise in their own way, had made some pretty obvious inferences. Fortunately for Tessie's peace of mind, she was nowhere near her home, nor did she expect to be for a six month at least.

Lord Cathgar was not entirely lighthearted about his high-handedness, for it weighed heavily upon him that his chosen one was as hardheaded as himself. She would need careful handling to be convinced of his good intentions. She was more likely, he knew, to fly into a pelter over his actions than to thank him.

For the first time in his life, he was uncertain, both of himself and of his ability to attach to the most desirable creature he had ever encountered. So hotheaded she was! More likely, he knew, to shoot him in the foot than to acquiesce meekly to his honorable intentions. But honorable they were despite the many overtures of several young debutantes, all *dying* to attach themselves to his fortune and rank.

He felt like he was running the gauntlet, for hardly a day went by when some young wisp of a thing didn't try coyly to trap him into indiscretion. Truly, he needed Tessie to save him!

Well, *one* of his actions, at least, was bound to please her bloodthirsty nature. Upon tooling his cattle down a country Hampstead lane, he was very nearly overturned by the merest whipster, occupying more than his fair share of the road, and driving his team into a lather. He might have let the matter pass had the whipster not then compounded his sin by shouting out obscenities and claiming to own half of Greenford.

Nicholas dismounted and waited for the gentleman to do the same. His lanky stature was quite striking, and all of a sudden, Nick was struck with a quite diverting notion.

"You are not Oliver Dobbins, of Greenford, are you?"

The gentleman looked quite smug. "I am. Heard of me, have you?"

"Indeed. And what they say is quite true. You require a hatter, your boots are indecent, and your waistcoat is an insult to any arbiter of good taste."

"Why, you . . ." Oliver lunged forward, but Nicholas was more than a match for such a paltry fellow. He delivered a marvelously flush hit, guaranteeing Mr. Dobbins a black eye for a sennight or more. Then, only half satisfied, he waited for Mr. Dobbins to return the favor. He did, but with weak, flailing arms and a neck far too stiff to see, due to the height of his ridiculous collar. Nick regarded this as fortuitous and blackened the remaining eye. Then with a merry whistle he doffed his hat and proceeded upon his way. Tessie could not quibble with *that!*

The return from Hampstead Oaks was dull and boring by comparison. Nothing at all like the first time he'd stopped at the posting station, buoyed up by the anticipation of snaring the notorious Luddites, led astray by the French spy, the Monsieur le Duc.

At worst, he had expected to die—that was the nature of his clandestine activities—but he had never, never expected to have his heart so mercilessly stolen by an impudent little chit of a thing with more sovereigns than sense.

Yet, she had single-handedly saved his life, a fact for which he was thankful, but not so thankful as she seemed to think. He was not offering marriage as a salve to his conscience.

He was offering for perfectly selfish reasons and, being a spoiled and cosseted peer of the realm, he did not intend to be thwarted! No, not even by sultry black lashes and lashings of tears sniffed back fiercely.

Nicholas, just passing the Postlethwaite toll, decided that patience was for fledglings. Despite all his good intentions and the countess's frequent little notes reminding him to bide his time, he would not. To hell and damnation with Delia's laughing epistles too! He was not surprised that Tessie had wriggled her way into their hearts—indeed, how could she not? But it was singularly unfair that he, who had discovered her, should kick his heels meekly in London.

The more he thought of it, the more he balked at the idea of Tessie being treated like a mere seamstress, working her fingers to the bone, and if he knew all his siblings, she would not be short of work! Yes, Lady Victoria Halgrove, the eldest of his many sisters, had already written of a feathered muff she was to have, embroidered all in the newest shade of blond floss, or some such nonsense. Apparently, Delia, too, was toying with a new spencer, and he would not put it past any of his beloved siblings to take advantage of the consummate opportunities Tessie offered.

And they were laughing at him! He knew it, for Delia had the most wicked sense of humor, and the tone of her last missive was suspiciously meek, almost as though she were choking on mirth as she penned it. But maybe he was being oversensitive. Where Tessie was concerned, he could not help it. Even if he could, that Friday-faced Joseph would not let him. There he was, walking now with his best Arab, his face sweeping the floor, muttering all sorts of dire epithets about allowing chickens to fly the coop, and about females "wot could teach un a thing or two," which he rightly inferred to be himself.

Even threats of instant dismissal did not stop the man, who looked at Nicholas with doleful, reproachful eyes until he thought he would scream. It was not as if he had not offered, dammit! More—insisted, even! What in the world could that contrary female wish for?

There was an attraction between them that he was perfectly certain she felt—indeed, it was her very responses to him that drove him crazier. Well, by George, he was going to find out! He was *not* going to meekly await another of his mother's merry missives and hope that Madame Stubborn had grown tired of her work. No! He was going now, to the Dower House at Chiswick, and to tarnation with the rest!

"Joseph!"

It took a moment for Joseph to halt the Arab and walk back to the chaise, bound for London.

"Aye, me lord?"

"You can stop looking so glum. I have had a change of plan."

"A change of plan wot includes snabbling the little mistress, me lor', or jest a change of plan wot some might say is chicken-hearted, like . . ."

"I am excessively interested to hear your theories on my chicken-heartedness, Joseph, but I have no time. You shall enlighten me when I return, however, having 'snabbled' the mistress. That is, if I haven't already dismissed you for impertinence."

Joseph righteously ignored the last part of Nicholas's sentence and allowed his countenance to brighten considerably.

"Good on yer, guv! We can take the Marlborough route—it is a shortcut wot I know across the downs, then into Fennimore—but wot are we goin' to do about the cattle?"

"*We* are going to do nothing. *You,* however, are going to stable the Arab and the mare with the ostlers at the next posting house. You are then to return to London at all speed on Juniper, returning with Jenkins and two of the grooms. Pay the shot and transfer the balance of the cattle to Cathgar House. That, I trust, shall keep you busy."

"Guv!" Joseph looked shocked. "I be missin' out on all the 'citement! Wot if she shoots yer?"

"Then doubtless I shall die."

"But . . ."

"No buts, Joseph. I realize my life is your chief source of entertainment, but on this issue I remain firm."

"Lawks alive! You might be wishin' for my 'elp, beggin' your lor'ship's pardon!"

"You apparently regard my . . . eh . . . private life to be as hazardous a mission as my . . . government activities. You may be right. However, I shall risk it, if you please, in peace. Besides, Pebbles is her favorite horse."

Joseph brightened. "Well, a rare goer she is, and that be fact! Orl right, guv, I shall do as yer say, but mind yer p's and q's and don't make a botch of it this time! I 'ave a fancy to see the little mistress again, and that be fact!"

"I shall endeavor to please you, Joseph."

Nicholas barely kept the irony from his tone. Joseph, however, saw nothing amiss in his master's words, and actually doffed his cap. Then he spoiled the effect by winking, shaking Nick's immaculate gloves mercilessly, and whistling as he returned to his duties.

Nick, free of those eagle eyes, sighed. He only wished he could be so sanguine. If Tessie was outrageous enough to dismiss his suit again, he would have to either murder her, kiss her, or abduct her. The trouble was, he really did not know which.

Miss Hampstead, the object of such musings, needed to clear her head. She had come to love the bustle about the great ivy-clad mansion, and even the comfort of her work, for while she stitched, there was precious little time to pine or muse. She had, of course, several times fallen into some happy daydreams but been rewarded for her pains by a needle pricking into her thumb or pins poking at her fingers. When the countess finally lifted an inquiring brow at such hamhandedness, she had colored and muttered nonsense about needing air and such.

The countess often obliged by ringing for a footman and having several of the windows open despite some inclement breezes from the east.

Then Tessie had shivered a little over her work but felt foolish asking for the great glass panes to be shut again. Once, when she was biting back an involuntary tear, the countess took her work from her and threw it—in a shockingly haphazard manner—on the bureau behind them.

"Come, come, is it so very bad, then, this life? It is very different from being a lady of fashion, perhaps—"

"No! Oh, no! You have been so kind. I never *dreamed* being in service could be so pleasant!"

"Then why are you crying? Yes, scrub at your face as you may, I can see there are tears! I may be as blind as a bat and need my monocle from time to time, but I am not in my dotage! Can you not confide in me?"

"You are kind to take the trouble . . ."

"Not as kind as you might think. I have my reasons, Miss Hampstead."

Tessie wondered what the reasons could possibly be, but she was too well bred—when not in a fiery rage—to ask.

"Is it a man? When I was your age, it was always a man!"

"Oh, he is not just *any* man!"

The countess smiled in satisfaction. "But it *is* a man that troubles you?"

Tessie blushed, knowing she should rather have held her tongue. The countess was too sharp to continue this particular discussion. But she showed no inclination to drop the topic, scraping great bolts of cloth onto the floor to make space for her ample being.

"Ma'am, they will be crushed!"

"Oh, bother the gowns! It is far more fascinating to meddle in other people's business!"

Tessie could not help but laugh. It was impossible to be angry with the countess, who she knew was nothing but kindness itself.

"I don't suppose you can really meddle, Countess. And my story is not unique enough to be fascinating."

"I shall be the judge of that, if you please! Now, tell me at once! Are you in love?"

Tessie was suddenly shy. "A little."

"A little? *A little?"* The countess's voice rose an octave. "Don't be a nincompoop, girl! One does not fall in love a *little!"*

"Well, a lot, then. Terribly. Hopelessly."

"Ah, now, *that* is better! I adore passion, and a smidgen of pathos. Adds spice."

Tessie nearly rather tartly mentioned that her life was not designed wholly to add spice to the countess's day, but she rather nobly refrained. She was fond of the countess.

"Don't glare at me as if you've swallowed a sour grape! Yes, I know you very likely want to throttle me, but you shan't. Though you undoubtedly have spirit, you are also very prettily behaved. So just resign yourself and tell me the whole."

"The whole?"

The countess's voice was firm. "The whole." She looked up from her great jeweled turban of russet silk.

"Go away, Delia. Tessie is busy."

Miss Hampstead, who had not noticed the door opening, looked up.

"Lady Ashleigh . . ."

"Lady Ashleigh is just leaving." The countess glared

at the indignant sister of Lord Nicholas Cathgar. They had the identical blue eyes and arrogant brows. Lady Ashleigh, however, had no scar to mar her handsome features. Tessie felt that wave of familiarity again, but she could not put her finger on it, certainly not now, when she was being trapped into confidences by her fierce—and kindly—employer.

"Am I?" Lady Ashleigh raised those lovely brows. "Why do I think I would rather not?" Her voice tinkled with laughter. Tessie wondered why, for indeed, the countess was being astonishingly rude to her morning caller.

"Because you are a meddlesome baggage. Come back later, if you must. Miss Hampstead and I are in urgent discussions."

"Regarding gowns? I rather have a fancy to—"

"Get out!" The countess threw an ink pot at Lady Ashleigh's head. She ducked rather expertly, but deep indigo stained both the bonnet and the floor. Tessie gasped, but Lady Ashleigh did not seem to take offense, merely discarding her hat as if it were of small moment.

"Thank God your aim is deteriorating with age. You missed this lovely sprigged muslin. Do you like it, Miss Hampstead? I purchased it in Chiswick. . . ."

"Go!" her ladyship positively roared.

"Pardon?" Delia asked innocently. Tessie started to giggle. It was a mad and delightful household she had stumbled upon!

"Oh, I can take a subtle hint. Yes, yes, I shall take my leave now." Delia smiled sweetly. At the door she turned and faced the countess once more.

"By the bye, you owe me a bonnet. A high poked one, I think, with spangles of ribbon . . ."

But the door was shut in her face.

* * *

Tallows grimaced in annoyance. Three weeks of skulking about the estate, poaching nothing but a jugged hare and a couple of trout, had done nothing for his temper. He now knew where the girl was residing, but not in the least how to kidnap her. The house was swarming with liveried staff, and if that wasn't enough, there were grooms and milkmaids, and heaven knew what all over the grounds. On the odd occasion—like when she visited that ruin of a church—she left the estate, but it was always with some grim groom in tow, or that modish woman who rode so disgustingly well.

If he was going to succeed, it would have to be with the girl alone. Two was too many for one person to overpower—and he had already seen what havoc the girl could wreak. More than enough of a handful, that one. Tallows lurked behind the hedges, pulling the odd weed when somebody passed. The only good thing about an estate like this was that there were always gardeners. One more pulling weeds would excite little notice, or so he hoped. He doffed a cap at one of the morning callers. So many there were, and all in fashionable rigs and phaetons. There had to be a way, there had to! His eyes sharpened a little as his gaze rested on something odd. He nodded in satisfaction. He had just the ticket.

Eighteen

"Oh, my dear! It sounds just like a fairy tale!"

Tessie smiled and shook those abundant dark curls so that they fell in a pleasing tangle about her elfin face. "No, indeed. My hero is not handsome enough, I am afraid. You forget the scar."

Lady Cathgar had done no such thing. Indeed, the scar had haunted her for almost a year, when her dearest son had refused to go about in society, or to take up his rightful place at Lords. It was still painful for her to think on it, for he had always been such a carefree, openhearted child, that the heavy irony he now adopted as a mantle was . . . difficult. She knew his reaction had been severe because of his reception back into the drawing rooms when the scar was still livid, and the memories of what had caused it vivider still.

Lady Cathgar had not been present, but it was rumored that several of the young debutantes had fainted from fright, and those who hadn't had been overcome by his pocketbook rather than by any real sensibility. Thus it was that Nicholas had adopted his customary sarcastic poise, had played hard, had used women shamelessly—his doting mama made no excuse—had become a rakehell but not so debauched that he ever forgot his cause, or his loyalty to king and country.

Tessie was exactly the miracle the countess had prayed for—honest, brave, and decidedly unmissish. If there was one thing the countess hated above others, it was prudishness, or young ladies given to spasms. If half of the tale she had just heard was true, Tessie was in no danger of falling into either of these categories.

"Ah . . . the scar. Yes, I had forgotten. Regrettable."

"Indeed, not!" Tessie was indignant. "It is noble. I cannot imagine his features without it. It maketh the man. Besides, it has an air. Piratical, I think."

"And that is a good thing?"

"But naturally! He is not an ordinary man, you know."

"I begin to think not, since he has engendered such obvious devotion!"

"He does not love me." Tessie's wide, adorable lips drooped. "I can't say I blame him, for apart from saving his life, I have been nothing but a trial to him! I ordered him about like a tyrant when he was ill, and I disappeared without a word when he had ordered me not to, and I have quarreled with him endlessly. . . ."

"Oh, do not let that make you too cast down! I quarreled with my husband until the day he died! We loved each other tremendously, you know!"

"Yes, but he was not forced to offer out of . . . out of . . . charity!"

"Oh, I doubt your young man did either. Men are strange that way, you know. Pigheaded. Never offer when they are not inclined!"

"Oh, but they do! Remember Lord. . . . eh . . . the *other* lord who offered for me? It is mortifying!"

"Now, don't get down in the mopes. I have a strange suspicion all will work out perfectly in the end. You have had two respectable offers and refused both. Very admirable, but next time, my dear, I advise you to put aside your scruples and accept."

"There won't be a next time, Countess. And I won't accept where I don't love."

"Ah, but naturally! Did I suggest such a thing? I must

be in my dotage after all. But, my dear, if you *do* happen to get an offer where your sentiments are involved, I assure you it will be perfectly permissible to succumb to your desires. No one can possibly fault you for such a thing, and if they do, they shall have *me* to answer to!" She glared balefully around the empty room. Tessie, in spite of her depression of spirits, laughed.

"Well, I *shall* promise, for it is highly unlikely I shall ever see my paragon again, let alone receive a third offer to throw in his face. I am sure he finds such a reception tedious."

The countess, who knew just how Nicholas found such a reception, nodded sagely. "Tedious" would not have been the term she chose, but "trying," most certainly.

Tessie was a perfectly trying person. Noble to a fault, prone to the most exceptional of scrapes, hotheaded, accident prone, and a darling.

All of these qualities absolutely necessary, of course, to the future Countess of Cathgar. The current countess could not abide simpering ninnyhammers or prudish Miss Prisms. Tessie, unstitching as much as she stitched, would be simply perfection itself.

The countess meddled with the floral arrangement in front of her. She simply *must* untangle her son and heir's amazing mull of things. He *must* tell Tessie that he loved her, sweep her up in his arms . . . she pulled off a perfectly good stem and turned to her listener.

"It is his own fault if he encounters such a reception! Tedious, indeed! Really, why, the man could not have stolen a kiss, swept you off your feet, murmured . . . gracious, my dear Miss Hampstead, you are blushing like a beetroot!"

Which was only to state the truth, of course, for Tessie hardly dared mention that all of the above had occurred in pleasing quantities. Naturally, the countess, eyeing her shrewdly, needed no further telling.

"Hmmph! I suspect, Miss Hampstead, you might have offered me an expurgated account of your activities!"

Tessie felt like sinking through the luxurious Axminster carpet, all delicate shades of lilac and pink.

"My lord was not . . . behindhand in such persuasions, ma'am."

"You relieve my mind! I did not think I could have produced such a . . . that is to say, I did not think a gentleman such as you described would have milk and water in his veins. Kiss well, does he?"

"Countess!" Tessie was crimson. "I beg you to leave off the subject!"

"Nonsense, we are precisely at the point that the tale grows interesting!" The countess murdered another poor rose.

"Well, *I* shall not say another word! All I have left, ma'am, is a few memories. I shall keep them, if you please, private."

"Bravo!" There was a clap from the door. ". . . And *that* should teach you, Mama . . . I mean countess!" Lady Delia Ashleigh tugged at her skirts and entered the drawing room once more.

"Did I not tell you to take yourself off?"

"You did, but I could not bear seeing you destroy that magnificent bouquet. You are perfectly visible from the garden."

"You mean you were eavesdropping beneath the window!"

"Well, not eavesdropping precisely . . ."

"Eavesdropping! Delia, you are shameless!"

Lady Ashleigh laughed. "Miss Hampstead, my compliments. You are able to rout my . . . that is to say, you glare at the countess to the manner born. She is used, I am afraid, to people kowtowing to her every whim."

"You don't."

"No, but then, I frequently have ink pots thrown at me for my troubles. Has he told you he loves you?"

Tessie groaned. "I suppose the whole of Chiswick has heard my troubles!"

"No, only me. Now, come on! Has he?"

"No." Tessie could manage only the one solitary word. Lady Ashleigh waved her riding crop about in disgust.

"Imbecile!"

"No, indeed! He is everything that is fine. . . ."

"He is a veritable clodpole!"

"Lady Ashleigh, I will *not* have you malign the man I love."

"So long as you don't actually shoot me! And he *is* a clodpole, whatever you may say!"

Tessie looked from the countess to Lady Delia. Again there was that strange wave of familiarity . . . she wished she could put her finger on it. A carriage rumbled to a halt outside. It was a large barouche, painted red, with the crest of an eagle upon its door. Lady Delia pushed the curtains back to see.

"Bother! It is Miss Hartleyvale. Can't we deny her?"

Lady Ashleigh turned toward Tessie in explanation.

"She thinks she owns the neighborhood, she being the daughter of the late Baron of Hartleyvale. She has never forgiven Mother her superior breeding or title."

Guiltily, Delia realized her mistake. Her hand went up to her mouth, but Tessie, already puzzling certain utterances, was more perceptive than usual.

"The countess is your *mother!* Good God, it is true, is it not? Lady Ashleigh is *not* a mere morning caller as I had assumed."

The countess frowned, then shrugged. "Trying, is it not? But yes, the impertinent little scrubster is mine, I fear. That is why I am so free with my ink pots."

"I should have known! There is something so *familiar* about her! It must be the resemblance to you!"

Neither lady mentioned the more obvious resemblance. Tessie would find that out in good time, when they had a thing or two to say to the son, brother, and Cathgar heir respectively!

Miss Hartleyvale was almost completely forgotten until, too late, the butler announced her in tones of righteous pomp.

"Miss Hartleyvale, your ladyship."

Miss Hartleyvale, of indeterminate age, twittered in. She was wearing a morning dress more suited to court than country, though the entire effect was ruined somewhat by a drab kerseymere cape she had thrown over the entire ensemble.

"Oh, I *do* hope you don't mind me dropping in, dreadful to stand on ceremony, I always say . . . why, Lady Ashleigh, I swear you have grown, and how are all your sisters . . . Lady Halgrove, that fine brother of yours . . . ?"

There followed a veritable stream of nonsensical pleasantries such as was guaranteed to appal the countess. Tessie, however, heard none of them, her mind a complete turmoil of shock. She could swear . . . yes, indeed, she could *swear* she had heard Miss Hartleyvale refer to the countess by her rank. She might be dreaming, but she vowed she heard quite distinctly the title Cathgar.

It was not until Delia winked at her, those familiar sapphire eyes agleam, that she understood, at last, the truth.

How many, she wondered, of those delightful morning callers had actually been Nicholas's high-spirited sisters? Lady *Halgrove* probably was, and she would bet her last farthing the others were too. Nick had spoken, had he not, of a dozen sisters or more—she remembered it clearly, though she thought he had been funning.

Was this the strangest of nightmarish coincidences, or was it some sort of cruel conspiracy? Oh, she felt like such a fool! How they must have been laughing when she divulged the inner secrets of her heart! Tessie blushed crimson. She simply could not bear it.

Lady Delia, eyeing her closely, took a step toward her. Tessie could not divine whether it was pity or compassion or plain merriment that compelled her.

Perhaps it was foolish, but without so much as curtsying to the countess or acknowledging the curious glance of Lady Hartleyvale, she turned from the room and fled.

It was sometime later, after refusing to acknowledge the fruitless knocking on her chamber door, that she'd decided to clear her head. Perhaps, she thought, the fair. At the fair she could lose herself among the silk mercers, the ironmongers, the jewelers, the japanners, the fine cutlery dealers. Anyone, that is, who was not associated with the regal House of Cathgar.

She desperately needed to think—it was impossible, here in this house, where every portrait now reminded her of Nick. How could she have been so stupid? Even the countess had his features and his curving smile. She should have known, she should have thought . . . with decision, she threw on her smart new riding habit, grabbed at her reticule—sadly depleted of guineas—and departed quietly through the little-used west wing. She had no wish to be accosted by Delia at the entrance.

The air was fresh and crisp, the clouds rather high in the sky. Tessie took long, great strides out, past the stables, toward the broad moors. She did not go unnoticed, as she hoped. Two pairs of eyes watched. Cal, the groom, ran after her, breathless. He had saddled Bess for her use. Tessie refused his aid up into the saddle. It was no good riding today. Riding would put her further in Lady Cathgar's debt. She shook her head at Bess, nuzzling her gloved hands beseechingly.

"Not today, dearest. You ask . . . Cal, is it?"

The groom nodded shyly.

"You ask Cal to sneak you a nice lump of sugar. I would myself, only I don't have any on me right now, just this great unfashionable reticule and my stout walking boots! There, you be a dear and go with Cal now. . . ."

The groom regarded Tessie doubtfully.

"You sure, Mistress Tess, like? The countess will 'ave my 'ead. . . ."

"Nonsense! The countess is perfectly delightful. Just explain that I wish to be alone. She will understand perfectly."

Bess hoofed the ground impatiently and snorted.

"Gentle, like, gentle, like!" The groom became absorbed in his duties.

Tessie smiled, though the effort was great, then lifted her skirts and ran across the fields. Watching her, the groom thought he had never seen a female "wot was such a spankin' great gun." Then he turned toward the cobbled path and turned his attentions to Bess.

Tessie did not know why she ran, only that she had to, or the enormous weight she felt depressing her spirits would crush her utterly. She had been tricked! She felt like a fool, but she knew she had to think things out clearly. Lady Cathgar was not cruel, but nor had she been open—even if it was a coincidence that caused her to hire her as a seamstress, she had still hidden her identity, and that of her daughters. That must mean some complicity, but *why?*

If only she could figure out why, she might come closer to an understanding. *Could* it have anything to do with Nicholas? Had they meant to disgrace her by ensuring she went into service? Perhaps they knew she would never have been hired, and so took the matter into their own hands? Did Nicholas know? Had they been protecting him or following his explicit orders?

Both thoughts made her so miserable that she hardly noticed the cold, and certainly not the trap that had been neatly laid by Tallows.

It had been a simple matter, really, of diverting a signpost when he saw her walking from the stables. A simple matter to keep watch, with enduring patience, and a criminal's intuition.

Somehow, he had known she would walk out alone sooner or later. He thanked his lucky stars he had noticed the ditch, dug for some reason other than the use he was now attaching to it. Perhaps it was to have been the foundations of an icehouse, or even a man-made pond. Tallows did not know or care. What was to the purpose is that it was deep and grown all over with grass. Doubtless the locals knew of it and kept their distance. Also, there had been the sign keeping wanderers on the footpath. . . . But not *this* wanderer!

"Oh!" Tessie shouted as she stumbled, not so much in fear as in surprise and pain, for she was positive she must have twisted an ankle in the overlong grass.

To her surprise, she tumbled, sinking deeper than she imagined, losing her grip on her reticule and squashing her bonnet most hideously. She winced from the pain, then removed her hat, determined to repair the damage at once before climbing back up to the footpath.

"Well met, mistress . . . Tess, is it?"

Miss Hampstead looked up with a start. Her heart began hammering idiotically, and she had the oddest sensation that despite the civil words, she needed her pistol. She had never actually seen the man Tallows, but his countenance was threatening, and the odd sibilance in his tone alerted her to danger.

"I . . . I am not sure I know you, sir!"

Tessie stalled for time as she calculated how far she had been thrown from her reticule. Too far, if the man meant mischief. The tips of his boots were pressing on one of its ribbons.

"You don't, but I know *you!* Lord Cathgar's fine piece you are, and me with a reckonin' to settle! Bloodied me eye, 'e did, aside from spoilin' a rare good plot. The Prince of Wales rests easy tonight, when the Luddites would as lief as 'ave 'im dead. Blame yer good Lord Nick for that!"

"You speak treason."

"Aye, but it is only your pretty little ears wot hears it. Now, get movin'. I 'ave a cozy little cabin for us, and a rare pot of green goose stew."

"I shall scream."

"Scream and Lor' Nick is as good as dead. We 'ave 'im, too, yer see."

Tessie's eyes grew wild with real fear now. She was not to know the man was lying through his teeth, shrewdly divining the best methods to control her. She knew only that if she screamed, Nick would die. She believed the man, for the Luddites had proven themselves again and again to be ruthless. Spiteful, even, for why they would they detain her, if it was Nick that they were after, Nick that they had?

She must stall him, go meekly, see how many of the original gang they were up against. Grange, at least, was gone. There were more, though, too many more. She must not lose hope. They would lead her to Nick. She must keep thinking that. They would lead her to Nick. If she could live to save his life once more, she ought to be satisfied.

So, meekly she allowed herself to be bound, to be perched upon a horse, to ignore Tallows's rank smell, to say nothing, though her fury knew no bounds, and above all to watch Tallows tip her pistol from her reticule and grind it into the grass-stained ditch. A cruel man, she thought, and shivered.

But not clever. If he were clever, he would have left no trace, spoken no word, instead of boasting ad nauseam of his triumphs. Tessie listened as she inwardly fumed, for every word might, she knew, be crucial. As they rode, she allowed her bonnet to be taken by the breeze. With her lips she prized off her gloves. These followed her bonnet across the plains. Not much of a trail, she thought grimly, but she would be damned if she did nothing!

Tallows, oblivious, chuckled in relief. It was true about the green goose stew. He had had rare pickings that day. And the huntsman's cottage at the edge of the estate was perfect, just perfect.

Nineteen

Tessie was still bound, but her mouth remained ungagged, thanks to Tallows's meaningful threat. Nevertheless, she said nothing, merely watched with observant eyes as Tallows stirred up his pot and muttered to himself about ransoms.

All the while, Tessie kept a close watch for any sign of Nick. She would have done anything to see him one last time, but not here, not like this! She hoped above all that Tallows had been lying, that Nick was safe and as happy as a grig somewhere, probably London.

Pride did not permit her to question Tallows, or to taste his wretched, ill-gotten stew that nevertheless smelled delightful in this cold, barren place. Yes, undoubtedly Tallows's observance had paid off. He had discovered this little thatched place and overnight made it home.

Or home in the broadest possible sense, that is, for save for the cooking pot and the fire, there was no redeeming feature to this dark, spider-infested place. The thatch leaked great drips of rainwater, and the couple of old sketches upon the floor were long past redemption, the charcoals having smudged mercilessly across the pages. Tessie thought she spied the imprints of boots upon them—one more indication that her captor lacked all sensibility. She tried not to watch him as he slurped back his meal and fetched out of his pockets a chunk of sourdough to soak up the remains.

"Fetch a pretty penny, yer will."

The first bit of satisfied comment Tallows had vouchsafed in over two hours.

Tessie, who had been working silently on her bonds, imperceptibly flexing her muscles to loosen them, looked up. Her hair, bonnetless, was all tangled again. She wanted to wipe the locks from her forehead, for they were sticking, but she could not.

"Beg pardon?"

Obligingly, Tallows's voice came louder this time.

"Fetch a pretty penny ye will, reckon Lord High-and-Mighty will pay something to 'ave yer back!"

Tessie's heart gave that sudden lurch she was becoming accustomed to. She decided to engage her captor in conversation. The more she could learn, the better. The more unguarded his tongue, the better.

"Which lord?"

"Lord bloomin' Nelson! I dunno, *you* tell me which lord will be payin' a pretty packet for your . . . wares."

Tessie, revolted at the implication, said nothing. But her mind worked swiftly, for in danger she was all up to the rig.

If this Luddite—and he was obviously that—everything he said screamed of it—if this Luddite was talking of lords . . . Tessie swallowed hard. There was only one lord whom the Luddites had a personal grudge against. One lord, who . . . but no! Tessie would *not* think that the debonair Lord Nicholas Cathgar might harbor some feelings for her! Some stray, misguided sense of responsibility perhaps . . . Tallows could be talking only of Nick.

She breathed hard. If there was talk of ransom, then Tallows had lied. Nick was nowhere in these rooms, in these small chambers, hidden in the loft, prisoner in the woods . . . he was not!

He was alive, safe, striding through his residence, riding his stallions . . . about to receive a ransom note. There was none of the gang in evidence, and Tessie was inclined to think Tallows had lied there too.

So what had she gained? Nothing but the miserable knowledge that she should have screamed when she could have. She had been duped like the green goose in the pot. The thought made her furious rather than cowed.

By God! If she were not to be saving Nick's life, then she was blessed well about to save her own! What was more, if this whey-faced mushroom thought he could cadge a ransom out of Nick, he was mistaken, very much mistaken!

Eyes flashing, she wondered what sort of ruse she could use to catch Tallows off his guard. Her wrists felt raw, but she believed that, if she needed to, she could free herself. But she had one chance, and she must not waste it.

Tallows peered at her.

"A right piece yer are, with all them pretty ringlets, like. Reckon if I were to cut off them curls, 'is lordship will send the ransom quick as a trivet."

Tessie's eyes blazed, then grew thoughtful. What, after all, were a few ringlets? They might prove useful. If she pleaded, doubtless the Luddite would be confirmed in his intentions.

"Oh, please, no! Not my hair! It has taken simply an age to grow and curl so!"

Tallows smiled grimly. "Well, it will take an age again! Let that be a lesson to the great Cathgar! Bless me if I don't slap on the handsome price of a coachwheel a curl. And seven hundred sovereigns for your person—'e should pay that easy, 'e should. Never say Tallows is greedy, like! But them curls . . . yes . . . them curls be a splendid idea!"

"Wicked, you mean!" Tessie tugged at her wrists again. Almost free, she was sure of it. And she would scream

if she needed to. There was no longer the threat of Nick's life gagging her. But it would be pointless here, in the woods, with no one but the odd poacher to hear her struggles. Here she must be silent, and pray that she could induce the witless Tallows to take her bait.

"Oh, please! I implore you! You simply cannot cut off these curls!"

Tallows smiled grimly. "I can, me dear, and I surely will. Just as soon as I have me a knife!"

And *that,* Tessie thought in satisfaction, was precisely what she wanted.

Nicholas was nearly home. He kicked in his heels and sent his horse flying over the hedgerow, ever alert for any signs of Tessie. He would not put it past her, he thought, to be wandering alone across his estate. It was just the foolish sort of thing she would do.

The next thing, it was not the horse, but he, who was flying over the hedgerow. The horse had stumbled in a ditch! He could have sworn it was the one dug by the first Lord Cathgar, a trench for dueling it had been, and such an eyesore that it had been abandoned for years, with nothing but periwinkle and long grass to mark the site.

Of course, all the signposts pointed away from the spot, though the locals knew to be wary. So how the dickens had the signpost been turned? Surely not on purpose? Who would do such a thing? And what in tarnation was that . . . that . . . *thing* lying filthy in the soil? Nicholas whistled gently to his horse as he brushed himself off and kicked at the piece of material. He stubbed his toe. He cursed in a most ungentlemanlike fashion, but then, he hardly looked a gentleman with his knees stained in dirt and his neckerchief more brown than pristine white.

Curious, Nick's eyes narrowed. There was something

familiar . . . he tugged at the reticule. Of a sudden, he knew why he had stubbed his toe. He was just thankful he had not shot it to pieces. He smiled rather ruefully. Tessie's pistol, snug in its dirty haven, was primed. He should have guessed.

Miss Hampstead waited, as her captor cursed, to undo her bonds. If she did so, she could flee, but she was uncertain whether she could be any match for Tallows. He was long and lanky and very likely could outrun her, especially in her skirts.

From somewhere—probably the sentry's box—Tallows had procured some writing equipment and old, crested paper. He wrote laboriously, tongue hanging out, occasionally asking for assistance, such as in the spelling of "ransom." Tessie's eyes would have danced with amusement had she not been concentrating so hard on her chances of escape.

When the task was done, Tallows sealed the missive with candle wax and looked very pleased with himself, obviously not doubting for a moment that Nicholas would be forthcoming with the blunt. He had brought with him a pail. His appeared to be filled with a variety of objects, not least of which was a plum pie. Tallows was obviously more adept at thieving than at kidnapping. For the first time, Tessie's lips curved upward in amusement. Tallows was no Grange, she was certain of it.

"What the devil do you mean, you can't find her?"

Lord Nicholas Cathgar, grimy, grim, and decidedly unfetching in town garb that reeked of the stable—and which moreover splattered mud across his Axminster carpets—glared fiercely.

Lady Cathgar, his mother, dabbed back a tear with an

enormous handkerchief sewn from spangled floss and shook her head.

"I tell you, Nick, she simply disappeared!"

"Ran away?"

"Not precisely, though I fear she was a trifle distrait. . . ."

"You shall be a trifle distrait if you don't speak more plainly!"

Nicholas glared at his mother and four of his beloved sisters. Two of them giggled, but the other two looked distinctly uncomfortable, not to mention genuinely concerned.

"Nick, number one, she loves you though you are clearly undeserving, since you have been a total blockhead throughout and not once thought to tell her you love her. . . ."

"Mama . . ."

"Don't mama me! I love Tessie dearly and I won't have her hurt."

"I! Hurt her! That is the outside of enough. . . ."

"Nonsense! You have hurt the poor child dreadfully with your high-handed ways! Did you woo her? Did you whisper soft nothings in her ear? Did you, while you were *kissing* her"—here Lady Cathgar stared at him balefully—"did you ever once mention that you loved her?"

"I asked her to marry me, for God's sake!"

"Yes, after you had ruined her! Not very romantic, Nick, you can do better if all the reports I hear are true."

"Mama, you listen to too much scandal broth!"

"Not enough, by all accounts! No one told *me,* my dear, *dear* Nicholas, that you are still acting government agent!"

"Tessie obviously did."

"I had to positively prize it out of her! Now, *do* be a good boy and find the chit, kiss her decisively, and don't forget to tell her you love her!"

"Where is she that I may carry out this admirable advice?"

"I don't know, I tell you! She sustained a severe shock today. It would have been fine, of course, had that *idiotish* Miss Hartleyvale not blathered out our names and titles before we could deny her entrance! If poor Tessie . . ."

"Where *is* she?" Nicholas's firm control was slipping. Finding her reticule had worried him more than he liked to say. She was a dear little scapegrace, but she treasured that damned pistol of hers. It should not have been lying in the mud like that.

"We think she went to the fair. Cal—that is, one of the young grooms—I think you know him—said she dismissed him, wanting the air. More like she did not want to ride Bess for fear she would be more beholden. A proud puss, your Tess."

"Then she was—is—unaccompanied?"

Lady Halgrove responded. "Yes, but it is only a mile or so to the fair, Nick! Surely she shan't come to any harm? We used to sneak out often enough ourselves, remember?"

Nicholas did not bother to reply. He simply strode out with nothing whatsoever in his ungloved hands but Miss Hampstead's famous reticule.

Out of the pail came a dram of red-brown liquid—no need to guess its identity—Tessie could smell it on Tallows's breath—half a pigeon pie, a shovel—curious, could be useful, but really rather small for her needs—and then the pièce de résistance, a knife. Miss Hampstead peered at it through the gloom. Yes, that would do. It was precisely what she'd been hoping for, in fact, with all this talk of curls.

It was growing darker and colder. Tessie hoped some candles would miraculously appear from the pail. They did not, but Tallows lit a taper from the fire. It was gloomy, grudgingly emitting a speck of half-light, but Tessie was grateful. That, too, could be handy. Time, she thought, to free her bonds, though she must sit with the ropes tied loosely upon her until her moment came. She counted on the moment, for it was all the hope she had.

It would be days before Nick received any ransom note in London. He probably never would, for she did not pin too much faith on Tallows's literacy or ability to frank the mail. There was no doubt in her mind that Tallows was a novice to the business of kidnapping. Good in some respects, but she must not rest on her laurels. Sometimes the stupidest criminals were the most dangerous.

She jerked her arms viciously apart, loosening the bonds so fiercely that they fell to the floor. The pail was too far on the other side of the room for her to make a dash for it. Heart beating, for should Tallows notice she would be quite undone, she picked up the cords and bound them about her wrists again.

How fortunate that her tormentor, occupied outside with the call of nature, and generally rather pleased with himself, did not suspect a thing. He returned and bade Tessie, rather curtly, sit by the fire.

"For there I can see ya as I cut at them curls. One at a time, like. Souvenirs for his lord worship."

Tessie said nothing, but did as she was told, taking care not to let the ropes fall from her wrists as she did so.

Fuming, she allowed Tallows to put his dry, mud-caked hands on her soft, tangled strands. They smelled of lemon and honeysuckle, but Tallows was too tipsy to really notice, or to appreciate this feminine nuance. He pulled at her hair—gently for such a large and lanky creature—and twisted a curl in his thumb.

Tessie did not move, her eyes focused almost entirely on the knife he'd removed from the pail. She thought of leaping up, taking him by surprise, pouncing on the knife, and making good her escape, then decided she was an addle-wit. Tallows would be at the knife in the twinkling of an eyelash, and all her hard work loosening her bonds would be for naught. No, she had one chance, really, and how she wished it was a gun and not a knife that she had to deal with! Still, beggars could not be choosers, and if she had to stab Tallows, she would, for undoubtedly he would not hesitate to do the same if he suspected trouble.

Nick would not just lie down calmly and pay the ransom. Even if he received the note, he would be concocting some cunning plan. If it failed, Tallows would not hesitate to kill her, or worse. He might seem a sorry sort of villain, but they were often the most dangerous. They worked on instinct rather than on calculation. Dangerous, dangerous.

Tallows let go of the curl. It twisted immediately into a little ringlet that framed her face. He pulled at it again, then watched it snap back into the same soft twist. Tessie did not say a word. Inwardly, she sighed, for she wondered how long her patience, never mind her famous temper, could stand this treatment.

"Quiet, aren't ye?"

"I have not much to say."

"That must be a first! You wimmenfolk blabber ten to the turrnpike, I always say! Bless me if them curls are not natural, like."

"Well, of course they are natural!"

Tallows regarded her suspiciously. "None of them curlin' papers, like?"

Tessie shook her head firmly, so the tangle of curls covered her face. She swept them back again with another swift shake. Nearly, nearly, she had used her hands. She must be careful. And she *must* incite him to make a move! The longer she dallied, the darker it got. She did not trust even a full moon to get her home.

"Please don't cut these curls! Please! Lord Cathgar would hate it!"

Tallows's eyes narrowed, and he stopped, to Tessie's relief, fingering her mass of silken locks. He stood up instead, galvanized into action. Yes, Tessie had been shrewd enough to realize that he bore Nick a deep grudge. Grudge enough to do something out of sheer spite. Tessie did not think of her curls—they would grow back—she thought of the knife. The long, lovely pearl-handled knife that Tallows caressed slowly.

He ran his finger down the blade and smiled. It was not a wicked smile, precisely, for "wicked" is left for more heroic, romantic villains—but it was mean and calculating. Tessie did not allow herself to shiver or take fright. If she failed, there would be plenty of time for such displays of misery. The knife was being sharpened now in front of the flames from the small hearth. Tallows had not forgotten a grinding stone.

Cal had nothing further to add to Nick's sisters' garbled story. Nick had to restrain himself from shaking the poor lad, for had he accompanied Tessie, she might, at least, be safe. Cal was near tears, trying to explain. Nick did not shake him, as he wished to, but pulled out a pristine handkerchief and muttered that no real harm was done. After all, Tessie was as stubborn as a cart horse. Cal would not have been able to resist her wheedling.

Now for no real reason other than the reticule, he had a distinctly dire feeling in the pit of his stomach. He prayed he spoke the truth when he said no real harm was done. The fair was full of unsavory characters—tinkers, peddlers—but somehow he did not think these were the problem. He was acting on instinct, but the instinct was strong.

He saddled Bess—for his own horse needed to be

rested—and set off, with Cal, in the direction of the ditch again. The sign was still pointing the wrong way. He slid down from the horse and examined it. There were small pebbles around it, and the mud on the post was fresh. Someone had deliberately turned the sign. A strong breeze, or even a horse cart brushing against the post, could not have caused those markings. Then there was the reticule . . . always, his mind dwelt unpleasantly upon it.

God, if something had happened to Tessie, he would never forgive himself. He should have followed her directly to Chiswick rather than allowing her to become a slave to his mother's whims! All those gowns—yes, even in his anxious state he could see how many bolts of material and half-finished garments were scattered about the drawing room—it was scandalous! He should have claimed her weeks before rather than meddling at Hampstead Oaks. He could have done that later, when matters were settled between them.

Nicholas's thoughts were bleak. Joseph was right. He was nothing but a cow-handed, rag-mannered, self-righteous rascal! Tessie should have been wed already, without the nosy Miss Hartleyvales of the world staring at her askance.

Well, if he could but find her, he would stick to his resolve. What was more, he was dashed if he would take no for an answer again! If Tessie proved troublesome—which undoubtedly she would, for that was her sweet, adorable, stubborn little nature—he would simply overpower her with his manliness.

Oh, yes, he would indeed. Nick's eyes were grim and mirthful at the same moment. Then they became merely grim as he noticed her bonnet and a tangle of ribbons close to an almost completely overgrown path. How he knew it was *her* bonnet, one could not say. Perhaps it was the gay feathers, all sticky and murky, or perhaps, simply, because the bonnet was squashed flat. Tessie's bonnets *always,* somehow, ended up looking like that! Whatever the reason, Nick decided it was Tessie's.

The path, however, was facing away from the fair, so he had to make a decision quickly.

"Cal, you go on to the fair. Search every stall for Miss Hampstead. Not the dancing bears—she would not be interested in that, I think. If you do not find her within an hour, return to this path and follow my tracks quietly. There might be danger."

"Aye, sir!" Cal's eyes shone. For him, it was an adventure. Nicholas found, when it came to his intended, he tired of adventure. But he nodded approvingly to Cal, hoping against all hope that Miss Hampstead would be found procuring pink sugar mice at the sweetmeat stalls. He would probably throttle her, then, of course, but Cal need know nothing of the matter!

He hardly stopped to watch Cal step off the overgrown path. He trotted down it silently, Bess sensing his need for caution. It took him a full ten minutes to remember the disused huntsman's cottage. This after finding a single grass-stained glove not far from the path. She was throwing out a trail, he was certain of it. Nothing more was found, for the second glove had been taken by the wind and was even now lying hidden beneath an elderberry bush. It did not matter. Nicholas, knowing the land as he did, no longer hesitated.

The only possible place for a villain—down *this* path at any rate—was the huntsman's cottage. Five minutes before he arrived, he tethered Bess to a tree. It was better, he thought, to arrive on foot. Tessie's pistol, though grimy, was still primed.

Twenty

Snip! It took just a moment of fumbling before the first ringlet fell to the floor. Tessie winced as Tallows hacked at it. The knife, sharp from its grinding, needed to slice into a hundred silken strands. Tessie's hair was abundant, gloriously so. Still, despite the tears that stung her eyes, the deed was done. The first twist lay forlornly on the stone floor. Tallows chuckled. That should make his lordship scarper up from London! With a great wad of notes, too, he should reckon.

"There, I do be afeared Lord What's-Is-Name will be alarmed! Wait still, missy, for I still 'ave the other to do."

Tessie said nothing as Tallows bent to pick up the curl. He laid the knife upon the table as he did so. The single moment Tessie had been waiting for! She leaped from the chair and grabbed the knife. Tallows whisked around suddenly and Tessie kicked him. Yes, it is very sad to report this, for it was in a most unmaidenly site, and Tallows yelled with a mixture of pain and outright fury. The bonds were on the floor again, for Tessie's hands were free.

Now was the moment she'd planned for—the perfect moment to lunge the knife into Tallows's back. He was still bent over, doubled in pain and fury. Tessie hesitated. Then she rushed to the door, frantically fiddling with the handle. She couldn't do it. She simply could not. It was one thing shooting a person in the foot, quite another stabbing him in the back. The door was not locked—Tallows had just come in from outside—but her panic made the dark timber stick, and she was holding the knife, of course.

Tallows, behind her, was grabbing at her skirts. She tried her best to keep calm, but panic enveloped her blindly. Tallows grew closer, his scrawny arm pulling at her waist in an impossible grip. Ridiculous, really, for a man so spindly. He grabbed at the knife. Tessie refused to release it, fury and despair making her stubborn. Tallows tugged at her arm; then, in a single moment of triumph, he eased the knife from her hand and pushed her back onto the floor.

"I'll cut orf *all* ya flamin' curls for that! Silly bleedin' wench!" He drew closer menacingly, his blade raised almost above his head in triumph. Tessie wondered how she could have been such an addlepated gape seed not to have stabbed when she could have. She watched Tallows carefully for a false move. She still had on her boots. She could do serious damage with those if only she were given the chance! But Tallows would be more careful, on his guard, now.

She heard a rustling outside. It was almost past dusk, past the moment where she could just run and find the village path. She could still scream though, and if for some happy reason there was a person outside, he or she would surely hear. It was her last and only chance, for Tallows was approaching her fiercely, and she doubted whether he would stop at one curl or even ten. She did not like to think *what* he might stop at.

She had not thought, while she was concentrating on escape, that Tallows would harm her. She was his only means to a ransom. But it was not just ransom Tallows required but revenge. She realized that now as he tugged at the first skein of her glorious, bountiful, ridiculously curly, long locks.

The rustling became more pronounced. Even Tallows released his grip a little and listened. Boot prints against pebbles. Stealthy, but audible if one happened to be praying for such a miracle. Tallows had not been, of course, but he was as alert as Tessie, though the ale made his reflexes less sharp.

Miss Hampstead opened her mouth and screamed. It was not so much a scream, precisely, as a blood-curdling shriek. Taken by surprise, Tallows started, then dropped the blade. He lunged toward her to stop her mouth—by God, he would gag her this time!—when there was a familiar report of gunshot. Tallows sank almost instantly to the ground, moaning in pain, and a great deal more Tessie could not understand. Just as well, for it was all most unsuitable for a lady's ears.

All this happened in the mere fraction of a moment, no more than a few simple heartbeats.

Above Tallows, Tessie still, for some incomprehensible reason, screamed. Perhaps in shock, she was hardly aware of her redemption.

"You may stop that caterwauling now, I believe."

The voice from the door was both mocking and amused. Tessie stopped, openmouthed, her heart fluttering so wildly, it was impossible to know whether it was from fright or from sheer, unmitigated relief.

It was neither, of course, for her heart continued to flutter long after the gentleman had stepped inside, had eyed his surroundings, had had the temerity to kiss her pretty little lips long and well—but neither long nor well enough—and hand her back her precious pistol.

"This is yours, I believe."

"You found it!"

"I did, and your hapless little bonnet—you should really stop wearing feathers, it is a shocking waste—and your glove. Not the other, I am afraid."

Tessie did not care about her glove, for Nicholas was

regarding her lips again, rather as though they were an interesting curiosity. Miss Hampstead hoped they were interesting enough, though Tallows still needed some attention. Her eyes must have flickered to the villain, for Nick finally allowed his gaze to wander to that quarter, too.

"I think he needs some help. He is losing blood. . . ."

Nicholas picked up a curl. "Did he do this?"

"Yes, it is nothing. Nick, he is an unscrupulous villain, but he needs attention."

"It is not blood he should lose, but a tooth. By God, let him just sit up and I will give him attention!"

Tessie laughed. Such ferocity! So different from the cool, languid, mocking man she had met. Over nothing more dire than a whisper of a curl too. Almost she could hope . . .

Tallows sunk into a swoon. Nicholas cursed, then drew some water to revive him. He stripped the man to his shirtsleeves to expose the bloody shoulder.

"He will live, but Cal should fetch a doctor. Then a magistrate. Can you help me bind him?"

"I don't want none of your bleedin' bindin's, Lord Whatsit!"

Tallows, reviving, was too annoyed to hold his tongue. Nicholas raised his brows as he bound the wrists firmly, then drew out an elegant silver bottle of French Madeira.

"A terrible waste, but I rather feel it is best if he fell into a stupor. At least until the magistrate arrives."

Expertly, he forced the drink down Tallows's stubborn lips. Stubborn, that is, until he had had his first taste. After that it was sheer simplicity. Tallows downed every last drop with nothing but a satisfied belch.

"A somewhat inept criminal, I find."

"Yes. Why do I have the strangest sense of déjà vu?"

"Perhaps because we seem destined to tie up criminals, you and I."

Tessie nodded. Perhaps it was relief, but she felt rather weak at that careless phrase, "you and I."

"Inept, but a terrifying criminal nonetheless." Nicholas regarded Tessie keenly. She nodded.

"Yes. I thought he might—"

Nick interrupted. He placed a finger over Miss Hampstead's mouth.

"Not terrifying for *you,* but for *me.* I thought I might lose you." Lord Nicholas Cathgar regarded Tessie meaningfully. Her heart did several quick somersaults. It was perfectly impossible not to look as though she was desperate to be kissed. She was, of course, only how utterly shameless to allow him to guess!

So she fiddled with her pistol—a hideous crime, one Grandfather Hampstead would have sent her to bed with no tea for a week over—and fussed over Tallows.

"Perhaps we should stay with him."

"Indeed we should not! I have better things to do! And by the bye, though I hesitate to mention it, I *did* reload the pistol as a precaution. . . ."

Too late! The report was deafening. Fortunately, since Nick ducked, it did no more harm than damage one of the cracked walls.

"You are a menace!"

"Good God, I could have killed you!"

"I think we can effectively say I have now scotched my debt of honor to you, Miss Hampstead. You saved my life, but I have just returned the favor with interest. You dashed nearly killed me."

Nicholas's tone was hard. Tessie's happiness evaporated with the last rays of the sun. It was suddenly dark and cold.

"Do you agree?"

What could she say? Tessie could, in fact, say nothing. She was too choked with tears. So she nodded. At least, she thought, she still had pride.

"Your reputation is still perfectly intact and you are not ruined, Miss Hampstead. No tattle has ever reached my ears regarding your progress to London. Since then, you have been the honored—and chaperoned—guest of my mother and my sisters. No possible blame can attach itself to you. The fact that you have chosen to spend your time sewing a great pile of impossible-looking ball gowns is no one's concern but your own."

"You are right. I thank you. My respectability is restored." So why did Tessie feel so miserable? Why was there a big lump in her throat, so large she found it difficult to swallow?

Nicholas relented.

"Step out with me, Tessie. I think I can hear Cal now."

His ears, acute as always, had not misled him. It was Cal, with a widening grin when he noticed Tessie trailing the earl. His grin widened even farther when he heard a quick account of events.

"Orl right and tight, guv! I will whip off to the old sawbones quick as a trivet, then off on to Mr. Townsend wot is magistrate of these parts. Sure ye'll not be comin'?" he offered generously.

Nick dryly remarked that he was perfectly certain. He had a *great* deal more important matter to bother with.

"What can be more important that securing a kidnapper and a Luddite charged with treason?"

"Step into this gentle night, Tessie, and I shall tell you."

Nicholas's tone was clipped, offering no immediate confidences. His hand negligently twisted Tessie's curl. She had no idea how he had come by it.

They walked in silence, stopping only to untether Bess, who waited quietly but whinnied on seeing both his lordship *and* Tessie restored to her.

"Can you ride astride?"

Tessie was taken aback by the question. "Of course I can. Grandfather Hampstead . . ."

The earl grinned. "I might have known. Grandfather Hampstead. The fount of all wisdom! Hop on up. It will be quicker if we both mount."

So Tessie, unwilling to disoblige Nick, and also rather pleased—in a thoroughly unmaidenly kind of way—to be so intimate with him, obediently mounted and put aside the fear that this would probably be the last moments of their great adventure. After that, she supposed, it would be off to Hampstead Oaks, to wait out the time before she came into her small inheritance. She would—could—think of none of that now. Her body was too close to Nick's to permit any other thought. She closed her eyes, dreaming that this short moment would last forever.

It didn't. She found herself in a clearing, close by the troublesome ditch. His lordship dismounted and bade her do the same.

"See that post? That scoundrel turned it so it pointed here, toward the ditch. Step in. I should like you to see something."

Tessie, curious, dismounted with ease and trod gingerly over the grass. Nick was already in the ditch. Sitting, getting his town breeches dirtier yet. Mystifying. Tessie stepped closer, and felt a strong arm pull her toward him so that she tumbled, for the second time, into that long and deceptive grass. She was but inches away from Nick, and her traitorous heart started thudding quite ridiculously, for he had made his intentions perfectly plain. There was nothing between them now.

Then why was Nick looking at her like that, with his mouth so tantalizingly close? Why had he shifted his body so that it almost towered over hers? Why did he kiss her like he did, oh so excruciatingly slowly . . . ?

He stopped. "Tess." The words were low and heart-stoppingly gentle.

"I love you. Can you hear me? I love you. I have ever since, I think, I saw you eat the strawberry trifle. Or maybe it was the cod's eye. Your revulsion, I mean." There was a peculiar, quirkish gleam in his eye, a bittersweet smile upon those masculine lips.

"Why did you not tell me?"

"Because I am a clothead! Or so my mother tells me, along with several other uncomplimentary terms! I thought you knew, Tessie. I was certain you felt the same attraction as I, the same passion, I could *feel* it. I naturally assumed you knew the other too. I couldn't love you more, Tessie. Not if you were the most untroublesome creature in all of England."

"Which I am not!" Tessie laughed. "Nicholas Cathgar, you have made me quite sick with misery!"

"Well, I shall now rectify that by making you quite the most dizzyingly happy young female. Yes, in all of the world. I can do that, you know."

"Coxcomb!" But Tessie's eyes were bright with happiness.

"Shrew! By the bye, how many gowns did you think you needed?"

Tessie gasped. "They were for *me?"*

"Of course. What other young lady is precisely the same measurements, height, tastes . . . oh, you *must* have known!"

"Not a thing, only that your bride had consumption."

"Consumption?" Now it was Nick's turn to stare.

"Yes. Consumption. Your mama, I am sorry to say, is a most undiscriminating liar!"

"But an extraordinarily *bad* one if that is all she could come up with! You look dreadfully woebegone, as usual, all covered in grime and hatless, but to say you are consumptive . . . well, now, that is the outside of enough! You are beautiful, a rarity, my brave little Tessie!"

"Could you possibly tell me the bit about loving me again?"

Nick grinned. "I suppose I shall have to get used to saying it a dozen times a day! If I don't, Joseph shall leave my service, Mama will have my hide, and a brood of nosy sisters will pester on about it in countless letters that I have to frank—"

"Gracious! They didn't!"

"They did indeed. Apparently, you have stolen many a heart, Miss Theresa Hampstead!"

"Only yours."

"Stuff and nonsense! What about Christopher Lambert? What about poor Lord Alberkirky? He shall be our best man, by the way. Recommended to me a very interesting stable for sale. Had to forgive him, after that."

Tessie's eyes grew wide, "A stable?"

"Yes, close to the village of Greenford. Hampstead Oaks, you know."

"You bought my stables?"

"Indeed. A wedding gift to you. Pebbles is already safely installed at my London residence. I infer your silence is happiness, not outrage?"

Tessie laughed. "How could it be? When it is the most thoughtful, glorious gift ever! I could hardly bear thinking of losing those horses. It has been a sad time."

"It shall not be anymore. You shall have your presentation at Carlton House, and I have been meddling, I am afraid."

"Meddling?"

"That is why I took so long to chase after you, my little baggage. I have been meddling in your affairs. Hampstead Oaks should be restored to its former glory by the summer. I met most of your tenants and dismissed Lawson, your land agent. I cannot *swear* he was stealing your profits but I suspect it. He was also consuming far too liberally of your grandfather's best burgundy when I came upon him."

"I hope you grabbed a couple of bottles for yourself, then. Excellent stuff!"

"You may gift them to me. I do not *grab,* Miss Hampstead."

What a pity, thought Tessie as she batted her lashes like a hopeless little hoyden. Nicholas's eyes sparkled, but he said nothing, merely pushing her back gently into the soil.

"My ensemble must be quite a sight!"

"It always is, Miss Hampstead! Thank God Mama did not stint on your wardrobe. The future Countess Cathgar must be impeccable, you know."

Tessie groaned. "Oh, my God, it will take me a century to finish those clothes! I have lost more blood pricking myself with pins than I ever did out hunting, or shooting, or fishing, even, with Grandfather!"

Nicholas laughed, then kissed her nose, which she found very pleasant indeed.

"That shall naturally have to be remedied, of course."

"How?" Tessie was curious but not particularly worried. The only thing that worried her just then was that Nick's arm was free rather than cradling the nape of her neck. She rectified this situation boldly, which caused the earl to grin rather wickedly. She liked that grin—it suited his scar.

"How?" Nicholas echoed her. He traced his fingers over her lips. "How very elementary, my dear Theresa! We shall consign the whole goddamn lot to Madame Fanchon!"

To which Miss Tessie made no further comment other than to mention accessories like bonnets.

"Milliners," murmured Nick.

"Gloves."

"God, I don't know! Miss Peeples of Bond Street! Now

let me kiss you quiet, for heaven's sake, and don't you dare mention fans, lace, clocked stockings, or corsetry to me again. You shall have them all."

Nick punctuated this remark with a gesture that Tessie found quite extraordinarily pleasant, though she was sure it was one Finchie—dear old Finchie, who was now Mrs. Moreton—would disapprove.

She mentioned this, between sighs of bliss, to her betrothed.

Nicholas nodded. "She is very right. It gets wickeder yet, I am afraid. You need a chaperone."

"No, I don't!"

"Yes, you do!"

"I do not, I tell you!"

Lord Nicholas Cathgar attempted something very salacious indeed. Tessie gasped, then blushed furiously. Nick, his breathing somewhat harder, looked smug.

"I am right, am I not?"

"Damn you, yes, but only until I am safely wed, and only because you are, you are . . ."

"A rag-mannered rogue?"

"I was going to say too devastatingly magnificent for your own good, but rag-mannered will do me fine."

Nick laughed. "Let me help you out of this ditch. I have a better idea."

"Better than a chaperone?"

"Much better."

"You are not going to be all horribly . . . *chivalrous,* are you?"

"Certainly not! I have not waited all this time in direst agony to be chaste, my dear Miss Tessie!"

"What, then?"

"We are going straight back to the huntsman's cottage."

"To the villain?"

"No, to Cal."

"To Cal?"

Tessie could do nothing more but echo the earl dumbly. She had no notion whatsoever about what he was on about.

"Yes. He should be arriving back soon. With the magistrate."

And still Miss Hampstead, renowned for her quick wit, eyed her love blankly.

"What a goose you are, Tessie! It is taking you an age to figure out what I figured in just a minute!"

"If you do not stop talking in riddles, my lord, I shall not answer for the consequences."

"Ah, that hot little temper of yours. I must learn to mind it. The point, my love, is that Cal is returning with Mr. Townsend."

"Yes?"

"I do not believe he will think it amiss, my love, to marry us. After all, you are ruined again. You are out with a gentleman—and might I say, a notorious rake—past dark. There is hardly even a moon to redeem you."

"How humbling. You say he will *marry* us?"

"I do not see why not. I posted the banns the day I paid you your wretched ten thousand pounds."

Tessie gasped. "Nicholas Cathgar, you are the outside of enough!"

But Nicholas only laughed. He had grown used, h thought, to Tessie's scolding. Fortunately, he thought h knew quite precisely how to silence her. He tested ou his theory almost at once.

The silence grew wonderfully, *scandalously* long. Nicholas Cathgar, as always, had been perfectly right.